LANDRIEN MORISET

A Novel

BERNETA L. HAYNES

Snake Doctor Press

First edition originally published in the United States in 2015 by Junior Deputy Press.

Second Edition: 2020 by Snake Doctor Press

ISBN 978-1-7359850-4-6 (paperback)

Printed in the United States of America

snakedoctorpress.com

For Mom and Doris

Acknowledgments

I thank my mother for buying me my first typewriter and always doing her best to make sure that I had food, shelter, and a room for my introverted self to flourish; my aunt Doris, for inspiring a whole generation in my immediate and extended family to value education and harness our inner strengths and talents; my grandmother and grandfather, Romineta and James Henry Haynes, for showing strength in the face of enormous obstacles; my best friend, Kimberly Rousseau, for being a loyal, honest, and quirky friend; Jamie James, for teaching me what it means to love without shame and without limit; Wanda Raiford, my lawyer buddy and othermother, for helping me understand the importance of black sisterhood and intellectual integrity; my aunt Queen, for showing me what it means to be bold and unafraid in the pursuit of one's dreams; and my English professors—Horace Porter, Peter Meidlinger, Ken Egan, Jo Van Arkel, Miriam Thaggert, and Lena Hill—for being supportive and wonderful teachers who really made college and graduate school worth the experience. As a technical matter, I cannot leave out my lovely and talented editor, Tameka White. You rock, Tameka!

In addition, I want to shout out all of the friends and acquaintances I met throughout high school and college, many of whom I am honored to still be in touch with, thanks to the wonders of social media and modern technology: law school buddy Lauren Tate; intellectual and artsy comrades Jessica Schneider and Cara Bates, Chinelo Okparanta, Gilbert Huerta, Krystle Oates, Bryan Wilson, Derrais Carter; filmmaker and comedian extraordinaire Zardon Richardson; all around renaissance man Alvin Irby; and Brooklyn queen Nicole Gainyard.

Last, but far from least, I want to thank Lornett B. Vestal, my feminist-atheist-afrocentric partner, for being the sort of man who gives me hope about the future of our species.

To you all and anyone I left out, you are awesome! This book might not have happened were it not for your influence. Many thanks and blessings!

PART ONE

"Home sweet home, or not." ~ Landrien

CHAPTER ONE

On a snowy evening in January, Landrien Moriset stood in the doorway and stared down at the dead woman lying against the wall. The woman peered out through wide, unblinking eyes. Her wrinkled hands lay palms up against the hardwood floor. Her head was wrapped in a red night scarf and resting against the wall. The body was so still and inanimate, like a doll. Snow blew into the house and the wind whipped at Landrien's back as she knelt down and brushed her hands against the dead woman's blotchy cheeks. Her mother was dead.

A few hours earlier, Landrien would have been willing to bet good money that her mother would live a long life, a life that largely comprised of making her daughter feel worthless. What a difference a few hours and a heart attack can make.

"Landrien, can you email me a copy of the interrogatories for the Muscatine case? I don't know where the hell I saved my copy," asked Jordan Sheehan on the other end of the phone earlier that evening. She put him on the speaker while she frantically rifled through a stack of manila folders on her desk. *Note to self, organize your desk tomorrow*, she thought, pushing a couple of folders aside and opening another.

"Sure. I'll send it in a few. Have you heard from the defendant's attorney, what's-his-face?"

"Larry? No. And we still need to respond to his request for Jennifer's prior employment records," he replied.

"Yes, we do, Jordan. Deadlines are coming at us faster than a teenage virgin, and we haven't even gathered our witnesses," she fretted, opening a folder and still tugging at her hair with her free hand. "I'm sorry. That was unprofessional." Her cell phone rang, and she glanced at it exasperatedly. "I gotta take a call, Jordan. Let me talk to you in a few, all right?"

"No problem."

She answered her cell phone. "Yes, Darren?"

"Have you been over to Mom's?" asked Darren.

"No. I'm busy."

"Come on, she's sick. You think you could let go of your attitude and make some time for her just this once?" he shot back.

"I'm really not interested in another one of your lectures right now." Landrien hovered over a letter and glanced at the clock on her computer screen. It showed a quarter to five.

"Look, I don't get off work for another six hours. Can you at least go check on her when you get off at five?"

Landrien sighed. "I don't know. I might be here kind of late, and anyway, I'm sure she's fine."

"Landrien," he groaned.

"But I'll try to check on her as soon as I can," said Landrien, relenting.

"Good. I just...I have a bad feeling."

She smiled. "You always have a bad feeling."

"Well, the doctor did tell us to keep an eye on her. Just in case," he reminded her.

She slid the letter inside a manila folder and made a note on a legal pad. "Yeah. But you and I both know Mom wouldn't give us the satisfaction of dying so soon."

"Don't joke like that. I gotta go. Just call me and let me know she's fine."

"Sure thing, big brother," she assured him. After the call ended, she switched the phone to silent and dropped it inside her purse.

She emailed Jordan, gathered her purse and jacket and turned off the light in her office. Considering the headache that had begun to brew around her temples, she figured it might be time to get out of the office for the day. "See you tomorrow," she called, waving to Mary Ann, the senior attorney in her unit, as she passed by. The woman stared sleepily at her computer screen and nodded to Landrien.

When she reached the end of the hall, she stopped at Jordan's office and lingered in the doorway.

"So, you're hanging around past office hours again. Could I convince you to leave this place at five for once?"

Jordan looked at her over his black-framed eyeglasses. He sat behind a large desk covered in papers and manila folders. He leaned back in his chair. "What're you offering?"

"Drinks. I need to unwind," she said, peeping down the hallway to ensure that no one was nearby.

"You always need to unwind."

Landrien placed her hands on her narrow hips. "And? You coming?"

He regarded her for a moment and then closed the folder in front of him. "All right then." He shut down his computer, gathered his briefcase and jacket, and approached her with a smirk on his face. His hand brushed enticingly across her waist.

***

While Landrien stared up at the ceiling, Jordan rolled over onto his back, his chest heaving up and down. She fluffed the pillow under her head and continued gazing at the cottage cheese ceiling. *Who thought up cottage cheese ceilings? What horrible person came up with the idea to do this to every house and apartment?* Perhaps the landlord would let her paint over it.

When Jordan began to put his arms around her, she inched away and, instead, pulled out a cigarette and lighter from the top nightstand drawer. She dragged in as much of the smoke as she could and blew out before she passed the cigarette to him. He took a long drag and passed it back to her. Leaning against the headboard, she watched him and listened to his heavy breathing and the sound of cars passing beyond her window.

"I thought you gave up smoking," Jordan remarked.

"I did." She passed the cigarette to him.

He smiled at her. "I guess it didn't take?"

"Not so much."

"Have I told you how much I love your apartment?" he asked.

"Only every time you've been here."

"I've been thinking about moving to West Philly, you know. I'm tired of the suburbs."

"I bet you are. All that nice yard space and low rent—"

"And nosy neighbors and overpriced SEPTA passes," he added. "It's hard to afford the city, though. I don't know how you afford it."

"I don't. It's called living paycheck-to-paycheck."

"That's no way to live," he said, running his index finger along the middle of her arm.

She breathed out more smoke. "No. It really isn't."

Jordan propped himself up on his elbow and faced her. "Well, here's a thought. How about we get married and split the bills on a place around here?"

She shrugged. "All right. Sure."

"Yeah?" he asked, his voice an octave higher. He sat up and considered her. "Seriously?"

"Sure," she repeated, her gaze fixed on the ceiling as she blew out smoke. She adjusted the pillow beneath her head.

"You know I was only joking, right?"

"Okay." She put out the cigarette in an ashtray on her nightstand and glimpsed the clock. 8:15 p.m.

"Would you actually do it?"

"Sure, why not? We like each other well enough, I suppose. And so far as I can tell you don't have any particularly unclean or otherwise unpleasant traits." She sat up and stretched her arms above her head, yawning as she did so. She slipped her arms through a blouse and buttoned it. She ran her fingers through the dark, tight curls that stopped just over her ears and patted the stubborn strays sticking up in bold defiance of gravity. "I have to go check on my mom. You can stay here if you want. I'll be back in a couple of hours," said Landrien, glancing over her shoulder at him and slipping her feet inside a pair of black leather boots that rose to her knees.

"Let's get married," he beamed, a big grin on his face.

"Great. Yeah, let's do it."

She stood up and went toward the closet, where she pulled out a red pea coat. At last, she turned to him. "I'll be back in a few."

Landrien dialed the police and the coroner to inform them there was a body at 4516 Belmont Road in Phoenixville and that it required removal. She was not sure why she called the police. After all, her mother was very much dead, and there was no longer any possibility of saving her. Did people call the police when they found an old person dead of natural causes? The question lingered in her mind until she remembered she needed to call Darren.

She rolled her eyes and held the phone away from her ear as Darren yelled at her on the other end, but she accepted his barrage of abuses without interjection. "She'd be alive if you weren't so fucking mean, holding grudges that don't mean shit anymore. All you had to do was go over after work like you said you would. What was so hard about that?" He needed to scream and blame her, and she did not see why she should deny him this opportunity. He was a grieving son.

As soon as he began to sob, however, she gave him the number of the coroner and rushed off the phone. "I'm very sorry." She ended the call without waiting for him to respond.

Landrien then sat a few feet away from her mother's body and leaned against the wall. She hardly took her eyes off her mother while she sat there on the floor in the dreary, quiet living room and waited for the police and coroner to arrive. Her gaze drifted over her mother's silk blue robe draped over her knees, which were bent back at a sixty-degree angle. Perhaps she had sat down on the floor to rest and catch her breath, not understanding that she was, in fact, having a heart attack. Her last heart attack. Noting the red head scarf, Landrien figured her mother had been preparing to lie down on the sofa and watch television in the living room until she fell asleep, her nightly post-seven o'clock ritual. This night, she did not make it to the sofa.

When the police officer and coroner arrived, she signed some papers and watched them drive away with the body. She shut off the lights in the house and locked the door. For a moment, she stood in the driveway and studied the modest two-story house where she had grown up. Then, she got in her Camry and backed out onto the snowy road.

That night was the first of many sleepless nights for Landrien.

A few days later, she stood next to her brother and watched him dump the ashes of their mother's body into the Schuylkill River. She gazed out at the murky water and up at the sky, and she wanted to believe in something. She was not sure what, but she wanted to believe in something.

CHAPTER TWO

Groaning and switching on the dim lamplight, Landrien sat up and reached for her cell phone. She watched Jordan, who was fast asleep and snoring, and then she dialed her brother's number. As she lay against the headrest, she closed her eyes until she heard her brother's voice.

"Hello?" Darren answered in a raspy voice.

At least one of us is not having any problem getting to sleep nowadays, she thought. "Hey."

"Do you know what time it is?"

"I can't sleep," she mumbled, pushing back the covers and standing up. Her bare feet carried her across the dusty hardwood floors until she stopped at her doorway. She glanced back at Jordan who was sprawled out on the bed, one hand above his head and the other across his stomach.

In the living room, she approached the window, pushed back the sheer curtains and stared out at the street three stories below. Two girls wearing matching black jackets walked arm in arm along the snow-covered sidewalk. "What do you think she left us in the will?" Landrien wondered, leaning against the window.

"I don't know, and I don't really see why it matters."

"It matters because when people die, someone gets stuck with all the dead person's shit. And if someone is lucky, that 'shit' ends up being a lot of money."

"So that's all you're thinking about? Money?"

"No. Actually, I don't want anything from her. I only asked because I'm curious. Aren't you a little interested in knowing what she might've left us?"

"Not really."

"Of course not. She probably left everything to you anyway."

"Look, it really is late. So—"

"I hated her, Darren. Do you know that I actually hated her at some point? Not just 'strongly disliked.' Hated. Sometimes I can't even remember why. You're not supposed to feel that way about your mother. And I tried not to, but it's like she just wouldn't let me in, at all. Now she's gone and—"

"And you don't have anybody left to hate," he interjected.

"No. That's not it."

He yawned. "Okay? So what is it?"

"Now she's gone, and it's really just us left. It feels weird to have no parents any more. I mean, as long as our parents are here, we're always somebody's baby, somebody's kid. But now with them gone…it feels weird, right?"

"Yeah, it does, especially when you put it like that," he replied, yawning some more. "But anyway, I gotta let you go. We can talk during the few hours when the moon isn't out. You know, day time?"

She looked out the window and watched the snowfall on the vacant street. "Yeah."

"I'll call you during my lunch break, all right?"

"All right."

"Oh, and do me a favor, Landrien?" he added. "Try to forgive her."

She closed her eyes and muttered, "Goodnight, Darren."

For a while, she sat in the dark living room, staring out the window. Ambivalent thoughts of her dead mother swam around her mind. After nearly half an hour, she returned to bed, where she lay awake with her back facing Jordan and her gaze on the digital clock until she drifted into a dreamless sleep.

Days later, she and Darren sat opposite Barbara Turner, their mother's attorney. They watched the attorney flip through a folder until she pulled out a piece of paper and leaned forward over her desk. The woman nodded, and her eyebrows went up as she examined the paper.

"Yes, I remember going over this will with Pamela. At the time, I thought it was a bit too colorful," said Mrs. Turner, removing her glasses and walking from behind her desk. She pulled up a chair and sat in front of them. Landrien watched her brother, who uncrossed and crossed his legs as he scrutinized the attorney. "As I mentioned, Pamela hired me to handle her estate."

"What's your fee?" Landrien asked.

The woman's eyebrows went up at the abrupt nature of the question.

"This is pro bono, Miss Moriset. Pamela was my friend. She helped my mother look after my father in his last year. I offered to do her this favor in return. It was the least I could do," Mrs. Turner explained.

"Wait a minute. Was your father Mrs. Rona's husband?" Darren asked.

"Yes," replied the attorney, in response to Darren. "Were you aware that Pamela had $10,000 in a checking account and approximately $270,000 in a certificate of deposit? This money was largely money left over from your father's life insurance policy when it paid out. She cancelled her own policy years ago, for whatever reason." Darren looked at his sister in surprise and then turned his attention to the attorney.

"No, we didn't know," he answered. Landrien shook her head to confirm that she, too, was unaware that her mother had so much money stored away. Darren sat up straight in his chair.

"She's left it all to Darren. I'm just going to read the will to you now. Pamela wrote it herself. I merely provided a few edits," noted Mrs. Turner. "I, Pamela Nelene Moriset, bequeath the full value of my checking account and certificate of deposit at the Credit Union of Philadelphia to my oldest child, Darren Thomas Moriset and his heirs, to do with as he sees fit," explained the attorney, reading from the will. Landrien shrugged, and Darren smiled as the attorney read on. "And to my oldest child and his heirs, I also bequeath my 2004 Chevy Impala, as well as my library and all of the furniture in my home at 4516 Belmont Road, Phoenixville, Pennsylvania to do with as he sees fit."

"Well, as I guessed, Darren, she left everything to you." Landrien didn't look at her brother but at the attorney. "Can we just sign whatever we need to sign? I really have to run some errands."

"I'm not finished, Miss Moriset. There's a bit more." She read from the paper again. "To my youngest, Landrien Bell Moriset, I bequeath my diary collection," Mrs. Turner went on, looking up from the paper resting on her lap.

Landrien chuckled. "How thoughtful. Are we done, Mrs. Turner? I can tell you right now that I don't want anything she's left me."

"I'm sorry. There's a little more. I'm obligated to make sure you know and understand the full contents before I wrap up Pamela's estate."

Darren apologized for his sister's rudeness and implored the attorney to continue.

"I also bequeath my home at 4516 Belmont Road, Phoenixville, Pennsylvania to my youngest, Landrien and her heirs," Mrs. Turner read.

Landrien and Darren ogled one another disbelievingly.

"So long as," the attorney continued, "within five years of the date of my death, she resides in the home continuously for at least one full calendar year; otherwise, the home shall go to the Phoenixville Greater Tabernacle Church of Christ." The attorney paused, removed her eyeglasses and wiped them with a cloth. "The language is a little bit clunky, but she wouldn't let me alter it much more than that. I suspect she read up about wills and imitated the language as best she could, or maybe she had another lawyer friend. At any rate, I'm unsure how well the language regarding the house would hold up in court, but she wouldn't let me make any more changes."

Landrien, who stared at the attorney wordlessly, now considered whether she should just get up and walk out or send up a few curse words to her mother before doing so.

While these thoughts raced around Landrien's mind, Darren cleared his throat and his gaze traveled from his sister to the attorney. "Is that the end of it?" he asked.

"Yes. I've just read you the full contents."

"Okay, so what happens next?" prodded Darren.

"She was hateful 'til the end," Landrien mumbled, almost inaudibly, her eyes fixed on the piece of paper on the attorney's lap. "Are we done?" asked Landrien, standing up. "I don't want any of it."

"Landrien," Darren chided her, grabbing her wrist. She sat down on the edge of the seat and tapped her feet. Darren smiled apologetically at the attorney. "I'm sorry, Mrs. Turner. We just didn't know what to expect."

"It's fine. I've had to break up fights during these types of meetings, and I have the bruises to prove it. Believe me, wills bring out the crazy in people." Turning to Landrien, she added, "I looked up the value of your parents' home. Its market worth is currently $340,500, based on its historic value and the increasing desirability of the neighborhood. As you know, your parents paid off the mortgage years ago. Also, Pamela paid up the property taxes for this year."

"I don't want it."

"I understand, Miss Moriset. I simply wanted to make sure you and your brother are aware of the monetary value of what your mother has left you before I begin the process of settling her estate."

Darren turned to his sister. "Landrien, she gave you the house. She obviously wanted you to have it. I don't understand what the problem is."

"I hated that house, Darren, and she knew it. My worst memories are in that house. She knew I'd sell it the next day and keep the money if she ever gave it to me. Don't you see what she's doing? Even from the grave, she's still screwing with me."

"Can we schedule another time to meet with you, Mrs. Turner?" asked Darren, standing up as his sister rose to leave.

"Sure," the attorney replied. Landrien left the room and headed out the building, while her brother scheduled another meeting.

When the icy air hit her face, Landrien pulled her cap down over her hair and ears. She tucked her hands inside her coat pocket, looked up and down the street and crossed over Baltimore Avenue toward the trolley stop.

"Landrien," her brother called from behind her as she picked up her pace. "Landrien," he said, his voice growing louder as he got closer.

As she made it across the street, he caught up to her. "Don't even start. I don't want it, not the house, not her diaries or whatever other bullshit she's left me." Her teeth chattered against the brutally cold wind, as she joined the people at the trolley stop and turned to face the street. Her brother studied her, his cheeks rapidly turning pink from the cold. He stared at her through large dark brown eyes that looked nothing like her narrower hazel-colored eyes. "I mean it, Darren. Spare me the speech because it's not gonna work."

"Sis, just think about what you're saying. Mom's given you the house. The *house*, sis. One year, and you can sell it and who knows how much you can make from the sale. Or you can rent it out. You heard Mrs. Turner: the neighborhood's still as desirable as it always was, even more so now. You're willing to give that up just because of some grudge? Come on, you're smarter than that, sis. I know you are."

She stared icily at him, and he winced.

"I didn't mean it like—"

"You want the house, it's yours. Take it," she groaned, stepping aboard the trolley.

"It doesn't work like that. She wanted *you* to have it. You heard what she put in the will. You can't just do this last thing for her?" he asked.

She glared at him and turned toward the window.

As Darren turned away, trying to figure out what to say next, his gaze fell upon a mother and little girl who were sitting near the middle of the trolley. The woman, who reminded him of his own mother, wore a bright purple hijab and a thick gray coat. Her eyes contained something akin to melancholy. He turned back to his sister. "Do it for Dad, then. It was his home, too. He wouldn't want to see it go to the church. You know how he felt about religion."

"Religion is where both God and rational thought go to die," she quoted her father, who repeated this phrase whenever their mother brought up church or religion, which had been often. She laughed a little as she thought about the number of times her father had uttered this phrase and the scandalized looks it always evoked from her mother. She recalled a conversation she had had with him one Sunday afternoon while the two of them sat out on the back porch and pieced together a puzzle. "Why don't you ever go to church with Mom?" she had asked one Sunday when she was ten years old. Her father's simple reply had lingered in her mind for a long time afterward: "Because I love your mom, and I don't want to lie to her. To love is to tell the truth."

"Landrien?"

"Yeah," she answered, snapping out of her daydream. "Fine. I'll do it."

Landrien sat on her sofa, sipping syrupy coffee, gazing around the airy room. A wide floor-to-ceiling white bookcase filled with novels and old photographs rested against the wall. One row in the middle remained empty but for a large candle and a silver analog alarm clock. Alongside the bookcase sat an old oak chair that she had purchased for ten dollars at the secondhand store a few blocks away.

The apartment, a 215-year-old Victorian house, contained four one-bedroom units, with oak floors that creaked at every step, deep clawfoot bathtubs stained from decades of use, tiny closets and abundant natural light flooding the living room from the large picture windows. As the light streamed in, she sipped her coffee while perusing a black and white photography book she had checked out from the library.

Once she drained her cup of coffee, she marked her page in the book and went to refill her cup. On her way back to the living room, she stopped in front of the mirror in the hallway and examined her reflection, the tight curls in her hair, the small dark brown birthmark at the crevice of her jaw and neck. "I need a haircut," she muttered, fussing with her hair.

Taking a step back, she examined her ensemble. She removed the gaudy belt and pulled the blouse out of her blue jeans. When she heard a knock on the door, she tossed the belt inside the hall closet and undid the top two buttons on her blouse.

Jordan smiled as bright as ever when she opened the door. She looked down from his black scarf to the wool pea coat and the gift bag he was clutching in his hand. "So you finally decided to use the main door key I gave you months ago? I thought you'd buzz in from the outside as usual."

"Maybe I just like to watch you come down the stairs every time I buzz in."

"Don't get cute. Who's the gift for?" she asked, returning to the living room. She resumed her place on the sofa, crossed her legs and picked up the cup of coffee.

"The gift's for you." He hung his coat on the chair in front of the bookcase.

He sat down beside her and handed her the small gift bag. Inside the bag was a small box. "Chocolates?" she guessed, just before opening the box. "Thank you. Dark chocolate, I hope?"

As she bit into the mint-flavored chocolate, she was on the verge of telling him how good it tasted when her teeth stopped against something hard, like metal. She pulled the object out of her mouth and swallowed the rest of the chocolate. In her hand was a small silver ring with a modest heart-shaped sapphire stone and diamond accent.

"I know we only just talked about it a little over a week ago, but I wanted to formalize it. I made that chocolate yesterday. Is it too much?"

"No," said Landrien, after a moment of surveying the ring. She chewed the rest of the chocolate and examined the ring, turning it over in her hand. "It's not bad."

"The ring or the chocolate?" he asked, with an uncertain smile.

"Both."

Jordan took the ring from her hand and slid it on her finger. "You like it?"

"Sure. It's pretty. Would you like to move into my apartment?" asked Landrien.

"Come again?" he replied, fidgeting in his seat and his eyebrows retreating further back toward his hairline.

"I'm moving out. Temporarily, I hope. I'd like for somebody to take over my lease for a while, as a sublet. You seemed like the logical choice, since I know you and I figure you won't destroy the place or skimp me on rent, which by the way is $940 a month, utilities excluded, but I'll take $870, utilities excluded. This would be a six month arrangement, possibly a year."

He ogled her in confusion. "What? Wait a minute. Slow down. Why are you moving out?"

"Okay. $850, electricity included, and you pay gas. Will you take it?" She fixed her eyes on him, watching him as he shook his head and fidgeted, and as he got ready to speak again but then seemed to forget what he was about the say. "It's my mom's will. If I live in the family house for a year, the title goes to me. It's a whole big complicated mess I don't really feel like going into right now. I can fill you in later. So, do you want my apartment or not? $850 is my best offer."

Jordan stroked his chin and scanned the room, as if he was surveying a used car. He went to the window and to the bookcase and drifted back to the window, where he leaned against the wall and gazed around the room.

"Do you want the apartment or not?" she asked.

After another quick sweep of the room, he turned to her. "Okay," he agreed.

Landrien sat at the bar and watched the place fill up with people. "So, when are you gonna show me some of your poetry?" she asked as she sipped the remainder of her beer and turned to face the bartender.

The bartender, a woman in her early thirties by Landrien's estimate, placed another mug of beer in front of her and scooped up the empty glass. "You know you're not interested in my poetry."

On her previous visits, Landrien had learned that the bartender was a published poet and worked only on Wednesday and Saturday nights at The Edge, a downtown bar where yuppie professionals often came to drink away the miseries of their daily grind. In fact, Landrien fast learned that at least half of the waiters in the bar were writers or artists of some sort, dreamers who reminded Landrien of her past self.

The bartender leaned forward and through full painted lips, said over the noise, "Do me a favor and pretend to talk to me, so this guy will stop trying to get my number?" The bartender glanced leftward, to where a balding old blond man was sitting a few bar stools away. He did not blink as he stared at the bartender.

Landrien winked at the old man, and his expression went flat. "I don't have to pretend." She smiled up at the bartender's dark face and surveyed the large red hoops dangling from her ears.

"You're almost as bad as some of the men in here, Landrien. And for the last time, I don't swing that way," said the bartender, smiling and running a wet towel along the bar top.

"They all say that at first," remarked Landrien.

"Didn't you come here with someone? Where did your little girlfriend go?"

"To the ladies' room, and she's not my girlfriend. We're exes."

She poured another patron a shot of tequila but continued smiling at Landrien. "I bet you've got a lot of those, don't you?"

"She's got a few," Elena Pierce chimed in. Elena leaned against the bar and kissed Landrien. "A heartbreaker, this one here."

"I believe you," said the bartender, shaking her head.

"Come on." Elena slipped her hand under Landrien's shirt.

As Elena grabbed her hand to lead her away from the bar, Landrien hastily placed forty dollars—with her cell phone number written on one of the twenty-dollar bills—on the bar top, gulped down the rest of her cider, and wished the bartender a good night. The bartender nodded and waved as Elena took Landrien's arm and led her through the crowd.

Landrien glanced at the clock on her nightstand and wondered how many more sleepless nights she could endure. Elena lay sound asleep on her back with the blanket half covering her and her long hair forming a circle around her head against the pillow. Landrien opened the drawer on the nightstand and fumbled around inside it until her hand landed on a small piece of metal. Clutching the ring, she brought it out of the drawer and slid it onto her finger. She extended her hand upward so that the light from the window hit the ring. The sapphire sparkled in the moonlight, and something about it made her smile. She admired it for a while, and once her eyes grew heavy with sleep, she removed the ring and placed it back inside the drawer. She fell back against the pillow, wrapped her arms around Elena and closed her eyes.

"Are you all right?" asked Elena, her voice raspy with sleep.

Landrien opened her eyes. "Yeah. I'm fine. Can't sleep is all."

Elena turned over to face Landrien and kissed the tip of her nose. "What's wrong?"

Landrien stared at Elena for a moment, wanting to mention Jordan's proposal, but she remained silent. She pushed strands of Elena's hair behind her ears. "In a few hours, I have to get up, pack and move into my mom's house."

"And you're worried that being there is gonna bring back all the memories, all the stuff you've tried to forget."

Landrien sighed. "Yeah."

"I know you don't like to hear it, Landrien, but maybe that's what you need. Maybe you need to remember it all and reckon with it. And anyway from what you've told me, it wasn't as bad as it could've been."

"You make it sound like I'm just whining."

"No, I'm sorry. That's not what I'm saying. I'm saying you should realize that your childhood was not nearly as bad as it could've been. You kind of had a decent one, all things considered. Okay, maybe I'm thinking too much about my own homophobic parents. But I would've loved to have had what you had. That's all I'm saying," Elena replied.

"Yeah, I guess you're right. But, still, I never thought I'd be back in that house."

Elena ran her hand along Landrien's lips. "I can move in there with you, so you don't have to be alone. The offer's still on the table."

They were silent for a moment and stared at one another. Landrien still wanted to mention Jordan's proposal, but she couldn't make the words form. "No. It's cool. I'll be fine."

"Because of Jordan, right? That's why you won't let me move in," noted Elena.

Landrien nodded. "Yes. And because I need to do this alone or at least give it a try by myself at first."

"Why are you with him, Landrien? I know you don't love him. So why do you do it? When your mom was alive, I assumed it was because you wanted her acceptance. But she's gone now. So why are you still with him?"

Landrien offered no response other than silence.

"I know it's not because of what he does. I know what you like, and he can't give that to you," said Elena, rising and thrusting her leg across Landrien. She leaned down and kissed Landrien's lips, neck, and shoulders. "So why do you stay with him? Why do you do it?"

"Let's not talk about Jordan right now," Landrien suggested, her hands resting on Elena's waist.

She stopped moving and stared down at Landrien. Just when Landrien was beginning to feel uncomfortable with the stillness and silence, Elena leaned forward and kissed Landrien's lips once more. In Landrien's ear, she whispered, "We're gonna have to talk about him soon."

Landrien nodded. She knew that conversation was inevitable, and she was eager to postpone it for as long as possible. "Soon." She lay back as Elena's kisses swept from her neck to her shoulders and everywhere else. In those kisses, Landrien was lost and perfectly happy.

CHAPTER THREE

Landrien stood in the yard of 4516 Belmont Road and surveyed the two-story redbrick house. Three brick columns lined the small unenclosed porch and extended upward, forming two square archways. Wood paneling began where the bricks ended. On each side, sage green paneling rose upward into a V-shape. She glanced over her shoulder and out at the vacant street lined with Red Oaks and Hemlock. After a deep sigh, she cursed her mother and proceeded up the three steps to the porch.

She gazed around the living room of the cold house and dropped her two over-sized suitcases along with her backpack and purse on the hardwood floor. A sense of inertia grasped her, and she found that she could not move. Instead, she leaned against the door and attempted to catch her breath. Her eyes continued scanning the room and fixed on the spot at the foot of the staircase, the spot where she had found her mother's body not so long ago. There was a dark circular stain just about two feet up from the floor. She approached the foot of the stairs, knelt down and brushed her fingertips against the dark circle. The oils from her mother's hair had seeped through the silk headscarf and left this circular stain imprinted on the wall. For a moment, she saw her mother's body there again, and she looked into the wide, horrified eyes. In the next moment, the vision faded, and Landrien was staring again at the dark spot on the wall.

When she stood up, she scanned the space and took in the dismal living room decor: the outdated floral-patterned sofa, the burgundy lounging chair and the old television her mother had had for decades. The television sat within a large and outdated entertainment center. She drifted to the sofa, which smelled like her mother's lavender perfume, and sat down. She put the sofa at the top of the list of things to discard.

She leaned back on the sofa and closed her eyes. The wall clock ticked and house and floors creaked. Then, silence. No noise of car horns, passing trolleys or people on the street talking or playing music.

After a while, she rose, grabbed her suitcases and carried them, one at a time, to her bedroom upstairs. She had not stepped inside her old bedroom in years, not since she had gone away to law school. The few times she had visited her mother after the second heart attack, she had not gone farther than the living room.

Landrien's old posters were strewn about the walls—Pam Grier, David Bowie, Angela Davis. Just behind the bed, there was a large autographed picture of Nina Simone, a poster Landrien had found inside her mother's closet. In the black and white photograph, Nina Simone wore a black jacket and black pants, with her afro picked out as she squatted and stared at the viewer with an impenetrable expression. She recalled passing many minutes admiring that poster.

"Mom?" she had said after she dug the poster out of her mother's closet one summer afternoon. Pamela Moriset, stretched out on the living room sofa, briefly looked up from her knitting. Landrien held up the poster. Pamela Moriset glanced at it and continued knitting.

"Yes, Bell? What do you want?"

"Who's this woman?" wondered Landrien.

"That's Nina Simone, a singer," she answered, watching the wooden needle weave through the loops of yarn.

"What she sing?"

"It's 'what *does* she sing'. And she sings music you wouldn't understand."

"What does she sing about?" She sat down on the coffee table in front of her mother and watched her with rapt attention.

"Pain and struggle, among other things. And don't sit on the coffee table."

Landrien stood up at once.

"Why are you so interested anyway? You've got more than enough dolls and toys to play with, instead of some dusty old picture of Nina Simone."

"Dolls are boring, and toys are for kids." Landrien turned her eyes to the poster. "I wanna be like her."

"A singer?" Pamela asked, looking up at her seven-year-old daughter.

"No. Brave. I wanna be brave like her," Landrien proclaimed.

Pamela chuckled at the excited look on her daughter's face and returned her attention to the knitting needles. "What makes you think she's so brave?"

Landrien studied the poster.

"Well, you won't be brave, I can promise you that. Brave women are fools. And I don't raise fools." Following this curious proclamation, they considered one another and shared an inexplicable moment that Landrien still puzzled over twenty-five years later.

Tearing her gaze away from the picture, Landrien went to the window and pulled back the sheer curtains. She took down the Nina Simone poster along with every other poster in the room, leaving the white walls bare. She folded each of the posters and placed them on the top shelf in the empty closet. Next, she changed the bed linens and replaced them with clean ones she had brought from her apartment. At last, she sat on the bed, fell back and drifted to sleep.

The next morning, Landrien rose and shuffled drowsily toward the bathroom suite that joined her room and Darren's room. Once she finished brushing her teeth and washing her face, she ran a bath.

Just as she was about to step in the bathtub, her phone rang from the bedroom. She figured only one person could be calling her at seven o'clock in the morning on the weekend. She hurried into the bedroom and grabbed the phone from the windowsill near the bed. "Yes, Darren?"

"Good morning to you too, Grouch. I was calling to invite you to lunch at my apartment today. I'm cooking for Irina's birthday. Can you come?"

"Maybe. I need to unpack and get settled in here, but I'll try to make it."

"How was your first night?" asked Darren.

"Oh, you know. Home sweet home, or not," she said, distracted as her eyes fixed on the spot near the window. She recalled seeing a female figure standing in the moonlight. It had been too dark to make out who the woman was, but the woman had unnerved her. Landrien had very few bad dreams, so she attributed this nightmare to the fact that she was back in her childhood home. "I'm already dreading my remaining 364 days in this place."

"What have you done with your apartment for the time being?"

"Jordan's paying me to stay there. Like a sublease." She turned off the water in the bathtub, removed her clothes and submerged herself in the hot bath.

"You know, if you want to invite Jordan to lunch later...?"

"He's busy. He writes on Sundays," she replied.

"He writes?"

"Yeah. He likes to write stories in his spare time."

"Oh. Interesting."

Landrien fixated on her feet sticking up from the water. "We're engaged now."

"That's...wow, sis. Congratulations!" shouted Darren. "When did that happen?"

"On the night I found Mom."

"Oh," he replied and fell silent before exclaiming, "And you're just now telling me?"

"It had slipped my mind."

He laughed. "Slipped your mind? You're a mess. Well, damn, that's some big news, sis. I'm happy for you. He seems like a good, honest guy. Better than all the other guys you've been with. I mean, not like you've been with a lot of guys. Not like you're..."

"A slut?" she asked.

Darren cleared his throat. "Of course you're not."

"Hey, I'm not ashamed. It is what it is."

"So, no more of that one girl, Elena?" Darren stammered. "I was never a fan of her."

"Why not? Because she's a woman?"

"No. Stop being defensive. I have nothing against lesbian relationships. In fact, I'm all for them," he teased, and Landrien rolled her eyes. *Typical man.* "She just seemed a little narrow-minded and cold. I knew you could do better. You and Jordan make a good pair."

"Yeah," said Landrien, closing her eyes as she sunk under the water.

"Anyway, I gotta let you go. I'm in the checkout line at the grocery store. I'll see you later. Call me if you can't make it?"

"Sure."

"Love you, sis"

"Yeah. Love you, too." She waited for him to end the call. She put the phone on the footstool next to the head of the tub, lay back in the tub and closed her eyes once more.

Grunting as she lifted a large box of shoes, Landrien staggered toward the front door and walked onto the porch. The heavy falling snow hit her face, forcing her to squint to keep it out of her eyes. She walked around to the right side of the house, where she had left the storage room door ajar. As the bitter, cold wind bit at her face, she regretted her decision to pack away her mother's stuff in the outdoor storage rather than in the basement. She had thought that the steep stairs leading down to the basement presented enough of a hazard without the extra weight of a fifteen-pound box of shoes and clothes.

She put the box down on the concrete floor of the storage room. The cobwebby room was about ten feet long by ten feet wide and already crowded with boxes, most of which contained Landrien's childhood possessions. Pamela Moriset had cleared out her daughter's room just shortly after her husband had passed away a few years earlier. She had taken all the shoeboxes in her daughter's closet—shoeboxes containing keepsakes, such as old theater passes, trinkets from their family vacations, photographs Landrien had taken with the camera her father had given her on her thirteenth birthday—and she had stacked them in this room.

She slid the box toward the back wall, closed the door and walked hastily to the front porch and into the house. She grabbed another box full of clothes and her mother's jewelry boxes. Once more, she staggered to the storage room. As she pushed the box to the back wall, she heard a hoarse but cheerful voice say, "Hi there. You must Pam's daughter."

Standing up slowly and rubbing her cold hands together, Landrien said, "That's me." She turned and faced a bright-eyed woman in her late sixties and who now stood in the driveway. The woman wore an ankle-length quilted purple coat and a matching knitted scarf and cap.

"I'm Rona. I live next door," the woman informed her, nodding at the one-story house on the other side of the driveway. She smiled and extended a gloved hand. "I'm sorry about your mother. I didn't believe it when I heard about it. I gotta say I was pretty disappointed that I didn't get an invite to the funeral." Her tone suggested that she was not only disappointed but outright offended.

Great. A passive aggressive, clingy old neighbor. Just what I need. "It was a small funeral. Just close family and friends," Landrien explained.

"Well, I honestly didn't think I could go on after my husband passed away. You can't imagine what it's like to be all alone after half a lifetime with someone at your side. My husband, bless his heart, he held on as long as he could for me. But you know cancer. It spares no one. Pam was there every day before he died and afterward, sometimes just to talk, sometimes to help me clean him or cook. You poor thing. What it must feel like to lose both of your parents so early. If you need anything or just want to talk, please just come knock on my door any time." She wiped snowflakes from Landrien's forehead. "I'm home most days."

Landrien nodded.

Rona smiled, her gray-green eyes watery, and she walked back to her house across the driveway. Landrien stood there for a moment, watching the woman depart, the wind hitting her face. Then, she hurried back inside the warm house.

The box containing her mother's diaries sat at the foot of the staircase. She squatted, lifted the box and returned to the storage room. She dropped the box on the storage room floor, and it tipped over spilling the diaries. She picked up each of the diaries and haphazardly tossed them back inside the box. But when she picked up the last diary, which had a brown leather cover, something shiny fell out and hit the cement floor with a clatter.

A silver necklace with a triangle-shaped locket hanging on it lay on floor and sparkled in the dim light. Upon closer inspection, she saw that the locket bore scratches and faded spots from age. There was a tiny latch at the right side. With her fingernail, she lifted the latch and peered inside at a small mirror. As she stood up to examine the locket, she pulled the string hanging from the ceiling and the light flickered on. Holding the locket less than an inch from her face, she attempted to make out the writing inscribed on the inside of the door.

The diary fell from her hands when she read the words, "Love Always, Bell" on the door of the locket. *I never gave anybody a locket...*

A quiet thud informed her that she had dropped the necklace on top of the diaries in the box. At once, she turned off the light and shut the storage room. She stood outside the storage room and looked from Rona's house to the quiet, empty street.

The cell phone vibrated in her coat pocket. "I'm coming, Darren. Give me an hour."

"Perfect. I made peach cobbler."

At exactly one o'clock, Landrien parked in front of Darren's apartment on 46th and Larchwood. With the snow coming down so hard, she wondered if she would be able to return to Phoenixville after dinner. At least she was only a few blocks from her apartment, in case the weather got too bad.

She trudged through the snow and up to her brother's porch. Irina opened the door and eagerly pulled her inside, took her coat and ushered her into the small dining room, where two other women and a man sat looking up in anticipation at the new arrival. She recognized the women as one of Darren's cop friends, Stacey, and the other woman was Irina's twin sister, Adina. She did not recognize the burly man who sat next to Adina. Landrien sat down and nodded at the guests who all smiled back.

"So, I'm surprised Darren never mentioned he had a sister," said the man, who introduced himself as Michael Reno, another one of Darren's cop friends. Landrien took in the man's tattooed and extremely ripped biceps and the WWE logo on the tight-fitting t-shirt that accentuated his chest muscles. She was sure this man had not spent a day of his adult life without a gym pass. Her eyes traveled upward to his youthful face and low-cut dark hair. Michael Reno was masculinity in all its confused glory, she concluded. *Who wears muscle shirts nowadays, anyway?* She sipped her water, feigned a smile at the man and averted her eyes from his hungry gaze. "You're a lawyer, right?" Michael Reno asked.

Before Landrien could respond, Irina and Darren entered the room, hand in hand, and the man turned his attention to them. Irina had changed into a yellow knee-length skirt that hugged her hips. Darren stood just an inch taller than Irina, who was short and more full-figured than Landrien could ever hope to be. The happy couple sat down at the head of the table and told everyone to dig in.

The lunch lasted about two hours, and afterward they went to the living room where Irina opened all of her gifts. Irina's face flushed as she opened Darren's present, an expensive-looking bracelet. She squeaked in excitement when Darren put the bracelet on her tiny wrist, after which he held her wrist to his lips and kissed it. Stacey and Adina 'ooohed' and 'aahed' while Michael Reno fixed a suggestive gaze on Landrien.

Everyone except Landrien had brought a gift. She apologized, but Irina just laughed and, with an animated wave of the hand that Landrien supposed was a Russian mannerism, exclaimed in somewhat broken English, "Oh, nonsense, sister. I don't care about presents and gifts." She got up from the sofa and pulled Landrien into a bone-breaking hug. While Landrien appeared to struggle for oxygen, Darren pressed his lips together to refrain from laughing at the pair.

After Michael Reno and the other cop had gone, Landrien decided to make her exit. She hurried out into the snow. At least two more inches had fallen since she had arrived hours ago.

"Be careful," Irina cautioned and waved as Landrien reached the car.

"Call me when you make it home," Darren hollered, and she waved to them before getting inside her car.

As she turned the corner onto Baltimore Avenue, she decided to stop at her apartment and visit Jordan. She walked along the dark hallway and up the staircase to the third floor. She looked around at the dark tan walls, at the antique still life paintings hung here and there along the walls, and she took in the dusty oak smell of the aging house. Had it only been one day since she had left this place?

She used her key instead of knocking. Sure, it was rude, but it would take some time to grow accustomed to knocking on her own door. When she opened the door, she stood face to face with Jordan, who grinned and folded his arms across his chest.

"Should I get used to unexpected visits?"

Landrien shut the door and closed the few inches of space between them. "Maybe." She dropped her purse and slowly pulled him toward her, burying her face in the crevice of his neck. As she looked up at him, he removed her cap and kissed her forehead. He smiled down at her, a smile that she thought contained more hope than she had ever seen in any other person. There was such an immense hopefulness in Jordan that she sometimes wondered—as she did while she stood there in his arms this Sunday afternoon—how he could sustain it. How did this intense hopefulness not crush him eventually?

She met his gaze as he raised her left hand up to his mouth and kissed the engagement ring.

"What? What's wrong?"

"Nothing," she said, a tense smile parting her lips. For a second, her mind had wandered to Elena. One day, she would have to break up with Elena, and she knew that day would be soon. *But was it a mistake to choose Jordan? How much does he really understand me?* These questions had haunted her ever since her last night with Elena. Sometimes, she wished she could be two separate people: the right woman for Elena and the right woman for Jordan. But that was unrealistic. She knew she had to make a choice, and she had done just that, albeit unwittingly, the night she said yes to Jordan's proposal.

"You're so strange sometimes."

She lowered her hands to his pants and held his gaze as she undid the belt buckle. "Normal is over-rated."

"I couldn't agree more."

They passed the Sunday afternoon wrapped in one another's arms, all worries temporarily forgotten.

When Landrien pulled into the dark driveway of her mother's house, she sat in the car for several minutes before she turned off the engine. Finally, she got out and headed to the front door but stopped halfway there and turned in the direction of the storage room. She stared at the box of diaries and, after a moment's hesitation, gathered the box in her arms and turned off the light.

Landrien carried the box of diaries up to her bedroom and set it inside the closet.

CHAPTER FOUR

She looked through the lens of the camera and focused on her brother who was sitting next to a honey-colored girl with bangs and freckles. Amma Shepherd's parents had moved in next door just a few weeks earlier. To her annoyance, Amma—fifteen years old, just two years older than Landrien—had started "going with" Darren. Landrien, who had not had the opportunity to get to know Amma before Darren claimed her, had a tough job of suppressing her jealousy. It seemed unfair that Darren always got all the interesting friends.

Amma and Darren, sprawled out in the grass in the middle of the backyard, pulled purple flowers from the grass and sniffed them. She watched through the camera as Amma brought a flower to her nose and inhaled. Amma could tell a story in a simple movement, and this captivated Landrien. Everything about Amma captivated Landrien.

On the way to school months earlier, Landrien had said offhandedly to Darren, "Have you seen the new girl, Amma Shepherd, from next door? She came over with a pan of brownies on Sunday when you and Mom were at church."

"Oh, that's where the brownies came from. I wondered," he had replied, making a quick left turn onto a tree-lined neighborhood street. Darren drove them to school most mornings once he had got his license.

Landrien stared out at the trees that seemed so vivid and bright all of a sudden. "I've never met a more perfect human being."

"You are really strange, Landrien," he had remarked, glancing at his sister and smirking.

Less than a week later, Amma and Darren had become a pair. Landrien did not speak to her brother for nearly a month.

She watched them as they sat in the backyard. Amma brought and held another flower to her nose. It was a slow, sensual movement, like something out of a movie—one of those scenes where a soft piano melody fades out at the end of a ballad. Holding the camera as steady as she could, she snapped a picture as Amma inhaled the second time. She snapped frame after frame as Amma's hands gently fell onto her lap, where the flower lay between her fingers.

When Darren laid his hand on Amma's thigh, she laughed and whispered something in his ear. Landrien, watching her through the camera lens, caught Amma's gaze and some curious, silent exchange occurred. In the next moment, Amma tore her gaze away from Landrien's and said something to Darren.

"What are you doing?" Darren glared at his sister. When she lowered the camera, his glare faded into a mischievous smile, one that said, "Go on, Landrien. Leave us alone. I think I might get lucky later."

She merely smiled and asked them to pose for the camera one last time. Per her request, they leaned against one another and grinned for the camera. She snapped the picture, turned off the camera and returned to the porch. For a few minutes, she sat on the sofa in the enclosed back porch and watched Amma and Darren. Amma lay across his lap, and he ran his fingers through her dark hair while she stared up at him, as if he was the only boy in the whole world.

"Spying on your brother?" came a low voice from behind her. Pamela had appeared at the doorway. She cast her daughter a suspicious look.

"No," mumbled Landrien, at once standing up and walking past her mother. Pamela stepped aside and let her daughter pass into the dining room.

"You could have a bit of respect and give them some privacy." She watched as Landrien passed through the living room. "I see the way you look at her. Don't think I don't know what's going on. You're not fooling anybody."

"Right," Landrien muttered.

"You'd do well to get yourself some friends of your own," Pamela added.

"We can't all be as popular as you, Mom," she muttered and walked up the stairs. Pamela was in the middle of food preparations for a dinner party that evening. She had invited all of the women on the block to attend. Pamela, a social butterfly in the neighborhood, headed a book club and frequently organized potlucks.

When Landrien reached the top of the stairs, she turned toward her parents' room instead of heading straight to her own bedroom. Her father was sitting in his chair—a faded old yellow chair he had bought from a thrift store—and reading a book. Anthony Moriset looked up at his daughter and smiled. Landrien sat down on the bed and lowered her head to see what he was reading. Toni Morrison's *Sula*.

"It's all yours once I'm finished," offered Anthony. He marked his page, laid the book on his lap.

"No thanks. I've already read it."

"You didn't like it?"

"Not really."

"I would ask why, but then that's probably a longer conversation than what you came in here looking for," he replied.

She stared at her father, at the gray in his curly hair, at his tired but lively eyes. "Daddy, how do you know when you love someone? Like really love them?" she asked.

He leaned forward and stroked the beard stubble on his chin. "That's a hard question. You just know. It's almost like a feeling you can't explain or define. But this feeling, it shows you what you always were and all that you can be. Why do you ask? I'm sure you're not just suddenly curious. Who's the lucky guy?"

"No one. I was just wondering."

"Well, I don't believe you. But that's fine," smiled Anthony. "Whoever he is, tell him. People like to know that they're loved."

"Yeah." Her eyes fell on the framed picture on the nightstand, a picture of her mother and father, sitting on the beach and hugging.

"You take any good pictures?" asked Anthony, reaching for the camera that she had laid next to her on the bed. "We can develop them this weekend, if you want."

She reached for the camera before he could grab it. "I didn't take anything worth developing. Do you think we can go to the lake this weekend? I wanna take some more pictures down there."

"Sure. Of course." He smiled warmly.

They sat in silence until she said, "Okay." Without another word, she went to her room, shut the door and lay back on the bed. As she lay there, she stared up at the ceiling and imagined the smell of purple flowers and Amma whispering in her ear.

***

Landrien shuffled through the folders on her desk as she searched for the most recent letter from the defendants' counsel in the Muscatine Manufacturing case. When she finally located the folder containing the letter, she sighed and cursed herself for not having scanned the document into an electronic file the moment it had arrived a week earlier. Yawning, she read the letter and every now and then glanced out the window at the falling snow. When she realized she was barely awake and had read the same sentence at least fifteen times, she gathered her purse along with the folder containing the letter and left her office.

"Here's the letter from a couple of weeks ago." She dropped the folder onto Jordan's desk. "Get the UPenn intern, Portia, to scan it and upload it to the client's file. Make sure she knows that everything we receive regarding a client should be scanned and uploaded as soon as it's received."

"Sure. By the way, I talked to our lovely client today," added Jordan. "She said she'd be willing to hunt around for more potential witnesses. People who worked on her shift, who were familiar with her work."

"Did you tell Jennifer it'd be good if we heard from her or could get in touch with her more than once every couple of months?" she asked, and Jordan simply shook his head in exasperation. "I'm going on a Dunkin Donuts coffee run. You want anything?"

"A glazed donut and a small coffee with cream, if you don't mind," he requested, eyeing her over his eyeglasses and flashing a smile. She told him she would be back shortly and headed toward the elevator.

Landrien slipped her hands inside a pair of leather gloves while she stood in front of the elevator. Just as she stepped inside the elevator, the executive director hurried inside and greeted her.

"How's it going, Sam?" She looked up at the tall, white-haired woman. Samantha Zinn was a striking woman. Despite being almost sixty years old, Samantha had never lost her figure, and she wore pencil skirts and red pumps regularly, even on colder days. She claimed that in Vermont, her home state, winter was not winter without a brisk cold spell and "southerners"—her umbrella term for everyone south of Maine and Vermont—were wimps about cold weather. Her disarming height and directness seemed matched only by her huge blue eyes, so bright and youthful as though they should have belonged to someone half her age.

"Oh, I'm doing all right, for a Monday," replied Samantha. "I'm glad I ran into you. Can you set up a time to meet with me during the next two weeks? You know Mary Ann is getting ready to retire in your unit. We need a diverse voice leading your unit. I was hoping you'd be interested in taking her place."

Landrien choked on her own spit and for an embarrassing moment actually struggled to breathe. The cell phone vibrated in her hand, and she fumbled around to silence it. "You want me take over Mary Ann's position?" she asked. "As Senior Attorney?"

Samantha nodded, and the door opened onto the second floor. "Think about it and email me with a few available meeting times," she said just before she exited the elevator.

The door closed, leaving Landrien in the heavy silence of her own disbelief.

***

At home that evening, Landrien continued reorganizing the house. Perhaps it was the fact that she had just learned she might be promoted, but she suddenly felt full of energy. Humming to this happy thought, she gathered a towel and a bucket from under the sink in the bathroom between the basement door and the staircase. She went to the laundry room in the basement and filled a bucket with bleach and hot water. Still humming and smiling, she put on a pair of rubber gloves and returned to the foot of the staircase.

As she got to her knees and scrubbed the dark circular stain on the wall at the foot of the staircase where her mother's body had lain, she stopped humming and fell silent. She wiped and wiped until the stain began to fade.

Next, Landrien went up to her parents' room and looked around at the large dusty space. It contained a king-sized high bed, a dresser, a few bookcases and her father's old yellow chair. She scanned the room, trying to decide what to move and throw away. In the room closet nearest the doorway, there was a shelf full of her mother's cookbooks. She counted at least two dozen cookbooks. She drifted to the center of the room, lay flat against the floor and searched underneath the bed. Large balls of dust had gathered under there, and she covered her nose to avoid breathing in any of it. She extended her arm as far as she could under the bed, and her fingertips brushed against a large square-shaped object. As she pressed her shoulder against the bed, she reached forward, managing to grasp the object and slide it toward her. It was a photo album.

She wiped off the thick film of dust, coughing as she inhaled a little and opened the photo album to the first page. It read, "Arkansas: 1975 through 1976." *Arkansas?* She hardly could point Arkansas out on a map, let alone imagine why her mother would have a photo album about

Arkansas. Landrien turned the book over in her hand, searching for other inscriptions. There were no words or pictures on the backside.

She got up, turned out the light and went to her bedroom, where she threw the photo album on top of the box of diaries in the closet. Just as she turned to exit the room, her gaze drifted to the windowsill, where the locket lay. She picked it up and reread the inscription: "Love Always, Bell." She said the words aloud a few times, as if doing so would trigger a recollection or a memory that would clarify the locket's origins. Not surprisingly, this was an exercise in futility. Landrien slid the necklace inside her pants pocket and went downstairs to put on a pot of coffee.

When the doorbell sounded an hour later, she hurried to the door and peeped behind the curtains. Jordan stood on the other side, covered in snow. He rushed inside and a powerful gust of wind and snow whipped at her face. It took a good deal of her strength to push the door shut. Jordan shook off and shivered, a puddle of melting snow dripping from his booted feet.

"It's a crazy world out there." She took his coat when he stood up and hung it next to the gas fireplace she had turned on earlier.

"You want some coffee? I made a fresh pot."

He was still standing at the front door, surveying the room. "This late in the evening? Is it decaffeinated?"

She smiled at him incredulously.

"Right. Of course it's not," he said, brushing snow from his hair. "I'll take a cup." He kissed her cheek before she scurried off to the kitchen. "This place isn't what I expected."

"What do you mean?" called Landrien, from the kitchen.

He gazed around the living room. "I don't know. It's so suburban and all-American, like the Brady Bunch house."

"We were far from the Brady Bunch," said Landrien, returning with two mugs of coffee.

While he sat down on the recliner chair and enjoyed his coffee, she took his small duffle bag and deposited it in her bedroom closet. When she returned to the living room, she found him standing at the fireplace, examining her family photographs. "I know I've said it before, but as far as physical appearances go, you and your brother are polar opposites."

Standing at his side, she saw that the photograph of their HersheyPark vacation had captured his attention. In the photograph, Landrien and Darren stood side by side. They were flanked by their mother on Darren's side and their father on Landrien's side, only a blue sky and parking lot in the background. Everyone except their mother flashed big, toothy smiles.

"I swear you two look like you shouldn't even be related."

"Well, Darren definitely managed to get the million dollar smile (from god knows who). Maybe Mom had an affair," she laughed. "Anyway, I managed to get the..." She looked at her parents' faces.

"Mysterious eyes. Every bit as mysterious as your mother's," Jordan noted, turning and staring at her. "You look just like her, you know, expressions and all."

"Speaking of my mother, why don't you help me pack up her room?" asked Landrien, taking the empty coffee mug from his hand and placing it on the fireplace mantle.

"What're you going to do with her stuff?" He followed her as she walked across the room and towards the stairs.

"She left the furniture to Darren. Whatever he doesn't take, I'm dropping at Goodwill."

"You're not going to keep any of it?" Jordan gawked at her.

"Nope. Do me a favor. Go look in my bedroom closet and bring me a couple of empty boxes." She pointed toward a room on the right as they reached the top of the staircase.

As Jordan entered the bare room, he looked around at the white walls and the small bed pushed against the wall. He opened the closet that was mostly empty but for his bag, a backpack, purse, two large suitcases and a couple of boxes.

Boxes in hand, he turned to leave the room when something buzzed. He spotted her cell phone vibrating on the nightstand and caught the phone before it hit the floor. It vibrated once more and showed a text message from Elena Pierce, a name that sounded familiar to him. The locked screen displayed a thread of messages. He typed in her password and after a few more moments of hesitation, opened the new message.

"You find the boxes?" Landrien called from the other room.

"Yeah. Hold on. I gotta pee." He went to the bathroom, where he closed and locked both of the doors. He pulled up the entire message thread, sat down on the toilet and read each of the messages.

2:15PM - ELENA

So, I've been thinking about our night together last week. And I guess I've realized that I miss you. I miss us. Maybe that makes me pathetic. But I don't know if I'm okay with us being together but not 'being together.' What do you think?

2:18PM - ME
It felt like old times, didn't it? It scared me.

2:20PM - ELENA
Scared you? Why? And, yes, it did feel like old times.

2:22PM - ME
Because it's not old times. There's a lot of new shit going on in my life right now. Can I call you this evening?

2:24PM - ELENA
Sure. Call me later.

2:26PM - ME
I think I love you, Elena. And I don't know what to do about it.

2:40PM - ELENA
*Wow. You've never said that to me before. Is that some of the 'new shit' in your life right now? *smiling**

2:45PM - ME
Yes. Some of it.

7:31PM - ELENA
Hey, I'm free now, if you still want to talk. For the record, I've loved you since the night of that Sade concert five years ago. I can't believe it's been that long. Do you remember what you said to me that night?

7:45PM – ELENA
You said maybe your mother was right. I don't know why, but I always remembered that. What did that mean, anyway?

Before Jordan could process what he had read, he stood up and looked around the room. He paced the bathroom for a couple of minutes, turning over the name, Elena Pierce, in his mind. Why did that name sound familiar? He stopped and closed his eyes. The nurse, the woman she was with before him. He remembered.

At precisely that moment, he decided to forget, as much as he could, what he had read. Whatever it took, he would push this into the back of his mind until it was gone and forgotten. Sure, such a task was a fool's errand, but he had to try. Determined and fixated on this impossible task, Jordan finally gathered the courage to leave the bathroom.

He put the phone back on the nightstand, picked up the boxes and walked to the room two doors down the hall, where Landrien stood amid a pile of books.

"Cookbooks. I never knew anyone more obsessed with cookbooks."

"Was she a good cook?" asked Jordan, sitting the boxes down next to Landrien.

"Well, she opened a small catering business just before Dad got sick, and she continued it until her last heart attack. I guess other people thought she was a good cook."

He turned over a Cajun cookbook and read the back cover. "Hmm, some of these might be interesting," he observed.

"Help yourself. Toss whatever you don't want in a box," she instructed him as she stood up and rubbed her dust-covered hands on her robe. "When you're done, you can join me for a bath." Flashing him a flirtatious smile, she turned to leave the room. As he watched her walk away, he caught a glimpse of the engagement ring on her finger.

Landrien looked over her shoulder. It was the second time she had heard it. She rose from the sofa and went toward the enclosed back porch. Snow fell in soundless bursts against the windows, and she estimated at least ten inches had accumulated over the last twelve hours. As she walked out onto the enclosed porch, her eyes traveled from the sofa and rocking chair, to the high table off to the left side of the room. After scanning the room a second time, she sighed and switched off the light.

"Get it together, Landrien," she muttered. She locked the door, glanced at the porch a final time, then turned around and went back to the empty living room. She looked up the staircase that seemed to lead up to an impenetrable darkness, beyond which Jordan lay asleep in her bedroom, while she suffered another night of insomnia.

She wandered toward the kitchen, having decided she could use a cup of herbal tea to calm her nerves. What she saw in the next moment brought her to an abrupt stop. She was not sure she would be able to move ever again. Landrien stared at the back of a woman who was standing at the refrigerator. The woman's hair, slender black braids, flowed down her back and stopped just at her bony shoulder blades.

The woman turned around and scrutinized Landrien through large, round eyes, accented by thick, arched eyebrows. The woman drew closer, and Landrien saw that she was thin and wiry, so much that her collarbones were visible but, not so much that she appeared ill or malnourished. Her femininity seemed affected, as if every aspect of it was a performance, Landrien observed. There was something boyish about the woman's facial features and demeanor, something wild that created an ambiguity and demanded recognition. Standing there, barefoot and wearing an orange summer dress, the woman smiled. For some reason, her smile acted like a dose of serotonin, filling Landrien with an overwhelming sense of peace. There was freedom in that smile.

"Summers under the shade, in the grass, nights lying next to nothing. I thought you would've have grown tired of thinking of me. Remembering loss. That's what you were doing, right, when you wrote to me? But loss is loss. Didn't I tell you there's some things you can't retrieve?" the woman said in a soft, distant voice. Her voice sounded as if it was there but not quite, and like the smile, her voice seemed familiar to Landrien.

At this point, Landrien began to evaluate the scenario objectively. First, she noted that the woman did not speak as people normally speak to one another in day-to-day conversation. This, coupled with the fact that she had never met the woman before, confirmed that she was dreaming. Of course, she was dreaming, which was a relief, given the number of sleepless, dreamless nights she had experienced lately. This was all a bizarre dream, and any minute now, she expected to wake up, yawn and say, "Wow, that was weird" and then go about her regular day. With this comforting, logical conclusion, Landrien relaxed and listened with a faint degree of amusement as the woman continued:

"Did you get tired of remembering me, Clem?"

"No," Landrien answered through no volition of her own. In fact, she felt somewhat like a puppet, although she had no idea where the strings were and who might be pulling them. Yet, of course, this was a dream, so regular rules of free will and such did not apply. She entertained the notion that this woman was indeed a ghost, perhaps sent to deliver an important message. She had read about how spirits sometimes found their ways into peoples' dreams to deliver important messages. As she considered this, she regarded the woman with curiosity.

In the next moment, a medley of emotions—grief, regret and shame—swept over Landrien. Covering her face, she turned away, and her body grew cold and achy. She sensed that someone else was inside her, someone else's feelings and emotions, and that person dwelled in a sadness more profound than any Landrien could know or fathom. It filled her nostrils and lungs, this despair, and she would have given anything to expel it, to breathe. "Fuck," Landrien muttered, clawing at her own arms and wrists, wanting desperately to rip this person out of her.

The woman's cold hands closed around Landrien's hands.

"I'm sorry." Landrien heard her own voice as if she was eavesdropping behind a closed door.

"What's he like?" the woman asked, after a while.

Hot tears rolled down Landrien's cheeks. "You."

The woman smiled. "And the other?"

Landrien said nothing but stared at the woman.

"You need to make peace with her," she insisted, pressing her hand against Landrien's cheek.

As she leaned her head against the woman's shoulder, tears trapped inside someone else forced their way out. She closed her eyes and clutched the woman's cold body.

"Landrien?" came a drowsy male voice. "What're you doing?"

She opened her eyes, and the woman was gone.

"What're you doing?" Jordan stared at her wet face and glanced around. "It sounded like you were talking to someone. Are you crying?"

She looked around. "The woman," she said. "The woman in the orange dress. She was...did you see her?" She turned back to Jordan and wiped her eyes, unsure of why they were wet.

"What woman?"

Chuckling and feeling hysteria creep in, she dried her face with the backs of her hands. "Okay." She looked around and upward, as if for an exit. "I wanna wake up now."

Jordan put his hand on her shoulder. "Landrien, you are awake. It's four o'clock in the morning. You're standing in the kitchen, crying and apparently talking to yourself. Are you all right?"

"Four o'clock? We gotta be up for work in two hours!" she exclaimed.

"No. We're snowed in, remember? Blizzard. Total whiteout. We checked the weather before we went to bed."

"What?" New tears began to cloud her eyes.

"It's all right. You're just tired, and you miss her."

"Who?" she asked.

"Your mom."

She said in her steadiest voice, "Believe me. I do not miss her."

He sighed and shook his head. "You need to make peace with her."

"What did you just say?"

"Nothing. Let's go to bed."

"There's something going on here, in this house," she muttered to herself. *Or I'm losing my mind.*

"Let's just go back to bed, okay?" Jordan repeated. He draped his arm around her and led her away from the kitchen.

CHAPTER FIVE

When Jordan fell asleep, Landrien slipped out of bed and went downstairs. She returned to the kitchen that was lit only by the stove light, and she stared at the refrigerator where she had seen the woman in the orange dress. She closed her eyes and opened them. She did this several times and scanned the length of the kitchen. *I am not crazy.*

After she drank an entire glass of water in a couple of swallows and refilled it, she peeked through the blinds. A hill of snow, about three feet high, lay piled against the house next door, and snow continued falling. She loved snowy days, even if they left her feeling a bit achy and tired. Snowy days were so serene and peaceful, as if the world was watching in quiet awe as nature performed one of her grandest acts. It snowed every year and, every year, she appreciated it the way a child appreciates her first snow. She did not know how people lived in places like Florida that never saw snow. Or Arkansas. Did it snow in Arkansas? She placed the empty glass in the sink and went to the living room.

As she dropped down onto the sofa, she grabbed the remote control from the coffee table and turned on the television. She prepared to fumble with the antenna on top of the television, but instead the picture showed clearly. The cable company had not cancelled her mother's subscription yet. She lay back and watched as a woman with blonde weave shoved another taller woman. The women yelled at one another, and the station bleeped out every other word. Eventually, the women grabbed one another's arms and began pushing and pulling one another. *The high culture joys of reality television*, she thought, remembering why she never watched television.

After she lowered the volume, she put the remote control back on the table, stretched out on the sofa and closed her eyes.

Gradually, the night slipped into day. When she opened her eyes again, some underfed actress was on the *Today Show* discussing Hollywood, sexism and the actress's upcoming romantic comedy.

Once she started a pot of coffee, she went upstairs to her bedroom, where Jordan lay sound asleep, the blankets bunched up across his waist. She cleaned herself up, put on a pair of jeans and a sweater and returned to the kitchen. She found a mug in the top of the cabinet, a mug she had had ever since she was a teenager. Darren had bought it for her during his summer with Uncle Dan in Tampa. Uncle Dan, her father's now deceased brother, had owned a glass and pottery store, where he sold local handmade dishes, vases and jewelry. At Darren's request, Uncle Dan had made the orange mug for her fifteenth birthday and engraved on it her initials, "LBM," in blue letters.

With the mug in one hand and a broom in the other, she left the kitchen and proceeded to the basement. She flipped on the light, peered down into the dreary basement and hesitantly descended the creaky wooden stairs. The Morisets had not replaced the stairs or remodeled the basement in all the years they had owned the house. As a result, it was as uninviting a place as ever, dark, frigid and dusty, with nails jutting out from the wooden ceiling. The washer and dryer sat just behind the stairs. Along the opposite wall, her father had placed three medium-sized bookcases, all packed with books.

As she kneeled in front of the smallest bookcase, which belonged to her father, she ran her finger along the spines of some of the books. The books appeared to be in no particular order. Her mother's books, on the contrary, were in alphabetical order by the authors' last names on the larger bookcases.

Landrien scanned the rows of her father's bookcase, until her gaze landed on a slender book with a dingy red cover, *Sula*. She pulled it from the shelf, sat down on the hard floor and opened the book to the first page. At the top right corner, there was a price handwritten in pencil and smeared, $1.50. Anthony Moriset always had bought books secondhand and had been friendly with at least half of the secondhand bookstore owners from Phoenixville to Philadelphia.

"I don't know what you like about dusty old books with faded pages," Pamela had said once while the three of them perused a bookstore in West Philadelphia near the University of Pennsylvania campus.

"The same thing you like about your cooking. The smell," he had said, holding Landrien's hand. He glanced at his eight-year-old daughter and winked.

Pamela smiled. "Nothing beats the new book smell. You're just old and cheap is all."

"Well, I am an English professor, Pam. I have a sacred sworn duty to like old libraries and, as you call them, 'dusty, old books.'"

Pamela chuckled and looped her arm through his free arm. The three of them, ever the happy looking family, perused the store and nearly an hour later left with a baking book, a copy of *Sula*, and a book of landscape photographs for Landrien.

When she graduated high school, her father gave her the copy of *Sula* he had bought that day. He had read the book several times before he finally bought a newer edition. It had been his favorite novel. Landrien had read it once when she was too young to appreciate the story. She left the book, along with most other things besides her clothes and camera, when she went out of state to college. She had thought she might read it again someday, just to satisfy her father, but then days passed into months and months into years, and then her father was gone, and she never came back for the book or anything else.

So on this snowy morning, on the cold basement floor, she sat for a long while, reading page after page and sipping warm coffee. After half an hour or so, she had to admit to herself that the book was fairly interesting, if slow and lacking in action. She was not much of a literature person, but she did not find the book to be impossibly tedious. The light flickered, and she glanced up once or twice at the one bulb in the center of the room. Sore from sitting on the hard floor, she abandoned her task, marked her page with a bookmark from one of her mother's cookbooks, stood up and stretched.

"Landrien?" He stared down at her as she arrived at the foot of the stairs. She ascended while clutching the book in one hand and the empty coffee mug in the other. "How long have you been up?" he asked, running his hands through his short dark hair as she reached him.

She checked the wall clock hanging over the back porch door. It was 7:43. "A little over three and a half hours," she answered and shut the basement door.

"Wait. You got right back up after we went to bed?"

"Sort of hard to sleep in a house that's haunted," she said in a matter-of-fact tone and smiled. Jordan flashed a worried look. *The man has no sense of humor.*

He followed her to the living room where she sat on the sofa and kicked her feet up on the coffee table.

"In a house that's what?" he finally managed to say.

She stretched out on the sofa and looked up at him. "Okay, I'm half joking about the haunted part. But I know what I saw," insisted Landrien. "And I know you don't believe me. That's fine. Don't worry, I'm not losing my mind."

He rubbed the back of his head, opened his mouth to speak, but then said nothing.

"I realize you don't believe in that kind of stuff, spirit stuff, and I'm not sure if I do either. But there was a presence here last night, Jordan. I didn't dream or hallucinate what I saw. That woman was there and creepy as fuck. There's some bad energy in this house, which really is sort of a relief, come to think."

"Why is it a relief?"

"Because I'll have absolutely no guilt about selling it next year. My brother thinks it would be sort of disrespectful for me to sell our childhood home. But after last night's little encounter, there is no way I'm gonna live here beyond the one-year period Mom stated in the will. No reasonable person would." With this proclamation, she opened the book and started reading.

He stared at her, his arms folded across his chest. "You do hear how ridiculous this all sounds, right?"

She shook her head and did not look up from her book.

"You just lost your mom, Landrien. Why can't you admit that you're stressed out and grieving, that this is all just stress? It happens to everyone. I don't understand why you have to come up with some nonsense theory to explain away your grief."

She closed the book and laid it on the coffee table. "Let me make you understand then." She sat up and stared at her fiancé. "Have a seat, Jordan." Once he sat next to her, she turned to him and began: "At dinner one night, when I was fifteen, my mom looked across the table at me with tears in her eyes. She told me that while she would pray for my soul, she couldn't wait for me to leave in three years and never come back. It was my birthday. A year before that, I returned home from a Halloween party, and she grabbed me and dragged me to the bathroom upstairs. She ripped off my costume and smeared red lipstick all over my face while I screamed and cried, and she yelled that she "did not raise fools and, least of all, dykes." She pulled my hair, slapped me around. I thought she'd finally flipped out. For a while, I wondered if she might even kill me this time, until my dad heard it and stopped her.

When I graduated high school, her graduation gift to me was a one-way bus ticket to Chicago. That was her present to me. I think she really hoped I'd never come back home. Every time I called during my first year, if she answered the phone, I couldn't get out two words before she hung up. But, masochist that I am, I came back during summer breaks and worked—not because I needed the money or couldn't get a job in Chicago. Part of me wanted to be home with her, since I figured someday she would have to forgive me for whatever I'd done wrong. Maybe one summer I'd get lucky, and she would forgive me and finally be nice to me. Every summer I went back, and every time she treated me like I didn't exist. I came back during holidays, year after year. Still, she treated me like I didn't exist. I don't even know how she managed it. It must've taken real effort.

My dad died in the middle of my senior year, and I thought his death might soften her, that maybe losing him would change her. It didn't. When I graduated college that year and came back here for law school, I visited her once and found out that she'd told the neighbors I'd married some man and moved off to Arizona or somewhere. (Apparently, she later told them the truth.) She wouldn't even open the door for me when I dropped by.

I never visited her again after that, not until she got sick anyway. But I sent her birthday cards and Christmas cards every year. She never sent me a card back or called to thank me for thinking of her. Nothing. It was as though I really didn't exist. I've always wondered what she did with those cards I sent her.

Years later, after her first heart attack, I started to visit once in a while, and she grew oddly warm toward me. You know how people can get real nice and Christian-like when they realize death is around the corner. Needless to say, I knew it wasn't genuine. She would never love me. And all the fake kindness in the world couldn't make up for the way she treated me all my life, like I was some sort of freak or mistake." She stared steadily at Jordan. "Is that enough? Or would you like to hear more?"

"You never told me…"

"I never thought there was anything to tell."

"She was horrible to you. I get it," he paused. "But it doesn't mean you're not grieving her death."

With an exasperated sigh, Landrien shook her head and stood up. She grabbed the coffee mug and turned toward the kitchen. "Forget it," she said, with her back to him.

When he began to speak, she raised her hand to silence him. "Jordan. I said forget it."

His warm hands grasped her waist, and she smelled the mint toothpaste on his breath. "I'm sorry," he whispered into her ear and pressed his head against hers. She closed her eyes as he wrapped his arms around her. "I'm sorry, okay?"

She turned to him and slowly brought her hands to his cheeks. There was such adoration in his eyes, she thought, such foolish adoration. As she leaned forward, she kissed him with a softness she usually reserved for Elena. In the next moment, she put her hand behind his head, grabbed a handful of his hair and kissed him roughly. She lifted his shirt with one hand and let the other hand slide downward. "Wait, hold on." He grabbed her hands and held them in front of her.

When he released her, she stepped back a foot or two and looked at him, at the river between them. Was there this river between all people, or was there something especially wrong with her? *Am I incapable of closeness?*

"It's not that I don't want to, but it just feels weird, Landrien. You're acting strange, stranger than usual."

She fastened her robe and turned to leave the room. "I'm going down to the basement to box up Mom's books. You can join me or not."

He watched her walk away. He scanned the kitchen, his eyes traveling from the orange coffee mug with the letters, "LBM," to the coffeepot that was still half-full. "I'll finish boxing up the books in her bedroom," he called but received no reply. When he picked up the coffeepot, it quivered in his shaky hand, and he sat it down immediately. "Maybe coffee isn't such a good idea right now," he mumbled, staring at his hands. He filled a glass with water and retreated upstairs. He needed a shower.

CHAPTER SIX

Landrien and Jordan sat at the dining room table, their laptops in front of them and the sun streaming through the window. She sipped coffee from her orange mug while she read through some documents on her laptop screen.

"I'm thinking we need to contest this," she mused, running her hands through her hair and reading the document.

"Huh?" Jordan's eyes were glued to his own laptop screen.

"The authorization form that asks Jennifer to release her prior work records. Have you looked at it? Muscatine sent the form with the first set of interrogatories. It needs Jennifer's signature. From what the form says here, Muscatine wants Jennifer's prior employers to provide any records of complaints she made, and wage and salary information, so forth and so on. Which I might understand, but they didn't give a date limiting how far back they want to reach into her employment history. Did you get the intern to do some case research on this issue?"

"No to both questions. But that would be an assignment for Portia when we get back tomorrow." He glanced toward the back porch and shook his head. Outside was a white blur of snow and blizzard winds. "*If* we get back to the office any time this week. Maybe we should just email her."

"Good, yeah. We have to know what authority Muscatine is relying on for this request. I mean, it's understandable that they'd want her work records since she left Muscatine. Any complaints of discrimination she filed since then, and so forth. But before Muscatine? That's reaching, don't you think? They shouldn't be able to dig back ten or fifteen years." She skimmed the document and scribbled on her notepad.

"I can see both sides really. But, in fairness, I agree with you. I know I've seen some federal cases that fall on both sides." He removed his glasses and looked at her. "I can do a case search right now, if you want."

She thought for a moment. "No, don't worry about it. We have time. Let Portia handle it. Just go ahead and email her and ask her to draft a memo within a week. Make sure you tell her to include only federal cases from Pennsylvania, New Jersey and Delaware. Tell her not to worry about New York cases unless she sees something particularly helpful, yeah?"

Jordan nodded, his eyes glued to his computer screen while his fingers pecked away at the keyboard. The lights flickered out, flickered on and then went out. "There goes the power."

"Which reminds me, I need to get the utilities turned over to my name."

"At least I have about an hour of battery life left. What about you?"

"About ten minutes. My battery's shot to hell," she moaned, saving her document.

"Well, I'll keep at it for another half hour. Let me know if you want to use my computer."

"No, it's fine. I might as well consider this a day off." She shut down her computer, stood up and went to the basement to retrieve a lighter and candles. A sliver of light from the two small windows illuminated the dark basement. She emerged from the basement with a box of candles and matches. She placed several lit candles throughout the living room, returned to the dining room, pulled out a cigarette and leaned against the back porch doorway, where she watched the snow fall.

After she took a few drags from the cigarette, she put it out in the ashtray next to Jordan's computer, and her phone vibrated in the pocket of her robe. She retreated to the living room until she thought she was out of earshot of Jordan.

"How are you?" asked Elena.

Landrien glanced over her shoulder at Jordan in the dining room. He was hunched over his computer. "I'm fine. Snowed in, and the power just went out. You?" She headed upstairs.

"I'm fine. You didn't call me."

Landrien shut the bedroom door and pressed the hot phone against her face. "I know. I'm really sorry. It's been kind of hectic, and I got sidetracked."

"You're always sidetracked."

As she sat on the bed, she closed her eyes. Her inclination toward blunt honesty made her ill-suited for these types of emotional conversations, she had told herself. "I meant what I said in the text message." This seemed a fair place to begin.

"Sure."

"I'm serious."

"Yeah, well. You like to talk a big talk. I'm used to it."

"I'm engaged," she said, walking to the window and pushing the curtains aside. "That's what I wanted to talk to you about."

"To Jordan?" asked Elena.

"Yeah."

"I suppose you love him, right? Does he know?"

"Does he know what?"

"That you're a dyke?"

"He knows you and I were together before," Landrien replied.

"But he's tolerant of your 'past lifestyle choices,' as long as you act like a good little straight girl when you're with him. Or let him get in on the action. Am I right?"

"It's not like that with him, Elena."

"Sure it is," Elena groaned. "I think you actually like pretending and performing this stupid straight girl role. Or who knows? Maybe I'm wrong. Maybe you do like men, too, and this is just you being so typically indecisive. With you, it's hard to say which is which."

She stood at the window and stared out at the falling snow. She offered no response.

"So? Men or women, Landrien? Why is it so hard to make a choice? I mean, is it just greed or sheer confusion with you bisexuals? I'd really like to know."

There it was. The familiar insult so many past lovers had launched at Landrien from that little arsenal of prejudice they all kept locked away for special moments such as this one. Eventually, they all said it—all except for Jordan—and it soured everything before and after. Five years of friendship had boiled down to this.

"Oh right, because bisexuals are the only ones who have problems with monogamy. None of the lesbians you've dated ever had that problem," Landrien blurted out before she could stop herself.

"That's your excuse? Everyone cheats?"

"Let's get one thing straight: I didn't cheat. We aren't in a monogamous relationship, Elena. I never lied to you about Jordan. I've always been honest with you. It's just that everything has to be one way or the other with you. I'm sure you'd be tolerant of my 'past lifestyle choices' as long as I put on my wife hat and acted like a good little lesbian with you. Right? But you don't get it. I'm not like you, and you've never accepted that. I can't be the good little lesbian you'd like me to be because I've been with men, and I may be with men in the future, and I don't give a shit about all these labels you cling to for security." She sat down on the bed and ran her hands through her hair.

"Fine. So then what now?" asked Elena. "I mean, clearly, you can't be happy with just a man or just a woman."

"Really? I was happy with just you, remember? I was happy and monogamous with you for years, until I realized we'd lost something along the way."

"Lost something?"

"Yes, something was missing, something we'd had in the beginning. Maybe it was just end of the honeymoon stage. I don't know. But I never lied to you when I decided to pursue other people, Elena. I never once lied to you about that, and you said you were fine with it. But I'm starting to realize that you were never fine with having an open relationship. You wanted monogamy, a wife. That's what this is about."

Elena snorted. "I've waited so long for you to come around, for you to figure yourself out. I don't think I can do it anymore. I'm getting too old for this."

Landrien inhaled and shut her eyes. "I understand."

"Let's just give each other some space for a while. And maybe, if we can be friends, then that's what we'll be. I guess."

She looked down at the ring on her finger and marveled at how heavy it felt now. "Okay."

***

Landrien screwed the top off the black eyeliner, examined her reflection in the bathroom mirror and carefully made thin short strokes above her top lip. She repeated this around her mouth with the black eyeliner. Once she finished at her chin, she stepped back from the mirror and, with curiosity and a sense of accomplishment, surveyed her face: dark mustache and goatee, hair parted just along the left side and slicked down, small stud in her left ear. As she closed her mouth, she ground her teeth slightly to make her lips appear less perky and round. She had heard from a group of girls at school that "aggressives" or "butches" ground their teeth to make their jaw lines and mouths appear more square and masculine. The lead girl in the group, Yazmine—a freshman at the high school—was having a Halloween party and had invited Landrien. She was determined to make a good impression on Yaz's circle of friends, who inhabited a special space in Landrien's mind. Yaz's circle included five girls, who at varying times had dated one another and did not run around chasing boys. Nor did they run around trying out for the cheerleading squad or trying to be the smartest people at school. They were just cool. As far as Landrien was concerned, they were real individuals, the sort who hung out in the courtyard at lunch and talked about all kinds of things, like politics, music, books, and movies. Foremost in her mind, they were gay and proud.

After she straightened the white collar on her shirt, she grabbed the striped blue tie that was hanging on the door and attempted to tie it. Although she had watched her father do his tie many times, watching was not the same as doing. Several minutes later, she gave up and hung the tie back on the door. Perhaps the ensemble looked better without a tie anyway, she reasoned. She straightened up her pants, buckled the belt, and pulled the pants down a little bit. This party was her introduction to a new set of friends, and it was essential she did not show up looking like a geek. Sagging was cool, according to the magazines and rap videos, right? As a last touch, she put a newsboy cap on her head, turned it slightly to the side and smiled at her reflection. On impulse, she grabbed the tie from the doorknob and headed downstairs.

Her father sat on the sofa, sipping tea and writing in his journal. His blue-gray eyes widened in surprise as he stared at his fourteen-year-old daughter. She stuck her right hand inside her pants pocket and stood at the bottom of the staircase. His lips formed into a smile as he approached her, and she waited for him to say something. "Well, well, well. Don't you clean up nicely," teased Anthony, grinning as he folded his arms across his chest and took in his daughter's outfit.

She smiled uncertainly and tugged at the jeans. "It looks all right? Darren's old clothes are a bit tight-fitting."

Anthony nodded. "Looks fine. He was a smallish boy, wasn't he? Never thought he'd end up taller than me, that's for sure." Anthony took the tie she held out. He tied it and fixed her collar.

"You're gonna have to show me how to do that later. Where's Darren, anyway?"

"In the basement, doing homework. Darren," he called out.

"No, you don't have to call him," she exclaimed. Her father looked down at her and was on the verge of replying when the doorbell rang.

Sweat rolled down her underarms as she grabbed Darren's old leather jacket from the recliner chair and ran to open the door. "Hey you," said Amma Shepherd, smiling. In a daze, Landrien sized up Amma's costume: black afro wig, teal pea coat, tight blue jean bell bottoms that left little to the imagination, shiny red heels, and huge dangling earrings.

"You ready?"

"Uh, yeah. Okay." Landrien nodded.

"What's up, Dad? Did you just call me?" asked Darren, before Landrien could shut the door. She turned around to her brother, who had a pencil behind his right ear, but he looked past her.

"You didn't have to come up. I was just asking Daddy where you were." The cold air from the door hit her neck, and she glanced at Amma, who smiled. "I didn't want to go to Yaz's party by myself, so Amma said she'd come with me."

"I'll have her back at a decent hour, Mr. Moriset. I promise." Amma smiled some more.

"Before midnight, all right?" Anthony's attempt at sternness was undermined by the amused smirk that curled his lips.

"No problem, sir." Amma pulled Landrien out the door.

Before the door closed, Landrien saw Darren frown and turn away. "He's gonna hate me." They turned the corner, toward Yaz's house just a few blocks away.

"Darren? Nonsense. He's too sweet to hate anybody," Amma reassured her, as if that resolved the problem. "Besides, he's your brother. He'll get over this."

"But you two..."

"Are exes. Anyway. You're a stud. I always knew you'd look hot as a dude." She squeezed Landrien's hand

and kissed it. For the next two blocks, Landrien walked with a strut.

They reached Yaz's house, a small one-story brown-brick house with an overly manicured lawn. "Let's get this over with, so we can enjoy the party, yeah?" Amma stopped abruptly. Before a confused Landrien could respond, Amma leaned forward and kissed her.

After what felt like several long, blissful days, she opened her eyes and stared at Amma. Neither said a word because, frankly, there was nothing to say. Amma grinned, took Landrien's hand, and they walked up to Yaz's porch, where the soft sound of pop music spilled out into the quiet night. For the rest of the evening, her thoughts lingered on the taste of Amma's watermelon lip-gloss.

"Hey, look at this," said Jordan, sitting amid a stack of cookbooks. Landrien was removing pictures from the wall in her mother's room, while Jordan continued sifting through cookbooks and commenting on recipes. He approached her and held out a small, faded piece of white notebook paper, folded in thirds. "Is it something you wrote to your mom a long time ago? It has your name at the bottom."

She opened the paper and examined the cursive writing. Most of the writing was faded and illegible, but she could make out the first line: "To Clem." The letter was signed, Bell. "It's not my handwriting. And I don't know anybody named Clem," she mused, remembering her exchange with the woman in the orange dress.

"Are there any other Bells in your family besides you? Maybe somebody you're named after?"

"She wrote it," Landrien muttered to herself, and she went to the window to get a better look at the letter. She held the letter to the light of the window and inspected it, trying to decipher the faded words written in pencil. "Her name must have been Bell."

"Uh, what are you talking about?"

She turned to him and held up the letter. "The woman I saw in the kitchen, she wrote this letter. She called me Clem. This is proof. Proof that I'm not crazy, Jordan. I remember the entire conversation in the kitchen. I need to call Marie." She paced the room.

"Who's Marie?"

"My mother's sister and my only family besides Darren."

"Only?"

"My dad's parents were racist pricks. They never wanted anything to do with us. We're the black sheep of his family, literally. And his only sibling, a much older brother named Dan, died ten years ago. Dan was always nice to us, spent holidays with us during which he usually introduced his new fiancé. Uncle Dan must have had a dozen fiancés. He married once, divorced within a year, and never married again." She paused. "Anyway, who the hell is Clem and Bell? That's what I want to know."

He watched her pace back and forth. "Landrien. Stop," pled Jordan as he grabbed her to make her stand still. "About this woman in the kitchen, I thought we agreed that you were hallucinating or something. You're not still on the whole haunted house theory, are you?"

"You bet I'm still on the 'whole haunted house' theory as you call it. What book did you find it in, anyway?"

He glanced at the pile of books. "Cajun Kitchen."

"That was Mom's favorite cookbook. That and the old faded one with the scribbles in it." She pointed to the faded brown notebook lying next to the pile.

Jordan sighed and sat down on the bed. "Landrien, this isn't healthy. I know you're tired of me saying it, but this is grief talking, and for whatever reason you refuse to admit that."

Her eyes narrowed on him now. "I'm done explaining to you how much I do not miss that woman. Apparently, nothing will make you believe me. So if you want to continue to psychoanalyze me, fine. But keep it to yourself." She stuffed the letter inside her pocket and left the room.

Landrien lay next to Jordan that night and stared upward at nothing in particular. Jordan's heavy arm lay across her chest, and she appreciated its warmth. The utility had not restored electricity in the neighborhood and, as a result, the temperature inside the house had dropped steadily throughout the night. They had buried themselves under two quilts and a blanket, their bodies pressed against one another to keep warm. Yet again, sleep evaded her. Pushing Jordan's arm aside, she sat up and stared out the window.

"You all right?" He turned over and rubbed his face.

"Yeah," she replied as she got up and walked to the window. She looked out at the backyard, at the canopy covered in snow. The snow fell lightly now, and she hoped that meant it would stop by morning so, perhaps, the utility would be able to restore electricity. The end of the snow meant the beginning of several days of unrelenting cold.

While these mundane thoughts flitted around her mind, her eyes drifted down to the locket lying on the windowsill.

"Clem?" A hand touched the middle of Landrien's back, and the woman said, "Come on."

She turned to the woman whose familiar eyes and face appeared strangely bright and visible in the dark room. She wore the same orange dress and the same inscrutable expression. This was Bell, she now understood with absolute certainty. She did not stop to consider what made her so certain.

Bell sat on the bed and regarded her. She did not blink once, as though she had no need for such an activity. For seemingly no reason at all, she suddenly smiled and revealed the biggest, whitest smile Landrien had ever seen.

From somewhere outside and separate from her own body, she watched herself draw closer to Bell, whose body radiated warmth and heat in the frigid room. *Why doesn't Jordan wake up and stop this?* But there was only her and Bell in the room, and this weird shit was happening for real, she realized. It was going to get even weirder, she tried to warn herself as she watched herself close the space between her body and Bell's, as she leaned forward and brushed her lips against Bell's mouth, forehead and neck. Peace and warmth resided in Bell's touch, peace and warmth that Landrien had known long ago, only once in her life. She laid her head against Bell's chest, and the two women were still and quiet for a while.

For the first time, she hoped Jordan was right about this all being a hallucination or a dream, although that would mean she had been overpaying her useless therapist for the last couple of years.

"You left me," Landrien heard herself say.

Unsure of what was happening and why, Landrien rose and felt her legs carry her out of the room. She drifted down the pitch black hallway, toward a sliver of light coming from Darren's room. She paused at the doorway of his room, her chest heaving in and out, and then walked inside. For some reason, anger began to flood and overcome Landrien as she looked around the room.

Filled with incomprehensible rage, Landrien swept her hands across Darren's bookshelf, upsetting books, candles, framed pictures and trophies. All of it crashed to the hardwood floor, an awful noise of banging and breaking. Her arms swept across the top of the dresser, and everything went falling to the floor. Pictures and trophies shattered and flew in every direction. Landrien ripped the covers from the bed and cast them to the floor. The sheets came next and then the pillows.

All the while, Bell stood in the doorway of Darren's room and watched Landrien with rapt attention and an expression that seemed to say, "Carry on."

At last, Landrien crumpled onto the floor at the foot of the bed and sobbed. "I lost everything I was." She lay against the bed and cried. After a few moments of hesitation, Jordan touched her shoulder, and she looked up blurrily at his frightened face. Her blurry gaze scanned the room and stopped at the doorway. The woman in the orange dress was gone.

"Oh my God." Wiping her face with the back of her hands, she looked around at the damage.

Jordan extended his hand to help her up, and her shirt snagged on the bed as she rose to her feet. When she tugged and pulled it out, she caught a glimpse of a white piece of paper lying on the floor at the edge of the bed. She picked up the piece of paper, and by the sliver of light from the window, saw that it was a photograph.

She let go of Jordan's hand and rushed to the window, where she held the picture up but still could not make out the image. She scanned the floor of the room for a flashlight—the one she had left there earlier when the power went out. She dropped to her knees and felt around on the floor, hoping not to cut herself on a piece of broken glass.

"Landrien?"

She ignored him and crawled around in search of the flashlight, until her hand finally bumped against it next to the closet door. The batteries had come out when it hit the floor earlier, but to her relief, the two batteries lay no more than a foot away from the closet door. Slowly, she got to her feet and held the light up to the photograph. The photograph showed a small house and a skinny, brown woman in an orange dress standing in the front yard.

CHAPTER SEVEN

Landrien lounged on the enclosed back porch the next morning and examined the photograph. The small wooden house appeared to be in the middle of nowhere. Only a field lay behind it. In front of the house, there stood a tall, slender woman who wore a pastel orange sundress with spaghetti straps and a V-neck that dipped low. Skinny braids fell down to her shoulders and brushed her collarbones. Everything on the woman's brown face was prominent: large, round eyes and lips, a modestly long nose, and a forehead that seemed to want all of the attention. The woman did not smile, nor did she frown. Rather, she regarded the viewer with a proud and self-satisfied expression, both hands on her hips. As far as Landrien was concerned, the woman was nothing short of stunning, but that was beside the point. The woman was Bell, she concluded. Yet one essential question lingered: "Who the hell *is* Bell?" Landrien muttered.

"Huh?" asked Jordan.

"Nothing."

He sat in the dimly lit dining room and worked from his computer. The utility company had restored power that morning. "Hmm. I don't think we're getting out of here for another day at least. Roads are closed all over from here to the city."

"Wonderful," she groaned, dreading another day cooped up in the house. She studied the photograph for a moment longer but then slipped it inside the pocket of her robe, stood up and walked into the dining room. "I'm going to go clean up the mess I made in Darren's room. Let me know if you get a response back from Larry about the work records, all right?" She ran her hand through Jordan's hair as she walked past him.

"For sure." He watched her walk away and silently cursed himself for missing his opportunity to broach the topic of last night's events. From what he could tell, she had no intention of discussing the theatrics of the past night. "Can we talk when you're finished?" he called, once she was out of sight.

"Okay," she said, climbing the stairs.

"Good. I'll get breakfast started."

She reached the top of the stairs and hollered back, "Thanks." Surveying the wreckage in Darren's room, she took a deep breath and went to work, starting with the bed. She picked the blanket and sheets up off the floor and remade the bed, careful to pull out all the wrinkles as her mother always had done. She folded the blanket and sheets back, fluffed the two red pillows and placed them at the head of the bed.

Afterward, she got on her knees and gathered all of the loose papers, books and unbroken trophies that had fallen to the floor. She placed them back on the bookshelf and dresser. After she gathered the broken trophy parts and pulled photographs from shattered glass frames, she placed the photographs and the broken trophies in a box and pushed the box inside the closet. Finally, she swept up the glass and remaining debris, opened the curtains and looked around the room.

The room looked quite different from what Darren's room had been like when they were young. Back then, he usually had notebooks and clothes strewn about the room, and she could not recall ever finding his bed made. His room always had appeared to her a space of sheer chaos. The absence of such chaos altered the entire aura of the room, but she supposed that other than that, many things about it were the same as when they were young. All of the same posters remained on the walls: posters of basketball players like Michael Jordan and Scottie Pippen, and Darren's favorite rappers, as well as one poster of a scantily-clothed Janet Jackson. It was a boy's room, through and through.

On her way out of the room, a photograph of Amma Shepherd caught her attention. The framed photograph was lying on the dresser, surprisingly not one of last night's broken victims. In the photograph, Amma had closed her eyes and was holding a purple flower to her nose. The background of the photograph was a greenish blur, bringing Amma and the flower into hard focus. Landrien wondered how and when Darren had obtained this photograph, one of the first photographs she had taken of Amma and one that she had given Amma on the night of Yaz's Halloween party during ninth grade. Perhaps Amma had given the photograph to Darren later, a thought that suddenly bothered her.

She pocketed the photograph and headed toward the basement to search for the other photographs she had taken of Amma. Just as she walked past Jordan and reached the basement door, however, the doorbell rang.

"I'll get it." Jordan rose from the dining room table and hurried toward the front door. She sensed that he was bored and experiencing a bit of cabin fever.

"Hello," said a familiar cheerful voice. "I'm Rona from next door. Is Landrien Moriset home?"

Jordan stepped aside. "Yes. Come in."

Landrien closed the door to the basement, buried her hands inside her robe pockets, and walked to the living room. Rona, whose face brightened into a sympathetic smile when she saw Landrien, was wearing the same ankle-length quilted purple coat and matching knitted scarf and cap. She was covered in snow. When she removed the cap, she revealed a thick head of dark hair pulled back into a ponytail that hung just past her neck.

"My goodness. I didn't see it before, but you look just like Pam," she exclaimed, walking toward Landrien as Jordan shut the door. "I'm sure you hear that all the time. You're the spitting image of her."

"How can I help you, Mrs. Rona?" The woman's smile faltered at the coolness of Landrien's tone. Jordan, who stood a few feet behind Rona, stared at Landrien disapprovingly.

"Would you like some coffee, ma'am?" he asked, stepping forward.

Rona turned to him, as if startled, but smiled. "Sure, honey. Thank you."

"This is Jordan Sheehan, my fiancé."

Rona winked at her, clearly pleased with her taste in men, as Jordan extended his hand.

"I'll go start a pot," said Jordan, taking charge of the situation and ushering the women into the dining room. "Landrien, you can clear the table. Do you take sugar or cream in your coffee, ma'am?"

"Both, thank you. Oh, and, uh, where are you from, honey? No one calls me ma'am but my nephews down in Georgia."

He flushed and his already pink cheeks turned pinker. "I grew up in Georgia, just outside Atlanta."

"Well, just like I tell my nephews, I'm not that old yet. So, it's just Rona for now. All right?"

He chuckled and flushed some more. When Landrien caught his eyes, he held her gaze for a moment, as if to communicate to her, "Be nice." Quickly, he returned his attention to Rona. "Sure thing, Rona." With that, he disappeared into the kitchen.

Rona and Landrien sat across from one another at the dining room table while they waited for Jordan to return with their coffee. "So, thank goodness the power's back on, right?"

"Right."

"How're you holding up, honey?"

"Fine," Landrien answered.

Rona looked closely at Landrien. "The last conversation I had with Pam, we were sitting at this table, having tea. We had tea during the afternoons a few times a week, and your mother, boy could she talk. Pam had so many stories."

"I bet," Landrien said in a low voice, but Rona did not notice.

"During our last conversation—"

"Hmm. That smells good." Landrien leaned forward and inhaled the aroma of the coffee as Jordan put the mugs on the table. "I'm a snob about certain roasts. Jordan likes his coffee weak. I'm more into strong, robust blends, myself."

Jordan brought Landrien's orange LBM mug to his lips and sipped the steaming coffee. Landrien's eyes followed the movement as he lifted it, sipped and sat the mug on the table, his hand still clutching the handle. She would need to set some ground rules about her mug.

"What's that you were saying, Rona," he cleared his throat, "about a conversation?"

"Huh? Oh. Well, the last time me and Pam sat down to tea at this table, we talked about our marriages. That's what we usually talked about, when we weren't talking about food and recipes anyhow. She even let me help out once in a while with her catering and everything. She was a wonder in the kitchen. But, anyway, she was awful quiet the last time we talked. She asked me if I had loved my husband, 'madly loved him' were her words, if I remember right. And I said, well you can't get much madder in love with a man than I was with my Gerard. You know, when I think about what me and Gerard had, and I see these young folks who think they aren't lucky enough to find that and so they settle, it really breaks my heart. It does. Never settle, I always said, and I'll keep on saying it.

Anyway, I asked Pam if she had loved her husband that way, too. She said she had, of course. But then, the strangest thing—she looked so sad all of a sudden after she said it. It confused me at first but then I figured it was probably just a rough topic for her because he was no longer around, and she didn't really have anybody else. So, I said something like, 'you can't change it. It's out of your hands.' I know the feeling, the guilt a person feels when they lose somebody so close. It was Pam who helped me through that guilt." Rona stopped and looked down at her coffee, before she continued more dramatically. "But Pam looked at me when I said that. She looked at me with a sort of pain, a hurt deeper than anything I'd known. And she cried. Right then and there. She just put her hands over her face, and she cried. I had never seen her cry before that day, never, not even a tear. You can imagine how startled I was. I didn't know what to say, quite honestly. So, I did the only thing I could think to do. I went over to her, and I just held her in my arms. She cried for what seemed like forever, big body-wracking cries from deep inside the soul. She was so broken. That was the last time I saw or talked to Pam, a couple of days before she passed on."

Rona talked nonstop, so much that Landrien wondered when the woman would stop to take a breath. She had met few people who talked as much as Rona.

Rona stared down at her cup and appeared to be on the verge of tears, Landrien observed. Jordan reached across the table and put his hand on top of her hand, and she looked up, her gray-green eyes clouded in tears that threatened to rain down her cheeks. Distracted, Landrien stuffed her hands inside her robe pockets while she listened to the sound of the snowplow beyond the front room window. Her hand brushed the photograph in her right pocket, and a thought struck her.

"Rona, did my mom ever mention someone named Bell?"

"She mumbled that name a few times when she cried that day, when I was holding her. I assumed she was referring to you. She called you Bell, right?"

"Yeah, sometimes. It's my middle name. So, she never mentioned a woman named Bell to you?"

Jordan stirred nervously in his seat, but Landrien ignored him and watched Rona.

"No. Not that I remember."

Landrien leaned forward. "Are you sure?"

"Yeah. I'm pretty sure." Rona nodded.

"So, thinking back to all the times she ever mentioned the name Bell, even if you assumed she was talking about me, is it possible any of those times she could've been talking about somebody else?"

Rona thought for a moment and shook her head. "I don't think so. I-honestly, I wouldn't remember one way or another. I always assumed—"

"You assumed she was talking about me." She slumped back in her chair and took a sip of her coffee. "I was just curious."

Jordan stood up. "Would you like more coffee, Rona?"

"Sure," said Rona, handing him her mug.

He refilled his and Rona's mugs, returned to the dining room, and for the next half hour the three of them talked about the weather, the utility company's exorbitant rates, marriage and home decorating. Landrien tried, to no avail, to keep the conversation away from her mother. Once Jordan and Rona started discussing cookbooks and recipes, the conversation inevitably drifted back to Pam. At this point, Landrien gave up and listened while they talked. When they finally walked Rona to the front door, she turned to them just as she was about to step onto the porch.

"It was lovely to meet you, Jordan," she beamed. She leaned in to Landrien. "You'd be wise to keep this one." Landrien blushed as the woman winked at her. "You two have a good day and pop over if you need anything, you hear?" With a final nod, Rona walked out onto the snowy porch.

In the dim light of the basement, Landrien sat atop the dryer and stared at the photograph of Amma. When she was a teenager, she had kept all of the photographs she had printed. Some were photographs of Amma, while others were of the parks or random people she had met during the infrequent family trips to the shore. She had kept all the photographs inside a shoebox under her bed. On prom night when she was sixteen, she wrapped the box of photographs in bright green wrapping paper, attached a note and gave it to Amma. She stared at the box now so many years later. It was still wrapped in bright green paper, now covered in dust. She had never opened the box after prom night, a night she remembered as vividly as if it had happened yesterday.

Dressed in a strapless sparkling blue dress that stopped at her knees, Amma sat on Landrien's bed that night and silently read the note attached to the box. One by one, Amma pulled out the photographs and admired them while Landrien stood near the window and watched. She watched Amma smile at some of the photographs and peer thoughtfully at some of the others. She watched her run her hand across her puffy hair she had teased up and adorned with a large sunflower. A slender silver bracelet dangled around Amma's wrist.

When Amma finished going through the photographs, she placed them inside the box, replaced the lid and slipped the note inside her silver sequined purse. She turned to Landrien, who stood with her hands at her sides and tugged at her pants, wondering why she had chosen to wear one of her brother's suits to Amma's senior prom. The pants were surprisingly snug in the crotch area. A dress would have been more comfortable.

With watery eyes, Amma put her arms around Landrien and kissed her but then refused to keep the gift.

"No, they're yours. I'll take plenty more photographs," insisted Landrien.

"I appreciate the thought. But I think you should keep them." Sad brown eyes, outlined with heavy black eyeliner, stared out from Amma's painted face.

After a while of standing there in silence, Amma pasted on a cheerful smile and suggested that they head to prom. "It's one thing to be fashionably late and another to be on 'cp' time," Amma joked. They hurried downstairs and rushed out the front door before Landrien's mother heard them. They took off in the station wagon Amma's parents had let her borrow for the evening.

As she sat on the cold basement floor decades later, she studied the photograph of Amma, the first photograph she had taken of Amma years before that prom night. She began to replay every conversation and detail of prom night, thinking perhaps she might spot the sign she had missed that night.

Her eyes lingered on the pink nail polish of Amma's short nails, the small black mole just below her pinky finger, the dark curls tucked behind her ears. She marveled at how carelessly Amma held the flower in her right hand, and how she was looking at something to the left and just outside the frame. She was looking at Darren, who had been sitting to her left outside the frame. Looking at him seemed to please her.

Landrien held the photograph closer to the flickering light bulb that hung about a foot above her head from the low-hanging ceiling of nails and screws.

"Hey, Landrien?"

"Yeah?"

He descended the creaky wooden stairs that threatened to collapse with every step he took. He looked around the dim room, until his eyes found her. "What're you up to?"

She replaced the shoebox lid and stood up, Jordan extending his hand to help her to her feet. "Nothing. I was going through some old stuff."

Jordan nodded at the photograph she was holding at her side. "What's that?"

She looked at it for a moment and then handed the photograph to him. "Just an old picture," she explained as he brought the photograph up to the light bulb.

"It's beautiful, especially the colors and the way the background is sort of blurred to bring the girl into focus."

"Thanks."

He ogled her in surprise. "Did you take this?" he asked, and she nodded. "Wow. Is this the only one?"

She shook her head as he handed the photograph back to her. She picked up the shoebox, and Jordan came forward and looked down at the box. "We developed and processed them down here."

"We?"

"Me and my dad. When he realized I liked photography, he bought a few books and taught himself how to develop and process photographs. He set up the tables and trays over there, so I could have a dark room." She pointed toward the area under the stairs. "Then, he showed me how to develop them, how to remove a film canister in a pitch black room, how to mix the chemicals, the whole deal. I hated the smell of the chemicals."

He watched her gaze drift toward the space under the stairs as she spoke, and she smiled.

"Who's the girl?"

"Amma." She looked at him rather than at the photograph. "Amma Carina Shepherd, one of Darren's ex-girlfriends. We were friends."

He examined another photograph. "She looks like she should've been a model or a movie star. Where is she now? Are y'all still in touch?"

Her eyes lingered on the area under the stairs. The tables where they had kept the processing chemicals were not there. She wondered when her mother had gotten rid of that table and the other darkroom equipment. "She's dead."

Jordan looked up at her and said what most people say at such moments because it seems like the only sensible response. "I'm sorry."

She stuck the photograph in the shoebox and replaced the lid.

"Do you mind if I ask how?"

She clutched the shoebox and proceeded toward the stairs. "I do, actually. I'm going to take this upstairs to Darren's room. I'm sure he would like to see some of these old pictures."

"Hey," Jordan added. "I think you oughta read your mom's diaries. Or, at least, go through the photo album you found. She left them to you for a reason."

"I'm not interested in her diaries or the reason she left them to me."

"But you're interested in the woman you keep seeing in your dreams, aren't you?" he asked. "This woman you call Bell? She's a big mystery that's bothering you right now and, I'm just trying to say I think the answer's in the diaries."

"They aren't dreams. And why do you think the answer is in the diaries?"

For a while, he stared at his hands, as if he was trying to decide whether to say anything more. "Because I read one of the diaries," he confessed.

Halfway up the stairs, she stopped and turned to him. He had not moved from where they had been standing a minute ago, next to the washer and dryer. "You what?"

"After Rona left, I got to thinking about the questions you asked her. And I got this thought that maybe the diaries might—you know—give some clues. So, I went upstairs to your closet and pulled out one of the diaries, and I just opened it and started reading. I only read one entry."

"You had no right."

"I know. I'm sorry. I just think she left you those diaries and this house for a reason, Landrien."

Without a word, she walked up the stairs and left him standing alone in the empty basement. Jordan sighed. Sometimes, he was not sure it was worth it. Was there no way he could get through this woman's walls?

He pulled the string to turn off the light. In the darkness, he stood for a moment and then walked up the stairs into the light of the dining room.

Landrien and Jordan sat on the sofa and watched the local news. The forecaster announced that the snow would let up during the evening and that snowplows would be out in full force trying to clear the main roads. "Thank goodness," Jordan mumbled, and Landrien nodded.

Afterward, Jordan cooked stir-fried snap beans and spicy rice, and they ate in the dining room in silence. He cast eager glances at her now and then, and she avoided his eyes whenever she caught him looking at her. Part of her hoped the roads would be clear tomorrow so that he could return to her apartment and she could be alone for a change. The other part of her was terrified of being alone in the creepy old house, so far away.

She joined him in the kitchen, where he washed the dishes, and she cleaned the cabinets and stove. They did not say a word to one another the entire time, although Jordan grunted now and then, and she rolled her eyes. When he finished washing the dishes, he folded the flower-patterned towel and hung it on the faucet. He leaned against the counter and watched her as she finished wiping the stove.

She glanced at him, laid the sponge on the back of the sink, and walked right past him without speaking.

They lay in bed sometime later, the light from the bathroom shining dimly into the bedroom. She lay on her side with her back to Jordan, while he faced her. His eyes studied her bare back, the curve of her thin shoulders, and the dark coils of hair low on her neck.

"Landrien, are you asleep?"

"No," she said, gazing out the window. The curtains were open, and she could see only snow beyond.

"I know you don't think I understand, but I do. I mean, I know how you must feel right now."

Yawning, she asked, "You know how I feel about what?"

"About your mother, about this house. For me, it was my dad. When he drank, he was an asshole, an even bigger asshole than usual. Fortunately, he didn't drink too often. But one day he had been sitting on the porch, drinking and listening to music. I was in the living room with a friend from school, a girl named Nathalie. She and I were sitting on the couch and watching a movie on tape. You remember that movie *Harold and Maude*? Nathalie had said it was one of her favorites. So I'd gone out and rented it and invited her to watch it with me, trying to impress her. I'd never expected her to accept my invitation, though. A few days later, I found out that she'd just broken up with her boyfriend and was on the rebound.

Anyway, while we were watching the movie, Dad came in and sat in his recliner chair next to me and Nathalie. He was drunk to the point of belligerence. I could see it all over his face, and I could definitely smell it on him. I knew what was about to happen, and I knew I couldn't do a damn thing to stop it. All I could do was sit there next to Nathalie and hope he'd fall asleep or just go back out to the porch.

Then, the thing I dreaded happened: the drunken, belligerent outpouring of hatefulness. It happened like it always did whenever he drank, and afterward, I wished he'd pass out and choke to death on his own vomit. I think I actually prayed to God that my dad would just die at that moment. That was the day I realized I hated my father. Truly hated him.

Let me tell you exactly what he did. In the middle of the movie, with no consideration for the fact that me and Nathalie were watching it, he just started talking. It wouldn't have been so bad if he'd just talked about regular things: school, work, things around the house, you know. But that wasn't the kind of drunk my father was. No, he liked to talk about other things. On this occasion, he started talking about all the times he had cheated on my mom and all the women he'd had. He talked about how I knew of his affairs, how I'd been a good boy and had never said anything to Mom about the other women. "Keeping my dirty little secrets for me, eh, Jordan? I suppose I should thank you," he said. I'll never forget that because I remember thinking that I might have hated him a little less had he shown some gratitude for my silence. So many times I could've spilled it all to Mom, but I didn't. The least he could've done was thank me.

Needless to say, Nathalie was horrified. She didn't say anything, but the look of disgust on her face was enough. I knew she wouldn't have anything to do with me after this, probably thought me and Dad were perverts. Part of me just wanted to run out of there and hide, and the other part of me wanted to get Nathalie out of there and explain myself, save my chances with her, whatever it took. But I couldn't move. I was completely paralyzed. It was like some terrible dream. I just couldn't believe what was happening.

Dad was on a roll, though, going on and on about all the sexual things he liked to do to his women. Explicit shit no kid would want to know. The worst part, though, was when he mentioned how I'd watched him one time with one of his women when I was ten. I never even knew he'd seen me watching. When he told that story, Nathalie looked at me in complete horror. You don't know how long it took me to wipe that look out of my mind. At the end of it, Dad turned up his beer and smiled, like a man who'd just won a game of cards. Most horrible fucking day of my teenaged life."

Landrien sat up and looked at him. "And? What happened after that?"

"Nathalie, not saying a word, got up and left when the movie ended," he continued. "She actually waited until the movie ended, which surprised the hell out of me. But she never spoke to me again really, other than to tell me at school the next day that she'd gotten back with her football player boyfriend and that we couldn't be friends any more, not that we ever were. I'd had a crush on that girl since I was ten, and I'd finally gotten her to speak to me, and my dad ruined it just like that. He knew how much I adored her, and he sabotaged me, simply because he was bored and it was easy.

When I got home from school that day, I exploded. I mean, I went off. I told him everything I'd ever wanted to tell him about how much I hated him and how he was just a jealous old man and a loser. The whole time, he just sat in his chair and looked at me while I ranted and hollered. Honestly, I think he was entertained. But when I was finished, he stood up, looked at me for a second like he didn't even know me, and he hit me. He hit me with his fists, with his feet. He probably would've killed me if my brother hadn't stopped him.

I didn't tell my mom about it. She thought I'd gotten into a fight at school. She never knew how horrible he was to me and my brother."

"You never told her?"

He shook his head. "When my dad's back went out and he started drawing disability, my mom had to work long hours at the factory. Before the injury, he worked as an EMT, and he was nice when he was home. I don't know what changed him after the injury, but he wasn't the same at all. That was when he turned into the mean-spirited jerk I grew to hate. He would sit at home all day and terrorize me and my brother, but never when Mom was home. When she was home he was still the perfect husband, always had dinner and breakfast on the table for her, the house was always clean. She was tired all the time and worried about bills and her job, yet she had the perfect husband and sons. I couldn't bring myself to tell her the truth, to ruin her fantasy image of this life she had created for us. I couldn't give her another thing to worry about. And I guess, if I'm honest, I was terrified of my dad. So, I don't know, I just focused on getting away from there, and that's what I did. I got away."

"But I've met your dad. You two get along so well."

"My dad and I have had years of practice in pretending to like one another. At this point, we're old pros. Look, I'm not trying to get pity by telling you all this. I'm just trying to tell you you're not alone."

"Thank you," she replied. It was all she could think to say.

***

Landrien crept out of bed, just after 6am, and headed downstairs to the living room. She stalked through the pitch black house, hardly able to see more than a few inches in front of her, and felt her way to the sofa. Reaching out to the table on the right, she switched on the dim lamp light and glanced around the room, not sure what or whom she expected to find other than herself. There was a faint tapping noise near the staircase. She focused her eyes, willing them to penetrate the darkness beyond the staircase. As far as she could see, there was nothing there. Yet the tapping, like distant firecrackers, continued. Creaking floors and walls, she assumed, though not entirely convinced.

As she leaned back against the sofa, she turned on the television and waited for the weather forecast. After a series of medicine and automobile ads, the weather forecaster reported that roads throughout Philadelphia were mostly clear and that public transportation was running in the city. "Towards the townships just west of the city, however, the roads are patchy at best," he said, warning of black ice and uncertainty about the schedules of the buses and trains connecting to Philadelphia. "We can expect more snowfall midday in the west, with around five inches more by nightfall. That will likely result in more black ice once the temperature drops to twenty-five around early evening. Driving is discouraged throughout the day and evening," cautioned the forecaster, before turning back to the anchors.

Landrien yawned and turned off the television. "No work today." She lay back for a while, dozing off now and then. As light began to come through the curtains, she rose and examined her disheveled appearance in the mirror hanging over the fireplace. She made a pot of coffee, set out her orange LBM mug, and went upstairs to clean herself up.

Afterward, she settled down in her mother's room with a steaming cup of syrupy coffee, the box of diaries and the photo album. For the first time, she sat on the faded yellow armchair where she frequently found her father reading a book, with his coffee or tea sitting on the windowsill next to him and his legs propped up on the gray ottoman. He would smile if she came to the doorway, put down his book and talk to her about whatever was on her mind.

As he got older and became more ill, she would find him sitting in his chair, an empty coffee mug on the windowsill, no book. "You don't want a book, Dad?" she had asked him once while he was sitting there with his body turned to the window behind him and staring out at the unpaved driveway between their house and Rona's house. He had shook his head and smiled at Landrien, who stood in the doorway. He had proceeded to talk about his mother and his father and Pam. On other occasions, he said nothing at all.

She placed the box next to the gray ottoman and sat down in the chair. Digging inside the box, she retrieved the photo album at the bottom, stared at the dusty leather cover and then gingerly opened the book.

She stopped at a photograph on the third page and stared at the image. In front of a 1970s cream-colored pickup, stood a gangly, thin woman with her hair flipped under in a short bob. Trees and shrubbery comprised the hazy background beyond the woman and the car. The woman wore a floral patterned blouse and a faded blue jean skirt that stopped midway past her tiny calves. She wore hooped earrings but no other jewelry. Her feet were bare against the patchy dry grass. With a rather understated sass and femininity, she placed one honey-colored hand on her hip, and her other arm hung awkwardly at her side. The age of the picture made it impossible to discern the details of the woman's face, but she imagined the woman must have been barely out of her teens. From what she could see, the woman seemed to be staring into the sun and probably wanted the photographer to hurry up and snap the picture.

"That's Clem right there. She didn't like wearing her hair like that. She preferred to leave it in a curly fro because she thought it made her look different and little less countrified," said a distant voice that Landrien instantly recognized. The woman in the orange dress stood at the window across the room and stared at her own reflection in the windowpane. "And she hated wearing skirts and dresses. She had her own way of doing things, I suppose you could say."

Surveying the room as if intrigued by her surroundings, Bell walked around and ran her hand along the dresser and then the bookshelf. At last, she moved toward the foot of the bed, sat down and crossed her legs. Smiling, she pushed some stray braids behind her ears.

"Who is Clem?" asked Landrien.

Absently, Bell kept staring around the room. "Clem's real name was Lorraine. Most of the time, I called her Clem."

"Okay. So who was she?"

"A girl I knew."

"And who are you?"

"Bell," she answered.

"I meant, who *are* you? I worked out your name already."

"Then I bet you'll work out the rest soon."

"Or you could just tell me now, save me the time."

"Where's the fun in that?" replied Bell, staring out the window. "It snows nonstop here, don't it? We never got much snow in Winchester, certainly not this much. It must be awful, living here year after year, so many cloudy days."

"Winchester?" Landrien asked.

"Southern Arkansas. Desha County, to be exact."

"Right. Okay, I still don't understand. What does Arkansas or this photo album have to do with my mom? I don't see Mom in any of these pictures, and I don't recognize any of these people, except for you anyway. How did you know my mom? She never talked about her family. Are we related?"

Bell stood up and walked toward the window. She pushed back the curtains and gazed out. "Something like that."

A creaking noise just beyond the bedroom door distracted Landrien for a moment, and she turned to find the source of the sound. She knew Jordan had gotten up and was making his way downstairs to find her. When she turned to Bell and started to ask another question, she did not get a word out. The woman was gone.

"Damn it," mumbled Landrien and leaned back in her chair. "I really wish she'd stop doing that."

CHAPTER EIGHT

When the snow subsided, Landrien returned to work the following Monday only to confront a mountain of work that had piled up during the blizzard. She managed to close two cases of clients with whom she had lost contact for several months. Yet those were only two cases out of her thirty active cases. To make matters worse, several of her sixty other inactive cases returned to the top of the active pile as she received an onslaught of calls and voice messages from clients she had been unable to reach for nearly two months. Not surprisingly, she took several coffee breaks before lunch.

As she pulled the wool cap over her ears, she walked out into the icy air. She dug inside her coat pocket, pulled out a few dollar bills and handed them to the old man in the wheelchair who frequently sat outside her office building. The wind beat against her face, and her teeth chattered as she walked down Chestnut Street with her head lowered to avoid receiving a face full of snow. She wove through the throng of people, women in thick quilted coats and men in long wool coats, another homeless man holding a cup, and another homeless man who merely stood with his gloved hand held out and his head bowed. Eventually, she arrived at a dark little Italian pizzeria, and her eyes swept around the crowded room. Waiters hurried to and fro taking orders. There was not an unoccupied table or booth in sight.

At a booth along the back wall, a middle-aged woman sat alone and fumbled with her cell phone. The woman glanced around once or twice.

"Marie."

The woman looked up through eyes remarkably like Landrien's. Positively glowing with excitement, Marie Carmichael stood up and clasped her niece in a tight hug. "It's so good to see you!"

"You too," she said as Marie released her. They sat down opposite one another, and the waiter arrived to take their orders.

Marie, still smiling as brightly as ever, put her phone down on the table and gave her undivided attention to her niece. Landrien watched her aunt's eager face and marveled at how much the woman resembled her mother, the same stern eyes, dimples, and perfectly arched eyebrows. "You cut your hair," Marie observed.

"Yeah. Just after the funeral."

"It looks good. It suits you. My goodness, girl, you look just like your mother. I never saw it before," smiled Marie. She pushed back her bangs and tucked some stray locks behind her ears. "So, how are you holding up?"

"Fine."

"You know, I was pretty surprised when you called and asked me to lunch. We haven't sat down and had a regular conversation in forever. Not since you were a teenager. Can you believe it? The way time slips away." A regretful smile flitted across Marie's face, and she sipped her water.

"What do you know about Arkansas?" asked Landrien.

A look of panic mingled with concern replaced Marie's smile. Yet the expression faded in an instant. Just like her sister, Marie was a pro at covering and concealing vulnerability, Landrien recalled. "Arkansas. Birthplace of Bill Clinton (not my favorite president, not that I like any of them, that is). Plenty of mountains and mosquitoes and blistering hot summers." From her tone, she might have been talking about the weather. "I lived there for a while. I can't say I know much more about it."

Despite Marie's pleasant demeanor, Landrien detected something lurking in her voice that had not been there moments earlier. Bitterness, perhaps? "That explains why you're in one of the pictures." Before Marie could respond, Landrien went on, briefly explaining the will and the Arkansas photo album. "Neither you nor Mom ever mentioned Arkansas. Why is that?"

Marie squeezed the lemon juice in her water and dropped the lemon slice in the glass. "I was a schoolteacher down there for a few years."

"Why? Why would anyone move all the way from Philly to backwoods Arkansas?" Landrien leaned forward some more, her arms resting on the table.

As Marie took a sip of her water and stared down at the glass, Landrien regarded her with increasing suspicion. "Your mother was from Tennessee. Our family's from the Memphis area of Tennessee and Arkansas."

"And neither of you ever thought it was important to mention this?"

Marie stood up and gathered her cap and scarf. She slipped her arms through the sleeves of her gray wool coat and signaled the waiter.

"After all these years, I thought maybe you asking me to lunch meant that you wanted things to be the way they used to be, back when you used to talk to me about everything. Remember when you told me you wished I was your mother? I never said it, but sometimes I wished I was, too. I did. But I was just the aunt, which you made very clear once you left for college and never bothered to contact me or return any of my calls. You know, I've never been able to figure out what I did to deserve that. Not that it matters anymore. But still. Anyway. Tell Darren I said hi, and I'll call him soon."

As Marie turned to leave, Landrien added, "Who's Lorraine?"

Marie stopped as if pulled by a string, but she did not turn to face her niece. "A woman who died a very long time ago," she replied, after a pause. She hurried away from the booth and out the front door.

After work, Landrien took the trolley with Jordan to her car that she had parked outside her old apartment on Baltimore Avenue and 48th Street.

"What's up?" asked Jordan, who sat sandwiched between her and a rather large woman.

Landrien shook her head. "Nothing. I'm good." She stared out the window, thinking about her aunt's reaction. Marie was lying to her, and she needed to know why. In fact, she hated to admit it, but her mother was beginning to intrigue her more and more.

A few minutes later, she got off the trolley, kissed Jordan and watched him go up to her old apartment. She got in her car and pulled away, turning on the radio to drown out her thoughts. To further distract herself, she dialed Elena and left a short message. She told herself when she hung up this time that she would not call again. She would not beg.

By the time she walked inside the dark, cold house, she felt trapped in her head, in her mother's secrets. This was supposed to be simple: stay in the family home for one year, get the title, and then sell it to the highest bidder. Why could things not be that simple? Groaning, she kicked off her boots at the door and turned the heat up from seventy-five to eighty.

She headed toward the stairs but stopped when her eyes fell on the spot where her mother had collapsed. The oil stain from her mother's hair was still there on the wall. She clutched her chest in fright. Once she got a grip of her senses, however, she knelt down at the spot as she had several times before and brushed her hand against the floor and the wall. She examined the oil stain on the wall, shrugged off her unease and headed upstairs. She ran a hot bath and, while the tub filled, studied her reflection in the bathroom mirror. She disrobed and stepped into the bathtub.

As she lay submerged in the hot water, the steam soothed her, and she slowly let the water cover her neck. The dim candle light from the sink flickered, and all was silent in the house but for the creaking of the stairs and the soft gurgling noises coming from the toilet every now and then. Only the lights from the two candles on the sink and the one on the back of the toilet illuminated the room. She shut her eyes, and thoughts and memories appeared to her, like sliding pictures projected on a screen. She saw herself wrapped in Elena's arms on the beach at Stone Harbor, her face lying in Elena's dark hair that smelled like raspberries. Next, she was lying on the floor of her apartment, laughing and looking up at Jordan who smiled over her. Her mother was pulling her up the stairs to the bathroom, her nails buried in Landrien's forearm, and her mother was pushing her to the floor, and they were both crying out for different reasons. When she looked up, her mother was sitting on the porch and wearing that tie-dyed t-shirt she liked to wear.

The orange and yellow leaves on the trees sparkled brilliantly in the sunlight, and she felt warm in her mother's arms. Then, there was her mother and father watching her from outside a Greyhound bus window on a cloudy August day, and her mother was looking away. Her father was waving and grinning, as happy and proud as a father could be to send his only daughter halfway across the country to college. One by one, the images appeared and faded, until at last Landrien opened her eyes and came up for air. Breathing deeply, Landrien stared straight ahead at the flickering candlelight.

After checking that she had locked all the doors downstairs, she turned the heat down to seventy-five, and turned on the stove light before she headed up to bed. She got under the covers and switched on the lamplight. Staring down at the box of diaries sitting next to the bed, she eventually picked up the diary lying on top, a brown leather diary with faded pages. It had no markings on the exterior and, except for the frayed spine, bore no indication that anyone ever had used it. She lay back and, after a few more seconds of hesitation, opened the diary.

On the first page, there was a date and a rambling paragraph written in small, slanted and closely spaced letters:

MAY 20, 1978. It all feels so meaningless, this living from day to day, these passing moments. Every moment is gone as soon as it comes, each moment bringing me closer to the one thing I try not to think about, the one thing I desperately want to put off and avoid for as long as possible. I shouldn't even write it, but if I don't write it I think I may do it, really do it, and that would be too much of a mess to leave for Anthony. To do it would be unforgivable. At least, that's what they all say. But I can't help myself. I think about dying sometimes, about ending it. Why not? This is not the life I was supposed to live. This is not my life. This is your life. No doubt, if I uttered any of this to Anthony he would try to commit me or something. Who could blame him? But I imagine that if I said these things to you as I write them here now, you would tell me to have some whiskey and mellow out to a good record. Wouldn't you? It's just like you to believe the meaning of life resides in a glass of poison and a good song. Who knows? Maybe you're on to something. I've thought about how I would do it, the details—the rope I stowed in the basement months ago in case I ever work up the nerve, the pills hidden in my sock drawer. I think about the home I left, the life I lost. But there's Darren and Landrien. There's you. My promise to you. So, I guess I have no choice but to do as you would suggest: drink some whiskey and put on a Millie Jackson record and live another day. There's always tomorrow and the day after, and that rope and those pills aren't going anywhere. I'll leave dying for another day, I suppose.

She reread her mother's scribbled left-handed writing and tried to hear the words in her mother's deep voice, tried to believe this was her mother's pain, her mother's thoughts of…suicide? She shut the diary at once and dropped it back into the box. She pulled the blankets to her chin and lay there under the dim lamplight, thinking about each word she had read.

Bell appeared near the window. She offered no strange words nor did her appearance frighten Landrien. She simply leaned against the wall and watched Landrien.

All the while, Landrien mulled over the words she had read in her mother's diary. *Suicide? What was so bad to make her to even consider that? What was so bad about a*

Susie homemaker life with a nice husband and a couple of kids? There are worse ways to live, surely. Maybe it was depression? But this simple answer brought her no satisfaction. So she sat up and took the diary out of the box again.

She opened diary to the one page she had read, and she regarded Bell, who smiled and nodded. At long last, Landrien emptied her mind as best she could and lost herself in the crisp pages of her mother's diaries.

PART TWO

"Misfits in a land of Jesus and cotton." ~ Reggie

CHAPTER NINE

She had driven past the dingy-looking shack many times but never stopped until today. When Lorraine walked inside the dusky store, she looked up at the towering shelves against the wall. A modest house that had been converted to a store, Mitchell's Produce was tiny and needed some paintwork. Several small shelves stood a few feet from the wall shelves and lined the center of the store. Her eyes scanned the rows filled with bags of flour, cornmeal, grits, pancake mix, sugar and all sorts of spices, all packaged up in small plastic containers. She walked through the center of the store and looked down at the cereal and loaves of bread on one shelf, and candy and junk food on another shelf. Because the store was so dimly lit, she had to lean in close to read any of the labels on the items.

"Good afternoon, ma'am," a young girl greeted her from behind the cash register as Lorraine continued down the aisle in the center of the store. The girl, no more than thirteen or fourteen years old, smiled brightly through a set of large round eyes. "Let me know if I can help you with anything, you hear?"

Lorraine nodded and smiled back. She arrived at the produce section at the end of the aisle and looked around at all the dazzling colors of the vegetables. Tomatoes, yellow onions, snap peas, a variety of peppers, collards, turnips, kale, cabbage, purple hull peas. Everything looked so delicious, and she was ravenous. No one, she realized, should go grocery shopping on an empty stomach.

"All the produce is mostly from the family garden," the girl hollered. "But we get the cabbages and tomatoes from the Morgan family up the way. That white family that lives across the bayou." The girl pronounced "bayou" as "bau," something Lorraine always thought was a curious anomaly specific to the residents of this small Mississippi Delta town in Arkansas.

Lorraine nodded. Staring at the produce, she noticed a door on the back wall. Noises emanated from beyond it, as if a crowd of people had gathered back there.

"The restaurant's out back, just through that there door," said the girl.

The smoky, dark restaurant looked like a combination bar and diner. Five round tables lined the floor, and a few feet across from the tables, there was a bar and five red stools. The black-and-white checker patterned floors clashed with the wood paneled walls but went quite well with the white tables and red chairs. Lorraine gazed around at the wood paneled walls, adorned with black and white photographs of famous black movie stars, singers and boxers. She watched a couple, a middle-aged man and woman, sitting at a table nearest the window and in front of a picture of Muhammad Ali. They were leaning in close to each other and talking inaudibly, every bit the happy couple.

The scent of chicken and onions stirred up a fury of hunger in her, detaching her mind from the couple and directing her feet toward the bar. Behind the bar stood a woman who was counting money at the cash register a few feet away from Lorraine. Unsure about whether to interrupt the woman, who appeared to be quite absorbed in her counting, Lorraine sat quietly and rested her arms on the bar top. The Dramatic's "What You See is What You Get" played softly from a set of speakers at the other end of the bar, and she bobbed her head as she mouthed the lyrics. Feeling somewhat awkward that she was alone in a bar, she busied herself by surveying the restaurant and peeking over the set of double doors behind the bar. "Um. Ma'am? Excuse me?"

The woman turned to her and a surprised smile sailed across her face. She stowed the money back inside the register and walked toward Lorraine. "I'm sorry about that," the woman said in a voice that reminded Lorraine of the sound that comes from rubbing one's hands against silk. "I didn't see you down here."

"I...yeah, I just walked in...it's fine." Lorraine stared at the woman's enormous brown eyes and the small braids hanging down to her slender shoulders. She was perfectly certain that she had not met anyone as beautiful as this woman.

"Would you like something? We don't have menus right now. We're still working on that," she said in a louder, fuller voice. "But we got some collards and macaroni coming out. You can get that, plus a thigh and hot water cornbread for our special today. I can get it out to you in ten minutes or thereabout. Or we can fix something for you. Let's see, uh, for meat, we got neck bones and chicken today. For sides, we got candied yams, fried potatoes, and green beans. Peach cobbler and a slice of pound cake for desserts. Oh, I'm sorry, I forgot we're out of cobbler today. But, like I said, we got pound cake. And for drinks, we got lemonade—fresh squeezed—and sweet tea, or I can get you a can of pop from the store if you like. Oh, I suppose I should introduce myself. My name's Bell. Well, that's what everybody calls me. Bell Mitchell. And your name is?"

"Lorraine," she answered. "Lorraine Clemente Sterling. But most folks call me Clem."

"Nice to meet you, Clem. You live around here?" Bell asked.

"No. Well, not Winchester, anyway. I live in McGhee. I don't get up here to Winchester much, besides when I'm visiting to buy peaches from a woman across the bayou," Lorraine explained.

"Yeah, well, you ain't missing much. Nothing but shacks, poor folks and stray dogs round here. Can't say I get out to McGhee much either, though. I usually go up to Dumas or Pine Bluff here and again, when I need to dance or drink away some blues. But, other than that, I never find much reason to get out of this old town."

"You should. There's so much to see, all kinds of places and people."

Bell gave a sad little nod. "Hey, let me leave you alone, so you can figure out what you want. I'll be right down at the register when you're ready."

"It's all right. I already know what I want," she insisted before the woman could turn away.

Bell pulled a notepad from her back pocket and the pen from behind her right ear. After she took Lorraine's order, she disappeared behind the set of double doors and quickly returned with a glass of sweet tea. Lorraine watched her as she went to the register and resumed counting the money. The ice cold tea tasted like heaven, especially after hours spent out in the humid August heat. As Bell counted the money, she glanced at Lorraine and smiled.

"You know anybody that sells cash registers?" she hollered.

The question was so abrupt that Lorraine almost laughed. "No. I'm afraid I don't."

"Doggone it." Bell stuffed the money inside the register. "This one here ain't worth a dime. Guess I'll have to go up to Dumas sometime this weekend and look around. Pa's tight with a buck and been avoiding buying another one. But this register has outlived its use."

"You can probably find one at a pawn shop for cheap."

"True." Bell nodded as she approached Lorraine. She rested her elbows on the bar and looked as casual as if she was talking to an old friend. "So, what you do in McGhee, anyway? For a living, I mean."

"Oh, nothing really. I live with a friend. I'm in college at the university in Monticello. I transferred from the University of Memphis."

"Wow. College girl, huh? I always wanted to go to college. Figured I'd study something to do with cooking—"

"Like Culinary Arts."

"Yeah, and then I'd open my own restaurant and write cookbooks someday."

"You still could. College is a different world. Can you believe that just a few years ago, it would've been practically unthinkable for you or me to go to most colleges?" Lorraine sat straight up on the stool. "It's a new era. There are lots of women in my classes, and I even have one woman professor. I mean, I'm the only black student. But things are changing, and there's nothing old folks can do to stop it. It's not like it was when our parents were young. White people are still funny acting, sure, and they don't really want us in their schools. I suppose that won't ever change. But the law's different now, and white folks have to accept us in their schools. So, as far as I can see it, black folks and women don't have any reason not to do better now. We can be whatever we want to be."

"Yeah, well, the more things change, the more they stay the same. At least, that's the way I see it. Anyway, we just can't afford it, college. Pa say ain't no need for college anyway. But I'm gonna get my restaurant one day, or maybe a catering business. I don't need schooling for that. And I'm gonna write some cookbooks. I'm working on one right now, but I don't have a title for it yet."

"Really?" Lorraine leaned forward. A squat, pot-bellied man appeared from behind the double doors, and Bell turned toward him. She moved aside as he sat a plate of food in front of Lorraine.

"Thanks, Pa. I forgot to go back and check."

He gave her a pat on the shoulder before glancing at Lorraine. "You let us know if you need anything else, now, ma'am." Lorraine nodded, and the man disappeared behind the set of double doors.

As she consumed her food, she marveled at the full flavor of the collards and macaroni. She could not remember when she had tasted collards more delicious, or a tenderer piece of chicken. Meanwhile, Bell returned to the register and rung up the couple that had been sitting on the other side of the room. The couple, walking hand in hand, laughed and talked loudly when they passed the bar.

"A bit too much whiskey for those two, I think." Bell grinned, approaching Lorraine. "They come in here almost every afternoon and Saturday night. May Rose and Jerry Taylor. A couple of drunks, if you ask me. But they're good people. Ain't nothing gonna tear them apart, not even May's affairs. (But that's probably cause Jerry messes around just as much as she does.) Just the other Saturday night, Jerry was drunk in here and threatening to shoot one of May's misters. Pa had to threaten to ban him, *again*."

Lorraine chuckled and sipped her sweet tea.

"How you like the greens and chicken? They're all my recipes."

"It's really good."

Bell seemed very pleased to hear that. "Say, you know that new movie *Claudine*, with Diahann Carroll?" she asked.

"Yeah. It's not that new, though. I saw it up in Memphis a couple months back."

"Oh, shoot," groaned Bell, snapping her fingers. "I was gonna ask you to come see it with me in Pine Bluff tonight."

"Really?" Lorraine's fork clanged against the plate as it slipped from her fingers.

"Yeah. I been dying to see it."

"Ask me." Her eyes fixed on the woman. Bell rested her elbow on the bar and leaned closer to Lorraine.

"Will you come with me?" she asked.

"Sure, I will," said Lorraine, grinning.

Lorraine pulled into her sister's unpaved driveway, which was muddy from the previous day's rain. Her car—an orange 1970 Volkswagen Beetle her father had bought used and passed down to her before she left Memphis—rattled and shook as she shifted the gear into park. "This damn car is going to give out on me before long." She shook her head as she shut off the engine.

Slinging her book bag over her shoulder, she shuffled out of the car and up to the small, unenclosed porch of her sister's one-story house. While teaching in McGhee, her sister had lived alone in the house, no children, her first husband dead from the war. Now she lived up north and was finishing a Master's degree to become a school counselor. Since it was the family's land, and she did not want to sell it, she only asked that Lorraine give her a little money per month to live in the house.

The cat, a stray named Willy, came to the door when Lorraine opened it and peered up at her with eager eyes. She knelt down and brushed her hand against Willy's back while he pressed himself against her ankle. "Hey there, you. You seen Reggie? Huh? Reggie!" she called.

As she stepped inside, she turned toward the small kitchen to the right of the front door. At the far left of the living room adjoining the kitchen, a narrow hall led to the two spacious bedrooms. The white walls of the living room and hallway were strewn with framed photographs and paintings her sister had picked up from her travels. Willy hopped onto the old brown couch that sat in the center of the room, two rocking chairs on each side. He stared at her and rested his head on his paws as she looked past him and toward the dining room. Just beyond the dining table, a white door with a screen opened out to a large, unenclosed backyard.

"Reggie?" she yelled.

Moments later, a tall man, wearing loose bell-bottom jeans and a pen behind his ear, appeared at the screen door. "Honey, you're home," he greeted her as she walked into the living room. He discarded his gardening gloves and came inside. "May I ask why you're hollering like all hell's broken loose?"

"I need you to proofread my paper tonight, so I can go to the movies. It's due tomorrow at noon," she answered, beaming. She removed her shoes and went to the kitchen.

Reggie collapsed onto the sofa and watched Lorraine from across the room. "Oh, is that right? And why would I do that? More importantly, why are you going to the movies tonight when you have a paper to finish?"

"Right, we'll just forget all the times I've proofread your papers when you were too busy to do it yourself?" She rinsed a glass and glanced at him before she turned to the refrigerator.

"Unlike you, I always have a legitimate reason for being busy."

"Oh, yeah," she said, taking a carton of orange juice from the refrigerator. "This demonstration, that protest, this petition. With all your activism, you seem to have forgotten that politicians tend to finish college first. And to do that, I'm pretty sure you have to do the class work."

"As long as I pass the class, and I can do that with my eyes closed. I ain't worried." He stood up and approached her. "But you still haven't answered the question. What's so important at the movies?"

"I'm going to see *Claudine*."

"We saw that months ago."

"Yeah, but I'm going to see it again with this girl I met at a store in Winchester. She said she hadn't seen it, and she didn't want to go alone. So I said I'd go."

He folded his arms across his chest. "Oh, I see. New friends are more important than work, now?" asked Reggie in what Lorraine considered to be a perfect imitation of her father's voice and mannerisms. She leaned against the counter, swallowed the last bit of the orange juice and turned on the water to rinse out the glass.

"In this case, yeah," she replied, grinning at him.

"So who's this girl?"

"Her name's Bell Mitchell."

"She in school?" he asked.

"No."

She walked to the living room and sunk into the sofa. Lorraine let out a long, exhausted sigh. "Fine. I'll proofread the paper for you," Reggie relented. He placed a hand on her thigh and patted it. "Go have your fun."

She planted a kiss on his cheek and jumped up to get dressed. Was this a jeans occasion or should she break out the black dress pants she had purchased in Memphis a few weeks earlier? *Or maybe that red button-down blouse and a pair of jeans, not too dressy.* She ran her hands through her fuzzy hair. *A blow-out. I have time to blow it out.* "Thanks, Reggie."

"Oh, I'm not doing this for free, honey. You owe me one," he replied as she sprinted toward the hallway and disappeared. Willy turned his gray eyes to Reggie and then decided to follow Lorraine. Reggie leaned back into the sofa, yawned and shut his eyes until he fell asleep.

Bell's mother had once told her that relationships and friendships have a tendency to form rapidly when two people are on a similar path. She thought about this over the next few days as she and Lorraine went to see *Claudine*, went drinking and dancing and sat out on Bell's front porch during a Sunday afternoon. It had been a long while since she had had any close friends. Usually, it was just her and her family, all cooped up in their small house, fussing and arguing or laughing and eating, when she was not working at the store. There had not been much time or room for anyone new. Sometimes, the simplicity of this routine brought her happiness and scarcely could she think of a better life. Yet sometimes she desperately missed her husband and wished he could return from the war, so they could get their own place together away from her parents. She never mentioned any of this to her father. She knew he liked having his daughter at home where he could keep a close eye on her, although he would never admit it.

On this Sunday afternoon, she and Lorraine sat in the rickety porch swing and sipped sweet tea. "Where is every one?" Lorraine asked.

"Church. Where else? They'll be there all day."

"Why aren't you there?"

Bell shot her an incredulous look and smiled. "Why aren't you?"

"I stopped going to church years ago. Generally, I think it's a bunch of nonsense and a lot of avoiding the real world. But to each his own, I suppose."

"I stopped going a few months ago."

Lorraine glanced sideways at her and, as usual, detected a hint of sadness in Bell's eyes. Bell put out the cigarette on the armrest, stared straight ahead and blew out smoke, then closed her eyes and inhaled.

"Are you happy?"

"I don't think we're meant to be happy," said Bell, not missing a beat.

"We're?"

"*We're*, as in people. Human beings," Bell replied, staring straight ahead. "I think people spend too much time chasing this thing—happiness—this thing that we ain't even sure is possible. This thing we ain't even sure exists. We chase it. We write about it and dream about it. We set our lives up around the little bit of hope that we might find it, when we don't even know what 'it' is, and when really happiness ain't the point, is it?" She stopped, gazed at Lorraine and lit another cigarette.

"I don't know. If happiness isn't the point, then what is?" wondered Lorraine.

Curiously, Bell smiled and then pointed upward toward the pear tree just in front of the porch. "You see that? Those two?" Lorraine looked up, searching for the object of Bell's attention. Two gray squirrels were chasing one another upward around the trunk of the tree. Perhaps it was a mating activity, or perhaps they were simply playing. Whatever the reason, the squirrels' interaction put a smile on Bell's face. "They're just living the only way they know how to. Maybe that's the point: just living. My mama used to say you gotta live and keep living. Of course, do any of us even know what it means to just live? It seems to me we try so hard to avoid living, what with all our thinking about heaven and happiness. Maybe living is just loving, fucking, growing, and all the pain that comes with that. Hell, maybe living is just feeling connected to everything, even those squirrels, and happiness is the little spark of joy in the midst of all of that." Bell blew out smoke and took another puff of the cigarette. "Or maybe I'm just full of shit."

"No. It's interesting. I never thought about it that way." Silence emerged between them as she considered Bell's words. For a long while, neither of them said a word but rather sat lost in their own thoughts, Lorraine sipping iced tea and Bell finishing her cigarette. "Why did you stop going to church a few months ago?"

"God ain't never heard nothing I said to Him. Either that, or He don't exist. But to put it simply, I didn't see no more reason to believe in Him. And besides, I got one Pa trying to run my life. I surely don't need another one."

"Can't say I disagree. Did something happen to make you stop believing?"

"Yes." She glanced coldly at Lorraine. "So, yeah, I don't see any point in attending church. Of course, my mama and pa think I've turned my back on Jesus. But I ain't stuttin' that, and they know it. They've given up trying to get me back in church, and so every Sunday I have the house all to myself for half the day. It's my favorite day of the week, the one day when I can get some relief and just have some peace and quiet. Sometimes I write or work on the cookbook. Sometimes I sit out here and take a nap or just think." Bell gazed out across the yard at the dirt road lined with trees, behind which lay a swampy stream.

"Do you ever write anything besides recipes?"

"Not really," answered Bell. "I used to keep a diary. You?"

"I keep a diary, and I write poetry. I'm not too good at it anymore, though, poetry. I've been thinking about writing a story."

She turned to Lorraine. "Yeah? What about?"

Lorraine yawned and covered her mouth. "I'm not sure yet. I'm just trying to finish up my teaching degree first. I'm so busy with school and everything. But I want to write. I suppose one of these days I'll figure out what to write about."

"Write about this," Bell suggested, staring out at the road and swamp. Lorraine rested her head against Bell's shoulders while they watched gray clouds pass and listened to the wind sing through the bare branches of the trees.

By the end of the month, Lorraine had spent more time at the store, on Bell's porch, or out walking than she spent in her own house. Reggie began complaining—"You're abandoning me for worldly vices, you and this mystery friend of yours"—particularly after she stumbled in drunk one evening and collapsed in front of the sofa, leaving him to clean up her vomit, change her clothes, and put her into bed. He threatened to tell her sister and parents, and part of Lorraine wondered if he was serious.

On a rainy evening during the first week of September, Lorraine finally introduced Bell to Reggie. Reggie eyed Bell with curiosity, and Bell returned his look with one of vague hostility. But the three of them sat down to dinner and toasted to Lorraine's twenty-first birthday. Lorraine, spectacularly made up in sapphire earrings and a bright sequined shirt over blue jean bell-bottoms, glowed throughout the entire dinner.

When she got up to bring more juice and cornbread to the table, Reggie sipped his water and surveyed Bell. She smiled nervously at him and forked some more green beans in her mouth, all the while humming to the Curtis Mayfield tune coming from the living room record player.

"So, how long have you and Lorraine been together?" she asked as she fixed her eyes on him and sliced the steak on her plate. Her somewhat stony stare lingered on him as she poured hot sauce on the steak.

He took a few seconds to swallow his potatoes before he responded. "A few years. Clem followed me from the University of Memphis."

"Oh."

He noted her unsuccessful attempt at nonchalance and had to fork more potatoes in his mouth to keep from laughing. "She didn't tell you?"

"Tell me what?"

"Well, let me just put it this way: you have nothing to worry about," he said, grinning and then forking some more potatoes in his mouth. He followed this with a piece of steak drenched in hot sauce.

"What do you mean?"

"He's sweet," Lorraine interjected. She held a plate of cornbread in one hand and jar of cranberry juice in the other.

"Sweet as a Georgia peach," Reggie added.

Bell looked from him to Lorraine. "You're...queer, you mean?"

"Ooooh, Lord. It's such a queer word 'queer.' You know some folks are even trying to reclaim that word. I say good riddance to it. But if you insist, yes, I'se as queer as a four dollar bill. Or is it a three-dollar bill? I never remember."

"Oh," Bell murmured and fell silent as she glanced back and forth between Lorraine and Reggie. She appeared to be putting together a puzzle, wiggling all the pieces into place, and it was requiring a great deal of concentration on her part.

Lorraine sat down and put a piece of cornbread on her own plate. "You didn't think...?"

"Yes she did. I wonder why," he said, toasting Lorraine. "I thought we were done with closets and whatnot."

"The truth is I dated Reggie back in Memphis. It didn't work out, though, for obvious reasons. I figured him out pretty quick." She smiled at Reggie.

"But I figured her out much earlier."

Bell turned to look at Lorraine. "Figured out what about you?"

"The gay civil rights activist and aspiring lawyer," said Lorraine to Reggie, as if Bell had not spoken.

"Dating the quirky bull-dyke writer-slash-aspiring school teacher. Talk about one radical couple. Half the people who knew us hated us, and the other half was practically obsessed with us." He glimpsed Bell's confused face and laughed.

Lorraine's eyes swept from him to Bell, and the three of them burst into laughter. Bell let out the loudest laugh of all as she bent over and held her stomach. Lorraine and Reggie laughed both with and at her. Lorraine later realized this laughter—or rather this moment of understanding—had created an eternal bond among her, Bell, and Reggie. Indeed, from that night on, Reggie dubbed them "the inseparable trio of misfits in a land of Jesus and cotton."

Just before they finished dinner, the trio made a pact to escape Arkansas as soon as Lorraine and Reggie's coursework ended and flee to some fabulous city up north or out west.

"All I know is I want to live some place where there are plenty of queens, homos, activists, lesbos and afros. Some place full of black folks who aren't afraid to be proud," Reggie exclaimed as he swirled the red wine in his glass. "Some place where I can strut."

"As long as there's no snow," said Bell, grinning.

"And especially no mosquitoes," Lorraine insisted.

Bell suggested San Francisco, while Lorraine and Reggie suggested New York and Philadelphia. They drank more wine, laughed some more, talked about their families, and the three of them toasted to their new friendship. Bell saw that, for the first time, she had friends who knew her secret and loved her because of it. Lorraine clasped her into a drunken hug, and the three of them sang to Marvin Gaye's "Ain't No Mountain High Enough," which Reggie noted was almost too sentimental and appropriate for the moment. He got up and switched to a Bill Wither's record.

A little past two in the morning, they sprawled out on the living room floor, where they talked and drank themselves to sleep. That evening, the world could have ended and even that would not have been able to disturb the peace Lorraine, Reggie, and Bell experienced, lying in one another's arms on the cold linoleum floor.

CHAPTER TEN

Both captivated and disgusted, Lorraine watched Bell attach a wriggling earthworm to the hook of the fishing pole and lower it into the cold water. Bell, who was wearing loose jeans, boots, and a corduroy jacket, used her free hand to hastily zip up her jacket and pull the cap over her ears. "Damn, it's cold," she muttered. It was a chilly Sunday afternoon, and the sun had taken a vacation for the last few days. The cool wind whistled through the bare branches of the trees and through the blades of dying grass. The October air held the sort of chill that hinted at the approaching winter but still contained residues of the summer just past.

Lorraine looked up at the white sky, saw her own breath in the air and shook her head. "I told you the temperature was supposed to drop today. I don't know how I let you drag me out here, cold as it is."

"Oh, we'll be all right," Bell assured her. "Besides, you gonna be singing a different tune when I fry up this catfish."

"Did I ever tell you I'm more of a trout person?"

Bell watched her in amusement and then nodded toward the bucket of earthworms. "You gonna bait your hook, or what?" she asked.

Lorraine peered down at the writhing pile of worms. She was certain she had never seen anything more repulsive. *Like big brown pieces of fat, moving around,* Lorraine thought, with a shiver. Bell, who was rocking the boat and mumbling in frustration, slowly reeled in something caught on her hook but still submerged in the water. Bell got to her knees in a continued effort to reel in the line, until finally a fish about nine or ten inches long and almost as wide, rose out of the water.

"Shit, the way you're acting I would've thought that joker was about six feet long."

"It's my fishing pole," Bell sighed, sitting down. "The line's caught." She pulled the fish off the hook and dropped it in the empty bucket reserved for the day's catch. While Lorraine glanced at the new catch flopping desperately in the bucket, Bell fussed with the fishing pole and muttered a few swear words. At last, she threw the pole down. "Cheap piece of crap."

"That's not a catfish."

Bell examined the struggling fish. "Looks like a small bass. I don't think I ever caught one before in this stream. I only ever caught catfish here. Hell, you might get lucky and catch a trout. Go ahead and bait your hook. I caught all I'm gonna catch today. I need to get a new pole."

Lorraine stared at the bucket of bait. Rather than succumb to the dread that suddenly had swept over her, she closed her eyes and dropped her hand into the bucket. The wetness and coldness of the worms, combined with the slimy texture and movement, made her dry heave a couple of times before she finally grabbed one between her index finger and thumb. She opened her eyes and attached it to the hook as her hands shook from nervousness. All the while, Bell held her stomach in pain from laughing so hard.

"You'll pay for this." She blushed and glared at Bell, who roared with laughter. Lorraine lowered the hook over the edge of the boat.

They watched the water for many minutes, but nothing happened as leaves fell onto the water and floated past her line. Lorraine looked up at the trees surrounding and towering over them like a canopy. Their little boat sat suspended in the middle of the stream, and on either side of them was a grassy, muddy shore. The stream ran on, curving this way and that, seemingly endless. Somewhere miles beyond where they sat, the stream emptied into the Mississippi River.

Lorraine turned to Bell, who had been watching her while smoking a cigarette. Recently, she had noticed that Bell liked to watch her for minutes on end, without saying a word. Sometimes, it made Lorraine uncomfortable, but mostly it just intrigued her. Lorraine was beginning to realize that as much as Bell seemed like an open book, much of her life remained a mystery. In fact, she often wondered how much Bell concealed about herself, about her past.

As Lorraine opened her mouth to voice these thoughts, the fishing pole jerked and nearly slipped from her hand. After a moment's struggle, she pulled up a large black catfish.

"Oh, God. Take it," she exclaimed, frowning and hastily handing the fishing pole to Bell. "Jesus Christ, it's disgusting."

Bell reeled in the fish, quickly removed it from the hook and laid the fish in the bucket with the bass that was no longer moving.

"I'm not eating that."

Bell picked up the paddle and handed the other paddle to Lorraine. "You are so girly and citified," she teased.

They paddled back toward land and docked. The two of them, after some struggle, managed to strap the boat onto the back of Bell's pickup. They dumped the bucket of worms, got in the truck and headed to Lorraine's house. That October afternoon in 1975 was the first of several fishing adventures they had at the quiet shore that Bell eventually dubbed "the spot."

Bell and Reggie sat at the kitchen table, engaged in a contentious game of chess. From what Lorraine could discern, Bell appeared to be a few moves away from winning the game, and Reggie furrowed his brow in intense concentration. He did not like losing and was the kind of person who would fight a losing battle to the very end. Lorraine, therefore, avoided playing board or card games with him.

"I got Millie Jackson tickets!" Lorraine shouted, shutting the front door and throwing off her coat. She held three silver strips of paper in the air.

"Really?" Bell said, not turning to her. Reggie nodded and kept his eyes fixed on the chessboard.

"That's it? That's all the reaction I get? Where's the love, folks? Don't you wanna know how I got them?"

"You bought them," said Reggie, staring down at the chessboard and waving his hand to silence her.

Lorraine tossed her scarf and cap onto the sofa and went to the kitchen. "No, smart ass. They sold out last week." She laid the three tickets next to the chessboard. "All right, not that either of you care, but I won them from the radio station. The concert's this Saturday up in Little Rock. I was thinking we could make the two-hour drive on Saturday morning and get a room. My sister knows an old woman who runs a B&B where we can stay for cheap. We can hit the town before the concert and then drive back on Sunday afternoon. It'll be fun. What do y'all think?"

"Check mate." Bell wore a victorious smirk on her face just after she moved her queen and took his last knight. She smiled up at Lorraine. "Sounds fun."

Reggie frowned at the board. But when he looked up at Lorraine, he seemed to turn something over in his mind. "Sorry, I can't go. I have to meet with the group to prepare for our demonstration on Monday."

Lorraine's shoulders dropped. "You can't do that on Sunday afternoon?"

"Nope. We have flyers to get copied, signs to draw, speeches to write—"

"Fine. I get it. Go ahead and work on your 'free the gays' demonstration." Lorraine shoved him. "I guess that means it'll be me and Bell."

"What's the demonstration about?" asked Bell, looking back and forth between Lorraine and Reggie.

"A little over a year ago, these two guys got caught blowing each other while parked along highway 70," began Lorraine. "They got sentenced to eight years in prison for sodomy. Reggie's organized a few demonstrations protesting their imprisonment—"

"And this state's ass backwards sodomy laws, excuse the crude pun. The defendants appealed all the way to the Arkansas Supreme Court, but they still lost. We want to get the guys some national attention, maybe convince them to challenge the law in federal court," he explained.

"Reggie even interviewed one of the guys."

"Sandy Carter, Jr. Unlike his partner, he was pretty eager to talk to us about the whole ordeal. On Monday, we're handing out pamphlets that have the interview. People need to know about this," he explained.

"They sure do." Lorraine nodded but turned to Bell quite abruptly. "So, you're coming to the concert?"

Hesitantly, Bell nodded. "I suppose Pa can cover my shift on Saturday. He ain't gonna be happy about it though."

"Great," Lorraine beamed. She kissed Bell on the cheek and, with a slight bounce in her step, retreated down the hallway toward the bathroom. Bell pressed her hand against her cheek where Lorraine had kissed her, and a dreamy expression sailed across her face.

Reggie stifled the urge to laugh. "You're in trouble," he said, gathering up the chessboard pieces and folding the board to stow it away. "That girl couldn't catch a hint if it hit her in the face."

"What? No, it's not..." stammered Bell. She stared at her hands and tried not to smile.

"Hmm-uh. You better open your mouth and say what you gotta say. You only live once. And Clem's not so good with hints and subtlety. One way or the other, though, I suppose your little trip this weekend is gonna be *real* interesting."

She regarded him and brushed her braids behind her ears. "How do you mean?"

"Clem might not be great at picking up hints. She's just innocent-minded like that. But don't let the innocence fool you: when she wants something, she ain't too shy about it. And that girl tends to get what she wants. Do yourself a favor and make sure it's what *you* want."

With that, Reggie placed the top on the chess box and withdrew to the living room, where he propped up his feet on the coffee table and began pouring through his gargantuan constitutional law book. Still sitting at the table and digesting his words, Bell looked down distractedly at her glass of water.

***

Thick, gray clouds rolled in on Saturday afternoon as Lorraine and Bell window-shopped in Little Rock's Park Plaza Mall. "I think we oughta hurry. I can smell the rain coming," said Bell, her braids blowing in the wind as they walked toward the entrance of the new Dillard's store. Lorraine smiled, took Bell's hand, and pulled her toward the glass double doors.

Once they entered the store, they perused the purses and coats, where Bell marveled at all the nice furs. Yet after ten minutes of shaking their heads and groaning derisively at the overpriced items, they decided to leave and visit the new mall in North Little Rock. When they got out of the car at McCain Mall, the sun was shining and accompanied by a light sprinkle. "Looks like the devil's whipping his wife." Bell gazed up at the sky and then at Lorraine.

Lorraine shot her a reproachful look. "That's a rotten thing to say."

"What? It's just an old folks' saying about when it's raining and the sun's out," replied Bell and shrugged.

Lorraine grasped her hand. "Let's hope this one has better stores than Park Plaza."

For hours, they walked around the mall, window-shopping and trying on clothes, eating hotdogs in the food court and talking about what they hoped Millie Jackson would sing at the concert later.

At last, they entered a high-end clothing store and wandered through the dress section. It astounded Bell that anyone would spend so much money on clothing.

"What do you think?" Lorraine asked, draped in an orange dress when she emerged from the dressing room. Bell, who had been sitting on a bench outside the stall, stood up and surveyed her friend. The dress had thin spaghetti straps, subtle white stitching, and with a slight flare fell down just above Lorraine's knees. Her bad posture and thin, bowed legs presented an amusing contrast to the simple yet elegant dress. Bell found it amusing to see Lorraine in a dress and suddenly wondered if she even owned a dress.

"It's pretty. But would you actually wear it?"

Lorraine poured over her reflection in the mirror and brushed her hands against the dress. "Nah, it's not really my style. But it sure is a nice dress, huh? Feel the material."

Bell passed her hand over the front of the dress and nodded. For a moment, they admired Lorraine's reflection. "You should buy it."

Lorraine turned to Bell and smiled. "Maybe. But I'm not sure orange is my color." She disappeared inside the changing stall.

While Lorraine changed, Bell hummed Millie Jackson's "I Gotta Get Away From My Own Self" and glimpsed the price tag on a shirt hanging on the changing room door. "Oh, man. This place is kind of expensive, don't you think? How much is that dress?"

"Thirty bucks, I believe."

"That's a lot of money for a dress. I bet we could find one cheaper in another store."

"Not one as nice as this one," Lorraine replied.

After examining a few price tags, Bell realized she could not afford anything in the store. One dress was worth half of her weekly wages at her family's store. With her other responsibilities, she was lucky to have ten dollars to spare each week. Ten dollars likely would not buy her anything in this store, other than a pair of socks. She scarcely could afford this weekend trip. The fuel for the car and the bed and breakfast alone was a full weeks' pay at least. Fortunately, Lorraine had insisted upon paying for both the fuel and the bed and breakfast for the night. Bell was too embarrassed to tell her friend that she had only a few dollars in cash. She was thankful she had been spared the need to confess her poverty.

Nevertheless, she wandered in and out of expensive department stores, and at Lorraine's insistence, tried on clothes she never would own or be able to afford. Yet Bell did not complain. She was with her best friend and away from work, responsibility and the worries of home. For one day, she would savor the feeling of freedom.

As they exited the mall, Lorraine glanced down at her watch and clicked her tongue dramatically. "We need to get to the B&B and drop this stuff off. The concert starts in two hours."

The bed and breakfast, a large early twentieth century two-story house, sat near the corner of Battery and West 15th in East Little Rock. A seventy-year-old black woman named Ethel Rose Taylor owned the home, which had passed to her through her father.

"So how does your sister know this woman?" Bell had asked on the drive up to Little Rock.

"Oh, Ethel is the grandmother of one of Marie's college friends. The first time Ethel and my sister met was at a sit-in civil rights demonstration in front of the capitol building years ago. Then, during junior year of college, Marie's friend got in trouble for having reefer in her dorm room. The school administration was ready to expel the girl right then and turn her over the police. Ethel had to come sort it all out. The girl's mother is dead, you see, so Ethel raised her. Anyway, Marie said Ethel was one of those little old ladies who seemed quiet until she opened her mouth.

Whatever Ethel said to the administration, it worked. Marie's friend didn't get expelled and never got in trouble again. Now the funny part is Marie said the woman's clothes reeked of reefer when she showed up at the dorm."

"Sounds like my kind of woman," Bell had replied, chuckling.

Ethel made her living by cleaning houses and renting out her two spare rooms to short-term visitors, primarily women visitors, though she did not discriminate if the price was right. This evening, Bell and Lorraine were her only lodgers.

When they entered the dark, smoky house, they found Ethel asleep on the sofa with her black cat, Evie, lying across her lap. Evie watched them as they proceeded as quietly as possible to the staircase across the room. The stairs creaked loudly as they crept up to their room. They stopped, however, when a cough sounded from the living room, and they heard Evie meow.

"Girls, is that y'all?" Ethel asked. Her hoarse voice revealed the damage of decades of smoking. The old woman looked up at them and stood with the cat in her arms.

"Yes, Mrs. Rose. It's us," answered Lorraine. They looked down over the balcony.

"I just wanted y'all girls to know my son called me an hour ago. Remember I told y'all he was going to that Millie Jackson show, too?"

They nodded.

"Well, he say the show been canceled," Ethel informed them, her left hand caressing the cat's back.

Lorraine's smile faded. "Is he sure, Ma'am?"

"He works for the radio station. He say Millie's people called and canceled the interview she was supposed to do tonight before the show. Apparently, she's sick with the flu or something."

"Damn," Lorraine cursed under her breath.

"Thanks for telling us, Mrs. Rose," said Bell.

"Y'all welcome." Ethel turned, humming as she went through the kitchen door.

When they entered their room, Lorraine plopped onto the bed and proceeded to sulk. For a while, Bell stood at the door and observed Lorraine's moping. Lorraine's body slouched, and her hands ran through her hair. "How inconvenient to announce this at the last minute, literally just hours before the show," she complained. Her hand came to her face as if to brush something off her nose, and her bottom lip poked out just slightly.

"Look, I'm still glad you asked me to come with you, Clem. It's nice to get away." Bell shut the door and leaned against it. "We can go out dancing somewhere tonight. Or just find a bar and have some drinks while men shamelessly hit on us."

A smile played across Lorraine's face, and her posture improved. "Yeah, I guess so. Might as well make use of this dress tonight." She reached inside one of the shopping bags and brought out the orange dress, which she caressed and then extended toward Bell. "Put it on."

"Me? Why?" Bell stared down at the dress as though it was the Pope's robes and touching it was unthinkable.

"Cause it's yours, that's why. And if we're gonna go dancing, we might as well go in style."

"But it cost a fortune, Clem. I can't accept—"

"You *can* accept it, and you will, or my feelings will be hurt," Lorraine urged her, still smiling. It was a slick smile Bell was accustomed to receiving from men when they wanted something from her. "So, go ahead, try it on."

Hesitantly, she took the dress and walked across the room to the vanity. She laid the dress across the chair and, with her back to Lorraine, hastily removed her shirt and pants.

"Slowly," said Lorraine, her voice commanding but gentle all the same.

Bell took a deep breath and slipped the dress over her head. Her hands stroked the silky material that hugged her waist and stopped just above her knees. The light silk of the dress felt like cool water on her skin, an immeasurably delightful sensation. She turned to face Lorraine and averted her eyes.

"I knew it." Her eyes, clearly pleased with what they were seeing, scanned Bell.

"Knew what?"

"You're perfect."

"It took me putting on an expensive dress for you to figure that out?" said Bell, grinning at Lorraine.

"No. I figured that out within five minutes of meeting you," Lorraine replied.

Bell turned to examine her reflection and chided herself for acting so shy. How pathetic she must look, blushing like a school girl at every little compliment. She buried her hands inside the pockets of the dress as Lorraine stood up and approached her. "I don't know what to say." Her eyes closed for a second as Lorraine's breath whipped against her neck. "I should've known you weren't buying it for yourself. Do you even wear dresses?"

Lorraine came closer, and they both stared at Bell's reflection in the wall mirror. "Not generally, but I do have a couple of skirts in my closet." Her hands came to rest on Bell's waist. "Does this bother you?"

"What? I mean, no. Well, a little."

She slipped her fingers through Bell's fingers, and they looked at one another's reflection. Bell had not noticed that Lorraine's eyes appeared bright brown rather than dark brown in certain lighting, and she had a small mole just at the corner of her right eye. It surprised her that she had missed these details. "Do you want me to stop?"

"No," breathed Bell. It was all she could manage to say as Lorraine's hands moved up the dress. Lorraine's fingers hooked on the spaghetti straps of the dress while her mouth pressed against Bell's right shoulder, against the indentation left by the dress strap.

"Take it off," Lorraine ordered her, peering at their reflection in the mirror.

Bell removed the dress while Lorraine watched. The dress dropped to the floor, soundlessly, and Lorraine's eyes traveled down the length of Bell's slender body. "Perfect." She said it as though no other word could capture what she was seeing. "You're so perfect."

"If you don't stop saying that, I might just end up believing it," Bell smiled.

Lorraine ran her fingers through Bell's hair and, for a while, they did not speak while they stood there in front of the mirror. "Have you done this before? Been with a woman?" she asked.

Bell observed Lorraine for a moment, as if she was not sure she should respond. "No," she replied, hardly above a whisper.

"I have. Several times. The last woman was married and desperately confused." Lorraine ran her index finger down the length of Bell's back. "She wasn't like you."

Bell turned to face Lorraine and fixed a blank stare on her. "What's that mean?"

She brought her hand to Bell's head and pushed back a few braids. "She was scared of everything, especially herself."

As she watched Lorraine's clothes fall to the floor— the yellow blouse, followed by the flimsy black bra and finally her jeans—she searched for a suitable response to this statement. But there was nothing to say. Nothing at all.

The next morning, they sat down with Ethel and enjoyed a breakfast that consisted of grits, bacon, and toast. Meanwhile, Evie, the cat, sipped milk from a saucer and fixed a yellow-eyed gaze on the three women. Ethel stole glances at her two lodgers as the three of them ate in silence. She had had their type as lodgers before, but these two seemed a little different from the others, for she never would have guessed on first meeting them that they were 'that way.'

While Ethel generally found people like Lorraine and Bell to be great mysteries, she avoided wasting her time hating them. She figured grown folks should do with grown folks whatever made them happy, and, besides, they had paid her well for the room. Their money was the same as anyone else's money, no matter their sexual predilections.

Ethel sat and ate quietly for a while, watching Lorraine and Bell exchange embarrassed glances throughout the meal. She studied the two obviously lovesick women and thought about how love often ended in misery. It had ended that way in her life and in the lives of many women she knew, yet what stunned her was that women felt so compelled to try it over and over again, foolishly expecting different results each time. Ethel hoped love would go better for these two. After she grew weary of these morose thoughts, she interrupted the silence and started talking about her son.

As Ethel essentially read off her son's credentials, Lorraine and Bell inferred that the old woman was hoping some woman they knew might be interested in her son. "What about that sister of yours? Marie done found her a man yet?" asked Ethel.

"I don't think she's looking for one right now," said Lorraine, unsure of what else to say and trying her best to appear cordial.

Fussing with the gray scarf tied around her head, Ethel eventually dropped the subject and launched into descriptions of some previous visiting guests to whom she had rented out rooms. Gossiping about her previous guests had become a pastime of hers, although she respectfully left out names. She prided herself on being the sort of gossip who at least had a fair amount of tact and respect for the privacy of her guests.

"Had a young fella traveling from Lafayette drop by here a few months ago. Had a ring on his finger, but I sure didn't see one on the young lady he had with him. She was big as a house, belly out to here. He did his best to make me believe that woman was his wife. I had to tell him flat out that as long as he paid me, I didn't care who she was. I suspect he was trying to take her somewhere to 'take care of it,' if you get my drift. All I know is that woman didn't look like she'd ever be happy again. You ain't never seen a sadder looking woman. Poor thing." Ethel spoke at ninety miles per hour, barely opening her mouth the whole time. She went on in this vein for a while, until the conversation managed to drift back to her son. At that point, Lorraine and Bell thanked her for the breakfast and excused themselves. They retreated to their room, gathered their bags and headed out to the car.

"Tell Marie I said 'hi.' And y'all don't hesitate to call me if you're visiting again and need a room," said Ethel, standing on the screened in porch and holding Evie in her arms. "Be sure to recommend me to any other traveling ladies, you hear?"

"For sure. Thanks again, Mrs. Rose," Lorraine hollered from inside the car. They both waved at Ethel, who waved back and watched them pull out of the driveway.

Bell and Lorraine remained quiet during most of the two-hour ride back to Winchester. The radio station played a few Millie Jackson songs, between which the DJ reminded listeners about where they should go to get their concert tickets refunded. Bell hummed along to the music while Lorraine tapped her fingers rhythmically against the steering wheel.

"So," Bell began as they arrived at her family's house.

Two people sat on the porch, a white-haired woman and a honey-colored boy whom Lorraine guessed was no more than two or three years old. She knew the woman was Bell's great Aunt Margaret. She had run into the woman in Bell's store one afternoon and found the woman to be somewhat mean. The boy was probably a cousin, since Bell had no siblings.

Bell turned to her. "So, what're we gonna do now?"

"What do you mean?" Lorraine asked. She parked the car in front of the house and turned off the engine. Aunt Margaret fixed her white-blue unseeing eyes on them, and the boy played with some sticks at her feet.

"I mean about us, about what we did. What're we gonna do about it?"

Lorraine smiled and rested her hand on Bell's thigh. "We're gonna have dinner. You're gonna come over to my house after work tomorrow. I'm gonna cook, and afterwards we can do 'what we did' again and again. We can do whatever we want."

Bell glanced at the woman and the boy on the porch. "We can't do whatever we want."

"Why not?"

"Because we live in the real world, Clem. This world, Winchester."

"Forget this place. I'll be leaving in a few months, anyway, and you can come with me. You *should* come with me. My sister in Philly said—"

There was a knock at the passenger door. When Bell opened it, the little boy stood there with a big, eager grin on his face and equally big eyes. "Mommy!" he exclaimed, jumping into Bell's open arms. She kissed his pale cheek, and he threw his arms around her neck.

"Mommy?" Lorraine repeated, staring at the boy with the large, familiar eyes. He was several shades lighter than Bell, but he looked exactly like her, right down to the smile.

"This is my son, Darren." She was looking down at the boy and running her hand through his tight curls.

"Oh." Lorraine was too stunned to say much else. To her surprise, the boy extended his right hand as if he wanted her to shake it. It struck her as a rather precocious gesture, one that made her smile at once and appreciate that someone had taught him good manners. Children with good manners were rare, in Lorraine's opinion. She shook his tiny hand and introduced herself before turning her attention back to Bell. "Why didn't you tell me?"

"I was waiting for the right time" explained Bell.

"And his father?" she asked, glancing at Bell's fingers. "Don't tell me you're married. You're not wearing a ring."

"My husband got called to service last year. Vietnam. I didn't hear nothing from him for a while. No news, nothing, until I got the letter six months ago saying he'd been shot and killed along with ten of his men. Darren's never even seen his pa. I stopped wearing the ring just before I met you."

"I'm sorry. That's...my God." They sat in silence, both staring straight ahead while Darren hummed and played with Bell's hands.

"Well, thank you for the trip," said Bell, unbuckling her seat belt.

"I'll see you tomorrow then? After work?" Lorraine asked.

Bell looked at her with curiosity and, after a while, nodded. "Yeah." She gathered her bag, held onto Darren's little hand and shut the door. Lorraine watched her walk up the porch steps and go inside the old house.

While she was on Hwy 65 heading home to McGhee, Lorraine gazed up at the blue sky and visualized the curves of Bell's body in the orange dress and the lavender smell of her hair. She was not certain of many things in her life, but she was certain of one thing that day: she loved Bell Mitchell.

CHAPTER ELEVEN

"Y'all are moving mighty fast, don't you think?" Reggie whispered to Lorraine one night, when Bell had excused herself to the bathroom. A bright-eyed Darren sat across the table and studied them with curiosity as he chewed noisily on his food. Lorraine winked at him and he returned the gesture with a wide smile that revealed a mouth full of half-chewed food.

Bell and Darren Mitchell soon became regular dinner and overnight guests at Lorraine and Reggie's home. In fact, Bell had all but moved in with her new best friends. Many of her belongings and Darren's belongings were stored in Lorraine's room or in the front room trunk. She spent maybe two nights a week at her own home with her parents whose behavior had grown increasingly hostile. Her father did not take kindly to his daughter's new friends who had become the central focus of town gossip, and he made sure to tell her so at every available opportunity.

"You got no respect for this family or for me. You keep this up, and I'll be out of business," her father had blustered one evening as she was leaving the store after her shift.

"Nonsense. I know for a fact don't nobody give a good darn. They're happy long as you feed them," Bell had scoffed and marched right out the back door to her pickup truck where Lorraine was waiting.

Yet even her father's vehement disapproval could not disrupt the peace she had found. "Pa'll just have to get over it," Bell told her mother while they ate breakfast one Sunday. Silent as usual, her mother just gave a sad little nod and said nothing.

So Bell spent more and more time with Lorraine and Reggie, avoiding her father as much as possible. It was easier that way, and Lorraine had never been happier.

"I'd say we're moving just fine." Lorraine shot a hard look at Reggie. She leaned forward and put another spoonful of sweet potatoes onto Darren's plate. He politely said thank you, and Lorraine marveled at the manners of the boy. If all children were so well-behaved, she might be inclined to have one or two of her own.

"I was just making an observation. You don't have to get a nasty tone."

She glanced at him with the same hard look. "Fine. Your observation is noted." To Lorraine's immense relief, Bell reappeared before he could respond, and the conversation ended.

The three of them lighted upon another topic while they watched Darren who appeared to find his sweet potatoes more fun than tasty. He mashed the potatoes and stirred them, then mashed them some more as if he was mixing up paint on a palette and, like children are prone to doing, sung some nonsensical words of a song he had made up on the spot. Lorraine observed him, and a smile curled her lips as she listened to the jumbled words of his song.

"Kids really have the gift of improvisation, don't they? Why do you think we lose that gift, eventually?" asked Lorraine.

Bell shook her head. "Not all of us lose it. I don't think most of us lose it. It just don't look the same the older we get." She took the spoon from Darren and told him to stop playing with his food. Turning to Lorraine and Reggie, she went on, "If you want my opinion, I say you gotta improvise the shit out of life. Do what feels right once in a while, so long as it ain't hurting nobody else. I mean, really, any of us could be dead tomorrow. What've we got to lose?"

Lorraine let Bell's last couple of sentences swirl around her mind for a while. She wondered if Bell's view was not an extremely immature way of looking at life. In all likelihood, none of them at the table would be dead tomorrow. In all likelihood, they would live long lives and die of a stroke or heart attack in fifty years or so. Furthermore, there was a lot to lose—freedom, family, friends, reputation, money, shelter, food, happiness. On the other hand, she could not help but respect Bell's outlook and see some truth in it. *Improvise...*

As they lay in bed later, Bell surveyed the room and Lorraine lay against her chest. Lorraine's outfit for the next day was folded on a wire hanger and hung from a knob on the top drawer of the oak dresser across the room. To the left, there were two bookcases, the smaller bookcase half-filled with Bell's cookbooks, and the larger one was filled with Lorraine's books, old diaries, novels, and a few books of poetry.

"I really want you and Darren to come with me after graduation," Lorraine said, jolting Bell out of her daydream.

"Clem," Bell began, sitting up and sighing. "Do you have to bring it up every time we're together? I told you I need to think about it."

Lorraine found herself confused by the contradictions between Bell's words and Bell's actions. *What about improvising life? Leaving this town and taking a chance in a new place would be an act of improvisation, wouldn't it?*

"I'm sorry. But it's been on my mind today. Reggie accepted the job in Philly. He mailed the letter today, and he's gonna get his brother to look for apartments for us. So he kind of needs to know how many of 'us' there'll be."

"I know. It's just that all my family's down here in Arkansas and Louisiana. I don't know nobody all the way up east. And we've only known each other for a few months."

"It's been way more than a few months. And what about improvising and all that jazz you were talking about at dinner earlier? That was just talk?"

"No. I meant all that. Look, it's just—it's asking a lot, Clem. I need more time to think about it."

Lorraine sighed. "It's your family. I understand."

"No, you don't," Bell argued, looking at Darren. "*All* of my family is down here. At least your sister is up north."

"Okay, you're right. I don't fully understand." She sat up and brought her knees to her chest. "But you'll have me and Reggie, and my sister will love you. I know that's not enough right now. I know you probably think it's all too fast. But I'm telling you, Bell, you'll never be able to be who you are, not down here. I mean, do you want to spend your whole life in this suffocating place, where you have to hide the most beautiful part of yourself? Do you want to raise your son down here? That's all I'm saying. And, besides, I looked up some culinary schools up there. Come on, let's do it! Let's improvise like you said."

"Clem. Just let me think about it."

"Okay." Lorraine leaned against Bell as they watched Darren break crayons and scribble in his book.

On Friday night, they went out with Reggie to Mae Anne's Cafe, a bar just outside of McGhee, to celebrate Bell's twenty-first birthday. Reggie and one of his classmates, a white boy named Bobby Eamon Murphy from Texarkana, accompanied them. "Now, ain't nothing but drunk and rowdy black folks at this establishment, you hear? They're not accustomed to seeing pale faces in this joint. Consider yourself warned," Reggie explained in the car, half hoping to frighten his classmate. Bobby just shrugged and said he knew how to handle himself, but Bell noticed he seemed rather distracted during the rest of the ride.

After some circling around the crowded bar, they found a table near the back, close to the restrooms. One of the waiters—a young woman whom Bell thought wore far too much makeup—cleaned the table, and the four of them sat down. Reggie ordered two pitchers of beer for the group. Meanwhile, Bobby peered around, and Lorraine realized that he was trying his best to keep his face straight in an attempt to appear relaxed. But his posture and silence betrayed his worry. He had not said a word since they entered the place. She scanned Reggie's posture and mannerisms as he eyed his classmate. He had placed his arm around the back of Bobby's chair, had turned his body halfway toward him and appeared to have eyes for no one else in the room. Bobby stared around, perfectly oblivious to Reggie's unwavering and—if Lorraine had to characterize it—lustful gaze. She kicked Reggie's foot under the table to get his attention and cast him a scornful look. It took her great effort to keep from laughing. Reggie's face contained a mixture of confusion and annoyance, as though she had woke him up from a deep and pleasant dream. "What?" he mouthed.

"That boy is not gay," she mouthed back.

Reggie shrugged and smirked. "We'll see."

Bobby suddenly turned to the three of them. "See what? What'd I miss?"

Lorraine and Reggie laughed. "Nothing," Reggie lied. I said we'll see which one of us ends up drunk enough to get out there and dance."

Bobby smiled and turned his attention back to the crowd. With a wink at Lorraine, Reggie turned up his mug of beer, before refilling it. Bell took this moment to change the topic to her cookbook. "I'm almost finished with it, and Pa said he might see about trying to sell some of them in the café. But it's just scribbles in my notebook right now. I don't know nothing about getting a book made."

This prompted Bobby to mention an editor he knew in Texas, and Bell's excitement at such a prospect rolled off her in waves. The two of them leaned in close for a while and talked over the music and noise.

"I bought you something," said Bell, turning to Lorraine.

"You bought me something for your birthday?"

"No. I bought you something just because." She sat her purse on the table and dug inside it. Eventually, she brought out a silver object and handed it to Lorraine as Reggie leaned in to get a closer look at it.

"A locket." Lorraine stared down at the triangle-shaped locket and turned it over in her hands.

"Do you see the writing on it?" asked Bell.

"It has an inscription?" Reggie leaned forward. "What's it say?"

Lorraine opened the door of the locket. "It's so dark in here. Hold on. Okay, I see it. 'Love Always, Bell.' Aww, it's so sweet." She threw her arms around Bell, who kissed her and held onto her. Once they released one another, they kissed some more, and Bell put the locket on Lorraine.

"Almost six months has gone by, yet we feel like we've known you forever, darling," Reggie addressed Bell, in mock formality. "Happy birthday to Miss Bell Mitchell on this here day, February 19, 1976. May you have many more." He held up his beer mug in salute. "And cheers to you, Clem, for bringing Bell into our lives. Now, drink up."

They all toasted, took big swallows of beer and refilled their mugs.

"So, what did you get me for my birthday?" Bell sat her mug down on the table.

Lorraine brushed her lips against Bell's neck and whispered, "A couple of things. But they're at home." In fact, after Lorraine's literature professor dismissed class early that day, she went to a small antique store in Monticello. A few weeks earlier, she had seen a silver tea set and a Cajun cookbook there. Fortunately, the owner had not sold either item by the time Bell's birthday arrived. Without hesitation, Lorraine handed the owner ten dollars and left the store with the tea set and cookbook gift-wrapped in newspaper. She was eager to see Bell's reaction later.

Bobby excused himself to the restroom, and Reggie rose to join him. "Just so nobody tries to bother him," added Reggie, when Lorraine cast him an amused smile.

"Sure," she teased, and he straightened the newsboy cap on his head as he turned to follow his classmate.

"Let me see if I can guess what you might have got me." Bell refilled her beer mug and drummed her fingers on the table.

Lorraine turned to her, but when Bell opened her mouth to speak, a male voice interrupted:

"Umph, umph, umph. You ladies sure are about the finest young things this side of the Mississippi. Gotdamn."

Bell and Lorraine looked up and found four men staring down at them. Two of the men sat down in Bobby's and Reggie's chairs, while the other two men stood behind and leaned against the wall. The man who had spoken placed himself directly in front of Lorraine and surveyed every part of her except her face.

"Y'all been here before?" the man said, looking only at her breasts. His loosely coiled hair was combed back and heavily oiled, a city look, a look that said he was not a local.

"Yes." Lorraine hoped the coldness in her voice conveyed her disinterest. But when she turned back to Bell and attempted to resume their conversation, the man interrupted.

"Nah, can't be. I'd never miss two good-looking women like yourselves," he declared, finally meeting Lorraine's eyes. He had arresting hazel eyes set in a pale yellow, freckled face. She did not like what she saw in his eyes. She glanced at the other men, who smiled and watched her and Bell closely. One of the men leaning against the wall took a drag of his cigarette and exhaled. *Here is a man who has watched one too many Ron O'Neal movies*, Lorraine thought.

"Look. We're flattered. But we're not interested," she replied, then rolled her eyes and turned to Bell.

"Now, hold on. You ain't even let me introduce myself and my fellas yet," he continued, chuckling. "Feisty something, ain't you?"

"Our friends are coming back," Lorraine warned the men. "And you're in their seats. Okay? It was nice to meet you. Good night."

"Your friends? The fag and the white boy that was sitting here with y'all?" taunted the man, smiling a horrible smile. None of the other men spoke.

"It's time for y'all to leave," Lorraine heard Bell say in a loud and steady voice. Bell stood up, and Lorraine's eyes followed her. The man who had spoken looked up at Bell, and she frowned at him. "You heard me," Bell told them.

The other man who had seated himself next to the hazel-eyed leader snickered and glanced back at his friends. This man, as fair-skinned as the hazel-eyed man but with sideburns so excessive that they deserved some sort of award, appeared to be in his late teens, younger than all the others. Lorraine felt an inexplicable foreboding when she stared at this man. He had a lot more to prove because of his youth, she surmised. He was just a boy, a pampered looking boy in fact, but far worse than the others, she realized. "I like this one. She got some fire in her," he smirked, casting a fleeting look over his shoulder at his friends. He turned to Bell. "Woman that fiery must give some good loving."

"You wouldn't know what to do with it if you got it," Bell replied. For a moment, Lorraine peered up at her in admiration. Lorraine never had been skillful with snappy retorts and envied people who had such skills. Quickly, however, the apprehensive feeling returned, and she watched the younger man.

"You got a big mouth, don't you? I like that in a woman," he went on, smiling at Bell and making implication of his statement clear as he spread his legs.

Not missing the implication, Bell fired back. "Fuck you."

"Be my guest," he mocked.

Bell moved forward as though she was ready to punch the man or jump across the table at him.

"Look," Lorraine broke in, her eyes darting between Bell and the young boy. "Just leave us alone, all right?" This was exactly why she had stopped going to bars in McGhee.

The young boy went on speaking, as if Lorraine had not said a word. "Y'all know what they say about women with big mouths," he remarked to his buddies, and they all laughed. He turned and looked intently at Bell without blinking or smiling, a look that sent shivers through Lorraine. She realized she never had seen such emptiness in anyone's eyes.

Lorraine started to stand up and pull Bell away from the table, but she stopped when she saw Bell bend down and reach inside her purse. Within seconds, Bell brought out a .22mm pistol and pointed it at the cocky young boy who had been speaking to her. The smirk on his face disappeared instantly.

"You wanna run that shit by me one more time? Huh, boy?" she snapped, holding the gun just a foot away from his face. Cautiously, he and the other man stood up. The two men already standing stepped back, their gazes fixed on the gun.

"A couple of bulldyke bitches. Just like I told y'all," snarled the boy, watching Bell. "I suppose this one here's the man in the relationship."

"Shut up, Eddie," the man with the hazel eyes said, not tearing his eyes away from Lorraine and Bell. Lorraine was pleased by the look of fear in his eyes. "Now, now, just hold on. We didn't mean no harm. Eddie here just run his mouth off at every pretty girl he see. That's all. Right, Eddie? We don't mean no harm. No harm at all." The expression on the other men's faces, all but the young boy, matched the fear in their leader's voice. Lorraine noticed that the cocky young boy named Eddie continued to stare coldly at Bell. Eddie did not appear frightened at all but perhaps turned on by the situation.

Bell, on the other hand, glared at Eddie. She held the gun steady and pointed it at his face.

The man with the hazel eyes stepped back, doffed his hat at Lorraine, grabbed Eddie's arm to pull him away, and forced a smile. His buddies, their eyes still fixed on the gun, followed him as he backed up and disappeared into the crowd. Eddie cast a final icy glare at Bell and Lorraine before the crowd swallowed him up.

Lorraine's gaze swept over the crowd of drunken and chatting people. No one had seen the altercation or, if so, they had disregarded it. She turned to Bell, who was stuffing the pistol back inside her purse.

"When the hell did you get that, Bell?" Lorraine watched Bell sit down and sip her beer nonchalantly.

"My pa gave it to me when I was eighteen. A birthday present. Have a seat, Clem. They're gone now," she said, and Lorraine gawked at her.

Frantically, Lorraine surveyed the crowd. There was no sign of the men, nor was there any sign of Reggie and Bobby. She sat down and scrutinized Bell.

"You want another pitcher of beer?" Bell asked.

"No. Where's Reggie and Bobby?"

"Probably somewhere screwing," Bell giggled.

She gawked at Bell. "Don't be so crass. What's with you anyway? Pulling guns on people?"

"People? They're predators, rapists. Believe me, it's only a matter of time before they attack somebody, if they ain't done it already. I probably would've been doing all women a favor if I'd shot the little bastard."

"And Darren? Would you have been doing your son a favor by landing yourself in the penitentiary?"

"Oh, just stop making a mountain out of a molehill, Clem. It's done now."

Lorraine stood up and grabbed her purse and coat. "Come on. We're finding Reggie and Bobby, and we're leaving."

Bell did not argue. She rose, finished off her mug of beer, picked up her coat and purse and took Lorraine's hand. Lorraine wove through the crowd, hoping not to run into the four men. She opened the door to the men's bathroom and yelled out Reggie and Bobby's names. No one answered. They walked around the tiny café and still saw no sign of Reggie and Bobby. At this point, Lorraine was furious and cursing the day she had decided to set foot in the café. Warily, she went out into the frigid air and rushed to the car.

"Are we just gonna leave them?" Bell asked as they approached Lorraine's car.

"I don't know. Depends on how I feel when I turn the key in the ignition." She looked left and right as they walked through the dark parking lot, making sure the four men were not lurking around.

When they reached the car, she saw that the windows had fogged up. Uncertainly, she wiped the windows, peeked inside, and discovered Bobby and Reggie in the backseat. The two men were wrapped in one another's arms, with Reggie on top and moving back and forth. "I cannot believe..." Lorraine knocked on the window, and both men stopped and looked up at her. "Reggie, you little tramp," she yelled, loud enough for them to hear her. She fumbled with the keys and unlocked the door. Bell got in and slid to the passenger side of the car that now smelled strongly of musk and sex. Lorraine frowned at the scent as she got inside and locked the door.

"Hello, ladies." Reggie pulled up his pants. "Leaving so early?" As he spoke, Bobby averted his gaze, shamefaced, and pulled down his shirt.

Lorraine glanced over her shoulder and frowned at him. "Yes, we're leaving. We were just harassed by a bunch of predatory men until Bell pulled a pistol on them. Of course, if you hadn't been out here doing you know what, those men probably never would've bothered us in the first place. You do realize that's why I bring you out with me, right? To keep the perverted men away?"

"Bell pulled out a gun? That's my girl!" exclaimed Reggie, high-fiving Bell. Glowering at both of them, Lorraine sighed in exasperation.

"Just buckle your seatbelts. And you're wiping out my backseat with soap and water tomorrow, Reggie." She put the car in reverse.

Bell and Reggie laughed. Lorraine pulled out onto the darkened road and listened while Bell recounted the incident to Reggie and Bobby. None of it was funny to Lorraine as she recalled the young boy named Eddie and his empty eyes.

Lorraine pushed back the covers and walked to the window, where she stared outside at the black night and the cloud-covered sky. Just a few stars were visible. The moon was the only source of light, yet the mysteries of the landscape seemed to hide from the moon. Vaguely, she could see the willow tree in the front yard and her

Volkswagen sitting next to Bell's pickup truck in the driveway.

She turned toward Bell and sat in the rocking chair next to the window. She gazed at Bell's face illuminated by the moonlight and thought about the locket's inscription. She felt anxious, but then realized that really it was worry that was consuming her. No, fear, she concluded at last. She had had an inexplicable fear gnawing at her all evening since they left the café, a fear as vivid as a vision. In this fear, she could see everything breaking and crumbling around her. Lorraine did not believe in God or anything supernatural, but she would have sworn that she was having a premonition of some sort. There was a storm coming.

For a while, she sat there and fell into her mind. She thought about her life, her future and the haunting feeling that had come over her. When Bell rose up and said, "Clem? Come back to bed," Lorraine silently obeyed. She slid under the covers, turned onto her side and shut her eyes as Bell's arms closed around her. "I'll come with you," whispered Bell, breathing against Lorraine's ear. "In May. Wherever you go, me and Darren will come."

Lorraine smiled at this sudden announcement and kissed Bell's hand. She closed her eyes and thought of the future, until she drifted to sleep in Bell's arms.

CHAPTER TWELVE

Over the next couple of months, Bell brought more of her belongings to Reggie and Lorraine's home. Bell brought boxes of clothes, cookbooks and Darren's toys, as well as one box full of purses she had made and used to store important papers and receipts. She also placed the draft of her cookbook, which was a notebook with a plain brown cover, and the Cajun cookbook Lorraine had given her inside the box. "What sort of papers you keep in there?" Lorraine had asked, sitting on the bed and watching her carry in boxes.

"You know? Social security cards and things like that," she had explained, after she pushed the box inside Lorraine's bedroom closet.

Every other week, she brought a few more items: shoes, her record collection, and photographs. In between all the moving and packing, they made love, took weekend trips to the mall or to the movies in Little Rock and went fishing at their usual spot. On Fridays, Bell cooked and they put Darren to sleep early. Afterward, they danced in the living room to Bobby Blue Bland, ZZ Hill, Earth Wind and Fire or whatever seemed appropriate at the moment, while Reggie and Bobby leaned close to one another in deep conversation or excused themselves to Reggie's bedroom. Lorraine marveled at how quickly days turned into weeks and weeks into months as she watched Bell grow happier, Darren learn more words and Reggie and Bobby split up and get back together multiple times. She watched leaves appear on the fig tree in her backyard as buckets of rain poured for days throughout April.

On some days, she sat on her porch next to Bell while Darren played with Willy the cat and the wind beat against the trees. Graduation came and went, and they packed and partied, or else lounged about listening to music, hardly noticing the passage of time. Days, months, it all swept by in one wave, as time often does when life is pleasant and free. All the while, the ominous feeling from that night at the café months earlier lingered like a gray cloud around Lorraine.

While sitting on the porch during a muggy day in late May, she watched Darren chase Willy around the willow tree. Darren laughed, falling onto the ground as Willy climbed on top of him. "You know, I'm surprised Willy's even playing with him this long," observed Reggie, appearing in the doorway.

She looked over her shoulder at him. He was wearing one of her aprons and holding a spatula, a combination that was altogether comical on Reggie. "I know. Considering how grumpy he usually is. I guess he's having a good day."

"We're all having a lot of those lately, huh?" he smiled, staring at Darren and Willy in the yard. Darren was lying on the ground and caressing Willy's back. "Call him in. The table's set, and I'm about to brown the chicken."

After she took Darren to wash his hands and sat him at the table, Bobby and Reggie joined them. In silence, the foursome dug into the fried chicken, baked macaroni and green beans. Lorraine watched Bobby, noting the gloom that had come over him during the last month. Frankly, she worried about Bobby and how he would cope while he finished his last year at Monticello without Reggie. She was not sure he had any other friends, and he had attached himself so thoroughly to them or rather to Reggie since that night at the café.

An idea occurred to her, and before she could stop herself, she blurted, "Bobby, you want to spend the summer with us in Philly?"

Reggie accidentally spit out a bean, and Bobby gawked at her.

"Are you serious?" said Bobby, his eyes wide.

She nodded.

He looked from her to Reggie. "Well, yeah. I don't know what to say. I can't turn that down. I've never spent any time up north." He grinned from ear to ear.

Reggie shot her a bewildered look, but she shrugged. "Wonderful. When do your classes end and—"

The door creaked open, and Lorraine stopped mid-sentence. "You're all sorts of late." She took in Bell's disheveled appearance.

"Mommy," Darren exclaimed. He ran to her, and she scooped him up in a tight hug. When she came into the light, Lorraine noticed that her eyelashes and the corners of her eyes looked wet. Bell put Darren on the floor, and he resumed his seat at the table.

"Who cooked this? It smells damn good."

"Well you know I didn't, since I can't cook to save my life. Reggie and Bobby cooked it, from your cookbook. It's really good."

Lorraine winked and smiled at Reggie, and he threw her a proud look before he resumed eating. "Everything all right?" she asked so that only Bell could hear her. Without waiting for an answer, however, she took Bell's arm, and they went to the bedroom.

"You've been crying?" she asked.

"It's nothing," Bell lied, wiping her face.

"Come on. How many times have I seen you cry?"

"Never."

"Exactly. So, what's wrong?"

"Me and Pa got to fussing about me leaving," Bell began as she sat down on the bed. Lorraine closed the door and joined her. "About me and you."

"What about you and me? You didn't tell them, did you?"

Bell wiped her face and appeared aggravated. "Oh hell, Clem, don't be so naïve. You really think they hadn't figured it out? The whole damn town knows. I *had* to fess up. Pa called me to the kitchen after I finished my shift, and he just went to hollering, wouldn't let me get a word in. The things he called me. I never would've believed he could think that way about me. Apparently, since I fuck women, I ain't fit to raise my own son. You know he wanna take Darren from me? That's why he's so mad about me going away. He don't mind *me* leaving. He mind that I'm taking Darren with me. I'm his only child, and he don't want me no more. His only child. Mama, she don't never try to stand up for me. Like always, she sit back and don't say nothing. She just let him say these terrible things. I can't wait to get away from here."

Lorraine put her arms around Bell. "It's just a couple more weeks, and we're gone. If you need to, you can stay over here until we leave. It'll be fine. I promise."

"I can tell you one thing, he ain't getting my son. I love my pa, but I won't let him take Darren from me. If anything happens to me—"

"It's okay. He won't get Darren. I promise," Lorraine assured her. As she held Bell's hand, she wondered why she was making a promise she could not keep. "Legally, I don't think he could take him anyway, but I'll ask Reggie."

They sat there wrapped in one another's arms while Bell sniffled and cried quietly. After a few minutes, there was a knock on the door, and they both turned to find Darren standing in the doorway. Bell quickly turned away and dried her face.

Looking up every now and then at Darren, who ran along the bank of the stream and dug holes with a stick, Bell hummed to herself and pasted Polaroid photographs into a photo album with a blank leather cover. She and Bell sat under the willow trees that drooped along the bank of the stream, providing welcome refuge from the spring sun. There was not a cloud in the sky, and the humid, hot air clung to their clothes. The May heat had made a surprising and spectacular entrance. Bell wore the orange summer dress Lorraine had bought her, and Lorraine wore a blouse and blue jean skirt. She tugged uncomfortably at the skirt, regretting that she had allowed Bell to talk her into wearing it. Bell had wanted one rare picture of her in a skirt.

"Look," Darren hollered, running toward them with something in his hand. As he drew closer, Lorraine saw that the thing clutched between his index finger and thumb was small, brown and wiggling. She shrieked and jumped back when Darren reached them, sending the boy into a fit of laughter.

"That's not nice, Darren. You know she don't like those." Bell suppressed her laughter. He laughed some more and took off with the worm. "All the times we been fishing, and you're still scared of worms?"

Lorraine shivered. "They're disgusting."

"They make things grow and live. Can't get less disgusting than that," Bell proclaimed, philosophically.

All the while, Bell scribbled on a small strip of white paper and taped it to the cover of the photo album. For months, she had been adding photographs to the album. She carried her Polaroid camera everywhere and had taken so many photographs of them, photographs of their fishing trips, their walks, nights out with Reggie. She had documented the last nine months of their life. "It's finished."

Lorraine leaned forward and read the words on the cover: "Arkansas: 1975 through 1976."

Together, they flipped through the pages of photographs. When they reached the last page, there was no picture. There was only a sentence written on a strip of silver paper that Lorraine recognized as the Millie Jackson ticket. Bell had placed it in the center of the page and scribbled on it, "Write about this."

"You like it?" asked Bell.

She kissed Bell's hand and looked down at the last page. "It's amazing. Thank you."

Bell wiped across the countertop with a soapy towel, and Lorraine sat at the bar and slurped lemonade through a straw. It was still early, not even 11 o'clock yet, and the place already had filled up with regulars and a few unfamiliar faces. The music blaring from the speakers had stirred up the crowd, but it hurt Bell's ears. Every time she turned the volume down, however, her father turned it up. He considered it a sin to turn down Muddy Waters and John Lee Hooker.

Lorraine yelled over the noise to Bell. "Hey, can I get a refill?" She pushed back her new braids in frustration, unaccustomed to letting her hair hang down. She usually kept it frizzed up into an afro or else pulled back into a ponytail. But Bell had insisted upon braiding Lorraine's hair a few days earlier, and both of them now had the same hairstyle. Reggie had joked that he hardly could distinguish them but for Lorraine's slightly lighter complexion, squinty eyes and narrower nose, compared to Bell's round nose and large eyes. "You want me to help you clean up? So maybe you can leave early?" she asked as Bell refilled the glass.

"No. It's fine. Pa don't want you here as it is. If he sees you behind the bar or in the kitchen, he might just have a heart attack." A sour smile crossed Bell's face, and she surveyed the crowd. She picked up several empty glasses and disappeared into the kitchen.

Lorraine sipped her lemonade and swayed her head to the music, mouthing the words to John Lee Hooker's "Whiskey and Wimmen." As she glanced at her watch, anxious for Bell's shift to end, someone's hot breath hit her neck, and it reeked of alcohol. *These damn men.* She looked straight ahead and remained motionless, as if she had no awareness of the man's existence or proximity.

"Looking just as fine as ever. I think the spring agrees with you," greeted the man.

At the sound of the familiar voice, she continued to look straight ahead towards the kitchen as she sipped her lemonade, never so much as glancing in the man's direction. She would not let them frighten her this time, she told herself. If she ignored them, she reckoned they would get bored and leave.

"Where's your friend?" the man with the hazel eyes asked.

"The mannish one," came another eerily familiar voice that Lorraine knew belonged to the cocky young one named Eddie.

Briefly, her hands tightened around the glass, and she prayed that Bell would not reemerge from the kitchen. On the other hand, she realized that she would quite like to see Bell put a bullet in the young one. Her mother had told her, "Some people ain't fit to breathe. That's just the truth." She stood up and turned to make her way through the crowd and toward the back of the bar. She wanted to get to the kitchen before Bell came out, before things got out of hand. She and Bell could slip out the back door, she figured, quickly strategizing in her head and hoping that Bell had left the gun at home.

As she began to push through the throng of people, Bell emerged from the kitchen and stopped when she saw the four men. She glowered at the men and met Lorraine's gaze for a moment before disappearing inside the kitchen. *Shit.* Lorraine moved faster through the crowd. *Shit, shit, shit.*

"Oh, so your little friend works here, huh? I think I'll have a drink, after all," taunted the hazel-eyed man. He turned to Lorraine. "What you having?"

She did not answer him. Instead, she looked in the opposite direction, and continued pushing through the crowd of patrons. Bell reemerged from the kitchen, with her father standing next to her. Mr. Mitchell wore a slightly too-small white tank top, a hairnet, and jeans. Were it not for his harsh gaze, Lorraine might have found his appearance laughable rather than intimidating. Arms folded across his chest, he scanned the four men, and the coldness in his glare surpassed his daughter's cold stare. "Is there a problem, boys?"

"Not at all. This a fine café you got here. I was just talking to this young lady." The hazel-eyed man nodded toward Lorraine. "And the young lady beside you."

"My daughter," Mr. Mitchell clarified. He moved closer to Bell.

"Well, how about that. She's a beautiful woman. Her and her *friend*," the hazel-eyed man went on. "I'm surprised ain't neither one of them married. I don't see no rings."

"That ain't none of your business," Bell shot back, and her father cast her a warning look.

"Where you boys from? You ain't from around here," asked Mr. Mitchell.

"Just visiting from Shreveport, in and out of town," the man replied, while Eddie watched Bell.

Mr. Mitchell noticed Eddie's stare, glanced at his daughter, and then fixed his eyes on Eddie and the hazel-eyed leader. "Well, I don't know how they do things down in Shreveport, son, but I don't tolerate no harassing of women in my restaurant, you understand? You either act with some sense or you can find yourselves another fine establishment to patronize, you hear? You ain't gone be starting no shit in my bar."

"Of course not," the leader assured them, smiling and doffing his hat in a dandyish manner. Lorraine watched Eddie, whose eyes were fastened on Bell with that same frightening glint as before. "We'll be on our way then. Ladies, y'all have a nice night," said the leader, still smiling as horribly as ever. Just as before, he doffed his hat to Lorraine, turned away, and was swallowed up by the crowd. His buddies followed him.

Lorraine walked around to the back of the bar and followed Bell and Mr. Mitchell into the kitchen.

"Are you okay?" Bell asked, hugging Lorraine. She nodded and pulled away at once. They turned to Bell's father, who stood a few feet away and watched them. His eyes lingered on Lorraine.

"Bell, you can leave early."

"Pa, I don't mind. I can stay another thirty minutes—"

"No," he insisted, and there was no arguing with him. "I got it. I don't like the look of those boys. I seen their kind before. Go get your pocketbook. I'll walk y'all to the car."

Bell slung off her apron, went to a closet in the back of the room, gathered her purse, and they exited through the back storage area. Mr. Mitchell, glancing left and right, walked them to Lorraine's car parked a few feet away on the grass. He kissed his daughter's cheek and shut the door after she got in on the passenger side. When Bell rolled down the window, he added, "Call me here at the bar when you make it to the house. All right?"

She looked up at him. "Pa?"

"Yeah?"

"Thank you," she smiled. Mr. Mitchell's face softened a little. He looked at Lorraine with an unreadable expression and stepped back. Lorraine reversed out of the parking lot, and Bell rolled up the window as they set out on the dark road.

Reggie was fully dressed to go out when they arrived at the house. He was sitting on the sofa and reading a James Baldwin book while he waited for them to return so that he could drive over to Bobby's house. Bell greeted Reggie and went to call her father from the kitchen phone.

"Darren's asleep in your bedroom. I'll be back in the morning," he informed them, kissing Lorraine on the cheek and practically bolting through the front door a few moments later. She locked it and went to the kitchen to get a glass of water.

When Bell hung up the phone, she leaned against the cabinet and smiled at Lorraine. "Maybe Pa's coming around," she considered.

Lorraine poured herself a glass of water and turned to Bell. "He's your father. He loves you, even if he doesn't like who you're with."

Bell took Lorraine's free hand and kissed it, and the two women stood there for a while.

Lorraine turned up the glass of water, drained it and placed the glass in the sink. She switched off the kitchen light and followed Bell to the bedroom, where they changed into pajamas and got into bed on either side of Darren. After Bell turned out the lamplight, she put her arm over Darren and drifted to sleep, grasping Lorraine's hand.

"Clem?"

Lorraine turned over and saw that Bell's spot was unoccupied. She sat up and looked around until her blurry gaze fell upon Bell, who was standing next to the window and peeking through the curtains. She moved to turn on the lamplight, but Bell hissed in the same quiet voice, "No. Don't turn it on." In the thick darkness of the room, her eyes searched Bell and stopped on the l-shaped object in her left hand. That's when Lorraine's heart began to race.

"They're here. All four of them," stated Bell. The calmness in her voice was altogether alarming. Her voice seemed distant, vacant. Sliding to the foot of the bed and standing up, Lorraine clutched her chest and hoped that she was dreaming, and that she would wake up in a moment next to Bell and Darren. Yet she was still standing, and Bell had turned to her and drew closer. "I need you to take Darren and leave."

"What?"

"You and Darren go out back. I'll distract them and draw them all to the front."

Instinctively, she now understood what Bell was staring at beyond the window. She wanted desperately to wake up. "Bell, there's four of them. I can't leave you."

"My son, Clem. Please, listen to me," she barked, hurrying toward Lorraine. "Do as I say."

Lorraine bent down and gathered up Darren, who was fast asleep. Meanwhile, Bell knelt, pulled Lorraine's purse from under the bed and thrust it at her. They both looked toward the window as they heard a sound at the front door that told them one of the men was trying to force it open. "Did you call the police?" Lorraine asked, looking at Bell's face, which she could not see clearly in the dark room.

"Yeah. A few minutes ago. But they might be forever getting out here," she explained. "Look, when I give you the cue, go out the back door."

"What's the cue?"

"A gunshot."

Lorraine stood motionless. She was sure she never would be able to move again.

"Did you hear me, Clem?"

"Yes," she gasped, staring at the gun in Bell's hand.

Bell leaned forward and kissed Darren. "Mommy will see you in a bit." She held Lorraine's hand, kissed it and stared at her. In the next instant, she cocked the pistol and stepped away. "Go now, to the back door. Don't open it until you hear the shot. Then give yourself three seconds before you open the door."

"How do we know one of them won't be back there?"

"We don't know. Just do as I say, Clem."

With Darren in her arms and a quick look at Bell, Lorraine ran to the back door and stood there. It was probably less than a minute, but she would have sworn it was an hour or something close to an eternity. She heard Bell's footsteps move away, toward the living room. Seconds later, Bell shouted something and the front door banged open and finally a gunshot sounded. Darren's heavy body stirred in her arms. Lorraine waited a moment, counted to three and crept out the backdoor as fast as she could without making any noise. She shut the door quietly so as not to make a sound, although she was sure they would not hear her over the banging and hollering that had commenced inside the house. She strained to tune out the sounds while her eyes scanned the vacant backyard for any signs of movement.

Darren grumbled and rubbed his eyes. Immediately, Lorraine leaned down and shushed him. "We're going to the store. Mommy'll meet us in a little bit," she whispered. He did not say a word but instead just looked at her. She walked to the right side of the house toward the driveway where her car was parked. While she stood under the fig tree, she looked out at the driveway. The men had left their car engine running, and she did not see anyone outside. More screaming and yelling sounded from inside the house, but she tried to tune it out and focused straight ahead towards her car. *Get Darren to safety*, she told herself repeatedly.

She ran out onto the driveway, crouching low to the ground as she approached her car. The keys were like butter in her hands, and she fumbled with them while struggling to hold Darren. At last, she stuck them in the lock, opened the door, put Darren in the passenger seat and started the engine, but she did not dare turn on the headlights. She reversed out of the driveway, as fast as she could and, by some impossible fortune, managed not to draw any attention to herself. As she pulled out onto the road, she glimpsed the front of the house: the door was open on the porch, the living room light was on, and she saw figures moving beyond the curtains.

Another shot rang out in the night.

As Lorraine's heart beat fast and tears streamed down her cheeks, she stared ahead at the dark road, pressed the gas and drove off. Once she was a half a mile or so away from the house, she remembered to switch on her headlights and turned onto Hwy 65. The dark road unfolded before her, but all she could see was the front porch and the shadow of the figures moving beyond the living room curtains.

At one point, she nearly ran off the road, and Darren squealed in fright. At the sound of his voice, Lorraine straightened up and did her best to focus on the road rather than on her thoughts.

Lorraine had not realized where she was going until she pulled into the gravel driveway. Terrified and her heart still racing, she grabbed Darren and hurried up to the house, all the while trying to be as calm as possible so as not to upset the boy.

"Who the hell is banging on this door at five o'clock in the morning?" she heard Reggie say from inside the house.

"It's me!" When he opened the door, she almost knocked him over as she hurried inside. "Bobby, take Darren to the back, please." Lorraine was surprised by the steadiness of her voice.

"What's going on?" asked Bobby, closing his robe and entering the living room.

"Now, please."

Without another word, he took Darren's hand and disappeared down the hall.

Lorraine clutched her chest and tried to catch her breath, but she felt as though water was rushing into her mouth and nose, suffocating her. "They—the men—they came," she managed and began waving her hands hysterically before her face. "She made me leave."

Reggie flipped on the lamplight next to the television and rubbed his sleepy eyes. "What are you talking about?"

"The men, Reggie. The four men from the café. They were at the store. They followed us home. They must have." He watched her pull at her hair, her face wet and contorted in terror.

"Clem." He extended his hand toward her urgently, but she recoiled. "Did you call the police?"

"They could've done anything to her. I gotta go back." Lorraine looked up at the clock. "How long does it take to get from our house to here?"

"We're in Gould. So, I guess about thirty or forty minutes." He paced back and forth, now just as panicked as Lorraine.

She pulled at her hair again and mumbled, "Oh God, oh God." She turned to run out the door, and he grabbed her arm. She shot him a murderous and frantic look that was more frightening than anything he had seen so far.

"I'm coming with you," he said, stepping into a pair of shoes.

It was dawn when they pulled into the driveway of Lorraine's house. The car that the men had come in was gone. The front door was still ajar, and all was quiet but for the crickets and birds. She leapt from the car and ran to the house, Reggie following behind her. There was a trail of blood on the porch, as if someone had been drug from the house. The trail ended just inside the doorway. Bell had shot one of the men, Lorraine realized with pleasure and a fleeting sense of hope. She hoped it was Eddie. *The little fucker.* This fleeting sense of hope vanished in a flash and was replaced by crushing fear.

Lorraine stopped and gaped at the trail of blood, suddenly feeling as though her feet had been nailed down to the porch. She couldn't move. Inertia trapped her as she closed her eyes and tried not to imagine the worst. *She's fine. We're moving to Philly this month. She's fine.* This refrain repeated in her mind until she felt Reggie's hand on her shoulder. She opened her eyes and took a few deep breaths.

Leaning forward at the doorway, she peeked inside the house. "Please, please," she kept mumbling, her eyes squeezed shut for a moment. When her gaze fell upon the bloody lump lying next to the sofa, Lorraine's knees gave way, and she sunk to the floor. A howl of sheer horror ripped through her as she stared at it and clutched her chest as her heart beat so fiercely she thought her chest might split open. This was a dream. How desperately she wanted to wake up. *This is not real*, Lorraine repeated in her head. She stared at the mangled, bloody lump on the floor and covered her mouth as her gaze stopped at the face that was no longer recognizable. It was more like a piece of raw meat that was every color but the normal, beautiful almond color of Bell's face. Lorraine turned her head and vomited on the porch.

Wiping her mouth, she leaned against the doorframe, looked up at the clear blue sky, at the blue and green dragonflies, and she listened to the birdsong and crickets. She hated it all.

Reggie, teary-eyed, knelt down in front of his broken friend and tried not to look at the dead and shattered body

Landrien Moriset

of his other friend. He did all that he could in that moment to hold in his own pain, for Lorraine's sake, and he held her as she cursed and moaned. "Nothing in this world is right." Holding her, he leaned against the doorframe of their home. "Nothing in this sad, fucking world is the way it ought to be."

Lorraine sat in her car and stared at the house, her mind a blank canvas of despair. Reggie came in and out, bringing box after box with him and packing them into the trunk and backseat of her car. Lorraine, who was in too much pain to question what he was doing, did not move but rather sat completely still behind the steering wheel and stared at the house. When he shut the trunk and walked past the driver's side, she finally spoke.

"What do I tell Darren? Bell's father'll have him now. Once he finds out. He'll have him. She was so afraid, Reggie. She was so scared that Darren would end up with her parents, stuck in this place. She wanted so much more for him."

"But that's his family. His family ought to have him."

She shook her head. "No. No, she didn't want that. She...I promised her."

Reggie studied her wet face while his mind lingered on the image of their friend, beaten and bloodied on their living room floor. The boy deserved better than this place, Reggie concluded, surveying the house and yard. But so did Bell's family. The sun had come out and was casting a piercingly bright light over the house. He had no intention of spending another night in this house, and he thought it better that they just leave early rather than stay another day there. What if the men returned? As he took in the beautiful blue sky, he did not understand how any day like this one

174

could be sunny. Then, it occurred to him: an idea, a wildly stupid, if not insane, idea. "I'll be right back," he told her and ran back inside the house.

In ten minutes, he reappeared, carrying two boxes and a purse. He placed the boxes in the back seat, shut the door and knelt down next to Lorraine at the driver's side. "Give me your purse," he ordered. She reached onto the floor of the passenger side, picked up her red purse and handed it to him.

Reaching inside her purse, he pulled out Lorraine's wallet. The wad of bills inside the wallet amounted to just over one hundred dollars. He reached inside Bell's small purse he had brought from the house and pulled out her wallet. He stuffed the bills inside Bell's wallet, shoved the wallet back inside the purse and turned to Lorraine. "You said she kept important documents, social security cards and things, inside old purses, right? That box in the backseat is the one with all her old purses."

"Yeah?" Lorraine stared at him in confusion.

He handed her Bell's purse. "Here. Take it. Then, go get Darren and leave," Reggie instructed her.

"What?" Lorraine asked and looked at the purse.

"Take it," he yelled, thrusting Bell's purse onto Lorraine's lap. He held Lorraine's purse in his other hand. "I put as many boxes as I could in your trunk and some of Darren's stuff in the boxes in the backseat. Take the boy and head up to Memphis. I'll come behind you in a couple of days, and we can drive on to Pennsylvania right away."

She studied him and her purse he was holding in his hand. She saw the fear and panic in his eyes. Slowly, she began to understand.

"I doubt anybody'll know the difference, Clem. The body's not even recognizable," Reggie snapped and paused, trying not to think about his friend's beaten body. "For all anybody knows, it's you in there, and Bell ran off with Darren and half your shit. Or they were snatched."

"Somebody'll figure it out. This ain't a movie, Reggie. The police'll figure it out."

"She's black and poor. The police won't care one way or another. Besides, folks knew she was getting ready to leave town with you."

"But the police, Reggie—"

"She called them hours ago, and they still ain't showed up. Clem, trust me. Go get the boy and leave. Get a hotel in Memphis. Call your sister when you get there and explain everything. I know Marie'll understand. But please don't call your parents. We need to figure that part out. Everybody's got to believe that body in there is yours, you understand? Call me at my brother's house in two days. I put the number inside Bell's purse. I should be in Memphis by then, and we'll leave together for Philly."

"And Darren? What do I tell him?"

"You're his mama now."

"Oh, Reggie—"

"Damnit, Clem. He's just two years old. He'll forget her." Reggie regretted his last words at once. Rather than apologize, however, he shut the door and looked down at her sternly. "I'll see you in a couple days."

Lorraine's gaze drifted from him to the house where their cat had appeared near the porch steps. "Don't leave Willy," she managed to say, and he nodded. It seemed the most appropriate thing to say. She shot a glance at Bell's purse on the passenger seat, forced herself not to cry and put the car in reverse. He watched as she backed out of the driveway and disappeared down the curvy, the swamp-lined road.

***

She sat on the bed and stared at Darren, who lay asleep and curled up under the sheets. So many emotions passed through her while she looked at him, this last living fragment of Bell. She wiped her wet eyes and cheeks and wondered what was happening back in Arkansas. What was Reggie doing? Was he talking to Bell's parents and to the police, lying to them about her whereabouts, crying over the death of his friend and the disappearance of his other friend? She could not imagine the horror Bell's father was feeling, to lose his daughter and grandson in an instant. No father deserved that.

Lorraine examined the driver's license and Bell's slender braids that hung to her shoulders in the photograph. She looked up at the mirror in front of her and examined her own reflection and the similarly slender braids that fell to her shoulders. She tried to forget the sensation of Bell's hand as she had braided her hair, and she laughed as she thought about Bell's proclamation once she had finished the braids: "You and I might as well be lesbian twins now, Clem."

She studied the driver's license card. Pamela Nelene Mitchell. She had not known Bell's middle name or married name. It had not come up in conversation, and now she wondered how her friend had come to be called Bell and why she had dropped her married name. It broke her heart that she had not known such basic facts about Bell. She wished she had asked. She wished she had asked so many questions.

She lay back next to Darren and looked out the window. The room was on the second floor of the motel, and Lorraine could see and hear the interstate traffic. Night was falling. The moon appeared, the streets and interstate grew quieter, and after many hours the moon retreated. All the while, she remained awake, afraid that if she slept she would dream of Bell's broken and beaten body or that she would awake to the police banging on her motel room door.

After a sleepless night, she got Darren up, dressed him, and they went to a diner for breakfast. He had not asked any more questions about Bell since the drive up from Arkansas. In fact, he seemed happy and carefree, and this bewildered Lorraine. As they walked out of a grocery store hours later with two bags of food—a loaf of bread, cheese, sliced turkey and juice—he looked up at her. "When Mommy coming?"

She pasted what she hoped was a believable smile on her face. "Let's get this stuff in the car first, okay? And then we can talk about Mommy."

He nodded and squeezed her hand. Lorraine's heart raced as she realized she had not thought about what to say to him. When they got inside the car, and she strapped him in, he repeated the question. His patience was running out.

"I don't know, honey." She could think of nothing else to say. "She's gone for a while, but she wanted me to take care of you right now. She wanted me to be your mommy while she's away."

He met her wary gaze, his expression a mixture of worry and curiosity. He looked as if he was on the verge of crying, but instead he nodded.

"Is that okay? Me being your mommy for a while?"

He halfway smiled and eventually gave her a slight nod, as if to say, "We'll see." She saw that he knew something was wrong but that he was too young to comprehend or articulate what he was feeling. Like most two-year-old children in moments of crisis, his options were either to cry or to go with the flow. To her relief, he chose to go with the flow, at least for now.

He did not ask any more questions for the rest of the day. She played with him, listened to him talk and barely understood anything he said, bathed him, and they watched *Soul Train*. He danced in front of the television while she applauded him and told him to "break it down." By ten o'clock that evening, he was fast asleep. Just as she had the night before, Lorraine watched him sleep and marveled at his ability to make her temporarily forget the pain and the horrors of the previous days. She watched his chest move up and down, and she realized with him she might actually be all right and maybe she could give him the life Bell had wanted to give him.

When she called Reggie the next morning, he and Bobby came to the motel, they piled into the moving van, and set out toward Pennsylvania. Bobby merged onto the freeway, and Reggie tried to find a radio station. Inside the van, all was quiet but for an occasional sniffle, which caused Reggie to look over his shoulder. He could not see her face, but he knew that she was crying as quietly as she could, to avoid upsetting Darren. Darren, on the other hand, bobbed his head and began to sing to the music from the radio.

"They'll get away with it," she muttered so that only Reggie could hear her. She looked out the window as she spoke.

He did not say anything but stared at her.

"They raped and killed her, and they'll get away with it because we ran instead of fighting. We're just running away."

Reggie surveyed her, wondering if he ever would see her smile again. All the years he had known her, all the things they had gone through, and he always had known the right words to ease her pain and grief. Yet his arsenal of comfort was useless now, so he said the only thing that seemed logical to him. "Sometimes the fight just ain't worth the price, Clem. Sometimes, maybe running away and getting lost is the sanest thing any of us can do."

She looked at him through bloodshot, wet eyes, but turned away and peered out the window just as Willy leapt onto her lap and stared at her through green eyes. She looked out at the cloudy landscape and rubbed her hand across the cat's warm back. Sitting completely still with her eyes fixed on the familiar landscape, the wide open fields and billboards, she thought about how excited Bell would have been to see this landscape. Lorraine stared at the world beyond her window. She never would see Tennessee or Arkansas again.

PART THREE

"Love is a hard thing to do." ~ Bell

CHAPTER THIRTEEN

Landrien dropped the diary into the box next to the bed and sat up. After a few minutes of staring at nothing in particular, she rose and went to the window, grabbing the pack of cigarettes she had left on the windowsill.

She looked out at the backyard, recalling the afternoons her mother had spent lying under the willow tree just to the left of the patio. She took a puff of the cigarette and closed her eyes. In the spring and early autumn, her mother would take out a blanket and spread out under that one tree, the only willow tree in their yard. Landrien knew not to bother her mother during those hours. She understood that those were her mother's private moments, flickers of time when her mother retreated to some other place in her mind and appeared utterly content.

When Landrien finished the cigarette, she lit another. *Why did I even read those damn diaries?* Disliking her mother had anchored Landrien for so many years that now she felt detached and more lost than ever. Perhaps, aimless was a more appropriate word. After all, how could she cling to that animosity, knowing what she knew now? How could she not empathize with Lorraine? This Lorraine was an intriguing person, somehow too interesting to dislike. With these thoughts swirling around in her head, she finished the cigarette, returned to bed, buried herself under the covers and lay awake until her eyes grew heavy.

But sleep eluded her. She simply could not empty her mind of the contents of the diary, of the story she had read.

She got up and lit up another cigarette. It was going to be a long night.

When she turned over the next morning and hit her alarm clock, she groaned and pulled the covers over her head to shut out the light. She hit the clock repeatedly, trying to silence it, until she realized the ringing noise was coming from her cell phone. She looked around, surprised to find that, at some juncture between all the chain smoking and glasses of wine, she had fallen into bed.

Groggily and with a yawn, she reached for the phone and forgot to check the caller I.D.

"Hey, did I wake you?" said Elena.

Landrien sat up at once and leaned back against the headboard. "Yeah, but it's all right."

"It's almost noon. Are you sick?"

"No. I was just up really late." She covered her mouth as she yawned. "How are you?"

"Fine. Just busy with work, as usual."

"Look, about last time, I'm sorry. It wasn't a conversation we should've had over the phone."

"Doesn't matter. Are you still staying in your family home way out in the boonies?"

"Yeah. I have to stay for a year before the title transfers to me."

"Oh. That sounds complicated."

"It is. I need to see you, Elena."

"I don't think that's a good idea."

"Fine," Landrien replied.

"But I can try to drive out there this evening," Elena sighed.

After the call with Elena, Landrien lay on her back and closed her eyes for many minutes, soaking in the waves of hope and possibility that had washed over her at the very sound of Elena's voice. Rona's Jack Russell Terrier began barking, which signaled that his owner was up and had let him out for a pee.

Landrien lay there in the quiet, still house and lost herself in thoughts about her mother.

As she knocked on the door, she looked around at the neighboring houses where a few people sat on their porches, some reading and some staring out at the street. One man, whom she assumed was in his sixties or seventies, nodded at her and she smiled. She remembered all the times she had sat on Marie's porch when she was a kid, taking photographs or talking with her aunt. It all seemed so recent yet so distant.

When Marie opened the door, she and her niece regarded one another for a moment. Marie, who was wearing jeans, a sweatshirt and house shoes, had combed back her hair and wrapped a black band around it. Neither smiling nor offering any greeting, she moved aside and motioned for Landrien to come in.

The air of the house was warm and thick with the scent of onions and peppers. The two women proceeded down the short, dim hallway and into the dining room where a mug of coffee and a book lay open on the coffee table. The television was off, and there was a soft hum of classical music playing from the ancient-looking stereo system next to the fireplace. Landrien remembered that her mother had been more of a jazz and blues person. Like Marie, Landrien preferred classical piano music.

Without a word, Marie sank onto the sofa, turned to her niece with an unfriendly stare and crossed her legs. She sat in the armchair opposite and tried not to wither under Marie's icy gaze. That gaze was one of the many things

Marie and Lorraine had in common. "So, how long's it been since you've set foot in here?" asked Marie, in a tone as cold as her gaze.

"Eighteen years or so," answered Landrien, glancing around the room. Little had changed. New record player, new curtains and new sofa. Same chair, same framed pictures on the wall and over the fireplace. "I like the curtains. What color is that? Lavender?"

"Or lilac, or something," replied Marie, with a wave of her hand, as if curtains and décor were the last things on her mind. "What do you want, Landrien? I've told you all I know." Marie averted her gaze briefly and seemed to preoccupy herself with staring out the window.

"No, you haven't. I asked you about Lorraine the last time—"

"And I told you she was a woman who died a long time ago," Marie interjected.

"If you consider 'a long time ago' just a couple months ago." She watched her aunt uncross and cross her legs, then avert her eyes and sip her coffee. "I know Lorraine Clemente Sterling was Mom's real name. Just like I know Marie Rae Sterling is your maiden name, but you preferred to keep the name Carmichael even after you divorced your second husband. For some reason, you're anxious to preserve this lie my mom created. But I didn't come here to hear about all of that. I want to know about Bobby Eamon Murphy and Reggie, Lorraine's friends. So, for starters, what's Reggie's last name?"

Marie leaned back on the sofa and folded her arms across her chest. Silence elapsed between them as Marie stared out the window again before turning back to her niece. "You got a cigarette on you?"

Landrien's eyebrows went up in surprise. "You don't smoke anymore."

"Things change. You got a cigarette? Or have you quit smoking after all these years?"

Landrien fumbled inside her purse. "I'm trying to quit. But I have one of those e-cigarettes." She pulled out a teal-tinted e-cigarette pipe and handed it, along with a lighter, to Marie.

Hesitantly, Marie took the pipe and lighter. She turned the pipe over in her hand, and her eyes narrowed as she examined it. From her confused expression, the pipe might have been some strange artifact. "What on earth is this?" she asked.

"I'll explain later. But it's better than regular cigarettes."

"Somehow I doubt that," Marie mumbled, lighting the pipe.

Amused, Landrien watched her aunt take a slow drag and then exhale the odorless vapor. Marie leaned back on the sofa once more, took another drag and exhaled, looking down with curiosity at the pipe.

"Now, what was Reggie's last name?" Landrien prodded.

"Dunbar. Reginald Dunbar." She watched Landrien take out a pad of paper and write down the name.

"Thank you. Are they still alive?" Landrien asked, pen in hand and eyes fixed on her aunt.

Marie nodded, taking another drag.

"Do you know if they're still together?"

"They are," Marie answered.

Images began turning over in Landrien's mind, and for a moment she was quiet and lost in her head. "They were at the funeral, weren't they? The two men all the way in the back? They left before I had a chance to say anything to them. That was Reggie and Bobby."

Marie sat the e-cigarette pipe next to the coffee mug on the table. "Yeah."

"Where are they?"

"Somewhere in Brooklyn, I believe. I don't know the address," Marie informed her.

For the first time, Landrien recognized the southern drawl Marie had covered for so many years. She recalled all the times she had eavesdropped on conversations between her mother and Marie, and she remembered wondering why they sounded a little different when they spoke to one another. She had assumed sisters had special ways of speaking to one another, and having no sisters of her own, she'd had no way of knowing whether this assumption was incorrect. Marie went to the fireplace and lifted up a small bowl that contained potpourri. When she returned to the sofa and sat down, she handed a white slip of paper to Landrien. "Reginald gave that to me at the funeral."

Landrien opened up the paper and saw scribbled on it a phone number with a New York area code. She looked up at her aunt, whose eyes had watered between the walk to the fireplace and the return to the sofa. She seemed so uncharacteristically worn down, Landrien realized, noting her aunt's thinness and the quiver of her hand against the coffee mug.

"I never called it," added Marie and sipped her coffee. She stared at the contents of her coffee mug.

"Why not?" Landrien watched her aunt fidget and close her eyes.

"I don't know. My only sister was dead."

"And they were reminders," Landrien concluded. Marie did not respond to this but instead finished her mug of coffee.

"Would you like some coffee? I'm about to make another pot," she asked, standing up. "And I suppose you can stay for lunch, if you'd like. I'm roasting a chicken and some potatoes that's got about twenty more minutes in the oven." It seemed as though it took Marie great effort to speak in a steady voice. She put one hand on her hip, pressed her lips together and looked down at her niece.

"Sure, I'll take a cup, and I can stay for lunch," Landrien replied. A question occurred to her just as Marie turned to go to the kitchen. "One more thing, Marie. What happened to your house in McGhee?"

"I sold it just before you went to college and gave the money to Pam. I mean, Lorraine."

"My college savings?" Landrien stared at her in shock. "But it was the family's property, wasn't it?"

"Yes, it was. Your college savings was primarily money I made from the sale of the house. Lorraine and your father didn't have enough to pay for your education after paying for Darren's. So, I used the money from the house. Half of it, anyway. Luckily for us, you got plenty of scholarships. The other half is in a cd, set aside for you." Marie did not frown, but she did not smile either. Rather, she regarded Landrien with an emotionless expression, like there was nothing else to say on the matter, before she turned and disappeared into the kitchen.

Landrien glanced down at the strip of paper and then stuffed it inside her pocket. She resolved to spend as much time with her aunt as possible from that day forward.

***

During the evening, as she waited for Elena to arrive, Landrien stretched out on the sofa with her laptop and a bagel, and she researched her mother's old friends. To her surprise, a quick Google search led her right to Reggie and Bobby. She was delighted to learn that they were married now after over thirty years together.

Reggie, who currently worked as an executive director at a legal services in Brooklyn, was on the brink of retirement after a colorful legal career that included public policy work, numerous academic journal articles on race and the criminal justice system, a few years as a columnist for a leftist political magazine based in Boston, as well as an unsuccessful run for city council in the early nineties. He was a striking man with big eyes and a bright smile. She smiled as she read more about him and thought about how her mother had described him in the journal entries. He fit her descriptions perfectly.

She could not find as much information about Bobby, other than the fact that he was a professor of history at a small college in New York. His photograph on the department's page revealed a good-looking man with lively green eyes. The biography below the photograph informed her that Bobby had been a professor at the college for ten years and had published a few articles on LGBT history and art. At once, she was not only curious but, in fact, excited about the prospect of meeting these two men.

As the night wore on, Landrien shut off the computer and turned on the television. Absently, she watched reality show after reality show while she browsed the internet on her smartphone. By the time she had spent a solid hour scrolling down her Facebook newsfeed, the phone's battery was almost drained. As she glanced at the television, she saw that the reality shows had gone off and been replaced by the evening news. She checked her text messages and voicemail.

Elena had not called or left a message.

Landrien got up and went to the window to peek through the curtains. The street was vacant but for a stray cat. *She's never stood me up.*

Landrien drifted back to the sofa and sat down as the realization began to sink in: she had lost Elena, finally and for good. She had sensed it ever since the conversation during the blizzard. Elena's voice had carried a sort of desperation and sadness during that conversation, Landrien now realized. This was for the best, she concluded.

After a few minutes, during which she tried to absorb the reality of her loss, she typed a text message to Elena and pressed "send."

10:15PM - ME
I understand, Elena. You deserve to be happy. Thank you. Love always, Landrien.

As she reread the message, it actually disturbed her how easy it was to say goodbye to Elena after so many years, how easy it was to release her and move on. She shut the phone, turned off the television and retired to bed.

When Landrien rose at dawn the next morning, she pushed the curtains aside to let the sun stream in and take in the view of the back yard. Birds flitted about and chased one another. Leaves were growing on the maple tree and the yellowish green grass, still partially laden with snow, sparkled under the sunlight. Spring had arrived.

Humming and whistling, she went downstairs to the kitchen. She turned on a pot of coffee, put on a pot of oatmeal, placed a few strips of bacon in the oven and returned upstairs to clean up. Landrien slipped into a pair of jeans and a sweater. She stuffed two of her mother's diaries inside her purse and padded downstairs to eat breakfast.

After placing the dishes in the washer, Landrien gathered the trash and the bag of bottles to recycle. She collected her purse and a light coat and headed out into the chilly March air.

Rona was backing out of her driveway next door but stopped and rolled down her window when she saw Landrien, who was depositing trash into the bin at the end of the driveway. "Good morning!" Rona hollered.

"Good morning, Rona," she smiled. "Where are you off to this time of the morning?"

"Grocery shopping before church. You need anything from the store?" Rona asked.

"No, I'm fine. But thanks for asking."

"I always do my shopping on Sunday mornings, so let me know if you ever need anything. Oh, and I see you got some bottles to recycle? I recycle on Wednesday mornings. If you ever want me to run your recycling down to the center for you just leave it on my porch in the morning."

"That's really nice of you. I'll try to remember to do that."

She gave Landrien a smile and a wave before backing out of the driveway. Landrien watched the woman turn and disappear around the corner. She looked left and right at the houses down the street and wondered if she should at least try to get to know some of the neighbors. *Note to self: stop being such a hermit.* As she headed to the car, she decided she would talk to Rona about the other neighbors.

Landrien made a stop at the recycling center a mile away, deposited the bottles, and then headed to a nearby coffeehouse. There, she ordered a decaf vanilla latte and found a table in a cozy corner at the back of the crowded coffeehouse. She sat down and sipped her coffee for several minutes, thinking about Jordan and what he might be doing right now. He was probably out walking, home sleeping, or else writing. Or he was thinking about her, too. Smiling at this thought, she stared out the window at the parking lot and finished her latte before ordering another.

When she returned to her table, she pulled the two diaries out of her purse, along with the strip of paper Marie had given her. She stuffed the piece of paper inside her pocket, looked down at the two diaries and took a deep breath.

After she had begun reading the first diary a couple of weeks ago, she had gone through the box and stacked the diaries in chronological order. They went from 1976 through 2010, thirty-two of them in all. The years 1977 and 2005 were missing. From this, she deduced that her mother had temporarily stopped writing every time she had lost someone she loved. The first time, in the seventies, she had stopped writing for a while after she lost Bell. In 2005, she had lost her husband and did not pen a single entry for the rest of that year.

On this day, Landrien sat and read entry after entry from the 1978 diary. Some of the entries were only one or two sentences, such as the entry dated January 10, 1978: "I am married now. The wedding was small." Other entries, however, carried on for pages, such as an entry about Darren getting sick with chickenpox in February. She stopped at an entry dated April 6, 1978. It contained only one sentence: "Two days ago, my daughter was born." As she read over the sentence a few more times, examining the curly handwriting, she was not sure whether she should be amused or a little hurt. That was all her mother had written about an event that Landrien, naturally, considered fairly momentous.

After she read a few more entries, she closed the diary, her mood less cheerful than it had been when she sat down. In fact, she had been in a good mood when she woke that morning, and she did not want to ruin a good day by taking in too much of her mother's words in one sitting. The woman had had a way of wallowing in the misery of life, and that misery was etched in every sentence throughout the diaries.

She slid the diaries back inside her purse and pulled from her pocket the piece of paper containing Reggie's number. With a deep breath, she replayed the conversation she had practiced and rehearsed in front of the mirror that morning. Then, she dialed her mother's old friend.

"Hello?" said a heavy male voice.

"Hi. Is this Mr. Murphy or Mr. Dunbar?"

"This is Reginald Dunbar. May I ask who's calling?" The man's tone was a little harsh.

"Hi, Mr. Dunbar. This is Landrien Bell Moriset, Lorraine Moriset's daughter." There was only silence on his end. Staring around the almost empty coffeehouse, Landrien pressed the phone against her face and waited for Reginald Dunbar to say something. "Are you still there, Mr. Dunbar?" she asked after a few more moments of silence.

"Yes. I'm sorry." He coughed and cleared his throat. "This is just, ah, out of the blue."

"I know, and I apologize, Mr. Dunbar."

"Reggie, please. Call me Reggie," he insisted.

"Reggie. Right. I got your number from my aunt, Marie Carmichael. You gave it to her at my mom's funeral—"

"Why did you call her Lorraine?"

She stopped and had to take a moment to understand his question. "It's her name."

"But nobody other than Marie knows about...did Marie tell you? She promised Lorraine—Clem she would never utter a word to anybody."

"No. Marie didn't tell me. My mother told me. Well, her diaries did anyway. In her will, she left me the house and a collection of her diaries. I'm calling because I'm going through the diaries, and there are holes in the story that I was hoping you could fill in. Honestly, I'd just like to talk to you and Bobby, so I can get a better picture of her life."

"I'm afraid Bobby's not available right now. He's out of town at a conference in Atlanta," he explained.

"No, I don't mean over the phone. I'd like to talk with you in person, if that's okay. Whenever it's convenient for you and Bobby?"

"Oh. Well, ah, the weekends are best. We live in BedStuy. I'm assuming you live in Philly."

"Yeah. Actually, I'm living in the family home right now, out in Phoenixville. But I don't have a problem driving to Brooklyn if that's what you mean. Does next Saturday work for you?"

"That's fine. Sure," he confirmed.

Unsure of what else to say, Landrien thanked him, took down his address and hung up. She sat there and stared at nothing in particular while making a mental list of things to ask Reggie and Bobby. When she finally got up and left the coffeehouse, she went next door to a florist and headed into the city.

***

194

The hall smelt of garlic and tomato, stirring up a fury of hunger in her. She told herself that she would have to stop for a hoagie at the sandwich shop on the corner on her way home. Her mind lingered on the thought of a hoagie until she stopped at her apartment door. She inhaled deeply and counted to ten. Despite how much she disliked having to knock on her own apartment door, she knocked three times and waited to hear Jordan's voice on the other side.

"Flowers? Really? I look like someone who likes flowers?" Jordan grinned and glanced down at the roses in her right hand.

She studied the red rose and two white ranunculus flowers she had selected. Sure she had chosen the beaten path taken by guilt-ridden lovers the world over, but was it not the thought that mattered?

He took the roses and kissed her and went to the living room. As Landrien shut the front door, she glimpsed the new table in the kitchen. He had gotten rid of her old, wobbly one. *I didn't tell him he could just throw away my shit.* But she let the thought drift away. *That raggedy old table was a piece of shit, anyway.* A large candle sat in the center of the new table.

She entered the living room where he was sitting on the sofa. The flowers were on the coffee table. On the table, he had placed two candles and an ivy plant where her photography and art magazines had once lain. Sheer curtains hung to the floor from the windows, and a standing lamp with a yellow shade was next to the bookcase. "I like the changes you've made. It feels like a different apartment."

"What's up, Landrien?" he asked, leaning forward and foregoing small talk. "You didn't just buy me flowers for no reason."

Remembering the point of her visit, she dropped all pretension. "I need to come clean with you about some stuff."

"Okay…" He stared at her.

"While we've been together, I've seen other people," blurted Landrien.

"People? Plural? Besides Elena?"

She blinked, surprised by the mention of Elena. She did not bother to ask how he knew about Elena. "Yes, but mainly her. I was always safe, always. Not that that makes it any better. It's just…with my mom's death and being back home, I've gained some clarity. I love you, Jordan. I didn't really understand that before, not fully. And I know I will probably lose you because of all of this, but it's past time for me to be honest with you. I would do anything to make this right, but I can't. All I can say is this: knowing what I know now, I would never fuck up so bad with you again." She removed the engagement ring and placed it on the table next to the flowers. "I don't deserve that ring or you."

He rolled his eyes and offered no response.

She stared at her hands on her lap while they passed several long minutes in silence. "Look, I know I have no right to ask, and you can tell me to go to hell, but I would like for you to come to New York with me next Saturday."

"Why?" he asked, frowning at her.

"I have to do something pretty important, and I want you there with me."

"What's so important?" he probed.

When she finished explaining the situation, to her surprise he agreed to accompany her. She had thought it would take more pleading and was thankful he had spared her.

At opposite ends of the sofa, they sat in silence for a long time, staring straight ahead and the scent of the flowers enveloping them.

CHAPTER FOURTEEN

SEPTEMBER 6, 1979. I'm twenty-four years old today, and apparently I should be pretty damn happy about that, according to Anthony anyway. For some folks, happiness is snow covered trees, an O'Jays song, or that nutmeg aroma on Christmas day. For other folks, happiness is simply sex on a Sunday morning. I guess I'm not any of those folks. Today is just another day, and I'm twenty-four.

When I stood at the stove this morning, thinking about all this and staring at the popping oil turning brown in the skillet, I listened as Anthony played with our daughter, who squealed and laughed. I listened to her joy as Anthony and Darren tickled her, and I was empty. Utterly empty. Does that make sense? Is that sound, the sound of your family enjoying one another's company, not the sound of perfection? I should consider myself lucky. Right?

I read somewhere that it's not unusual for mothers to harbor feelings of dislike toward their babies and that it eventually fades. Marie said that it's normal for some women and that it always passes. "Just give it time, sis," Marie said. But Marie has never had children of her own. She has never had something that lived inside her for months, something she never wanted there in the first place, a little person of her own flesh and to whom she must now dedicate her life and love. Marie is just a wife, living in a big house with her husband and no other responsibilities, with all the time in the world to enjoy her life on her own terms. I envy her sometimes.

Anyway, I'm straying from my point, and I honestly don't know why I feel the need to make this point. I don't even know if I should write this, and I don't know why I'm telling you, but Marie and that author are wrong. I would give everything I own, including the clothes off my back, just for Marie and that author to be right, just to believe that it will pass. This...aversion. But it won't pass. When I turned to look at Landrien, whom Anthony had sat on the countertop next to the bowl of pancake batter, I knew in my heart that Marie and that author were wrong. Just as I knew I'd never forgive myself for wishing I could rewind the last three years of my life. Erase my daughter and Anthony and this place.

As I stood there and watched them, I reminded myself that I couldn't afford these thoughts. I am a mother.

After taking three plates out of the cabinet above the stove, I piled fried eggs, potatoes and three strips of bacon onto each plate. I handed one to Darren, and he followed me as I carried the two other plates to the dining room table. He had been nosing about the kitchen periodically as I cooked, trying to help. I think he likes to cook, surprise, surprise. Maybe I'll teach him some of the recipes from the cookbook I just started writing. Anthony has an agent friend at a publishing house in Philadelphia, who wants to see the draft when I finish it. Are you surprised? Me, writing cookbooks now? Anthony told me I should try starting a catering business. Maybe I will someday. You just never know where life will lead, the way it winds and bends in this and that direction, a little dizzying life can be at times.

Darren grabbed my hand as we returned to the kitchen for orange juice and cups. I put the leftover pancake batter in the refrigerator, handed Darren the cups and took the jar of juice. We returned to the dining room, and I watched Darren set out the cups. He seemed so eager for everything to be perfect, and he grinned at me when he sat down, a huge smile that always makes me feel a little better about my life.

Anthony joined us, carrying Landrien on his shoulders. He placed her in the high chair next to him, while she giggled and reached out for him. Darren looked wide-eyed and ready to dig in. Our regular morning routine.

Anthony reached across the table and laid his hand on top of mine. "Happy birthday, Pam," he said.

To my left, Darren bent down, disappeared under the table and resurfaced with a medium-sized, gift-wrapped box. He slid it toward me and said, grinning as wide as ever, "Happy birthday, Mommy."

All this time, and I've never gotten used to hearing him call me that word. Landrien's words so far are limited to "ball," "no," "want," "daddy," and "three." Her first word was "ice," according to Anthony, but I haven't heard her say it. Anthony said that when he was sitting on the back porch with her in March, she pointed toward the window and said "ice." There was snow on the ground. She wasn't even a year old yet. Now, she just stared around at the commotion and excitement and managed to shout, "Want three!" Or I suppose that's what she said.

I turned and hugged Darren, who blushed violently. When I looked at Anthony again, I think I smiled. At least, I intended to smile, graciously. Gratitude was the least I could give Anthony, although he deserved much more. "I'll open it when we finish eating," I said.

Of course I should be grateful for all of this, for everything I have, for my husband and children and this home. You would be surprised to see the quaint little wife

I've become. Sometimes, even I am surprised. I'm not sure why I even bother to write about my life, other than I fear I might just fade away—more than I already have—if I didn't write about it.

    Don't feel sorry for me, though. I'm not writing this as a plea for sympathy. I have a husband, two kids, and a fancy suburban home with several nice private schools and shopping centers nearby. Today is just another day. Perhaps I'll convince Anthony to buy a dog, since Willy died just a few days ago.

Landrien slid the diary inside her purse. Yawning, she put on her coat and cap, and got up to leave the coffeehouse. That was quite enough of her mother's morbid thoughts for one afternoon. She figured it was time to enjoy the weather for a change. The weather was unusually warm for the second week of March. Over the last couple of days, the remaining snow had melted to reveal dead, yellow grass that, within the next few weeks, would become lush and bright green. The temperature was supposed to reach the mid-60s by Friday, and she awaited this change with great anticipation. After the onslaught of snowstorms during the last two months, she welcomed the warm weather. She would be happy if she never saw snowflakes again for the rest of the year.

    Unfortunately, just as the weather became more pleasant, her body started rebelling against it. For three days, she felt nauseated and overly tired, so much that she found herself bent over the toilet bowl each morning. Initially, she wrote it off as stress and resolved to rest for a few days. Yet when she rose from the toilet bowl this morning, an intense fear gripped her.

Once she arrived at the contraception section in Walgreen's, the fear wracked her whole body but subsided as confusion set in. Never had she bought a pregnancy test before. At her age, she considered this quite an accomplishment. Until recently, she had lived her adult life according to plan, never veering too far off course, never having to deal with many unexpected events. Barring sudden illness or death, she maintained firm control over her life and made sure to trim away any excess people who might throw a kink into her routine. But sometimes shit happens, whether we like it or not. So there she was standing in front of the collection of pregnancy tests and feeling altogether overwhelmed.

She had not realized that there were so many brands. She suddenly wished she had stayed on "the lesbian track," as her brother had teasingly referred to it, that she had started in middle school, or the celibacy route she had rode for a few years after college. *Jordan just had to come along and disrupt everything*, she thought. *Fuck.*

Landrien stood in the contraception lane for a while, reading the labels, and eventually picked a brand she had seen on a commercial. She whipped out her smartphone and quickly researched the brand on the web. Satisfied with her choice, she went to the pharmacy checkout counter, and a blond freckle-faced man about her age greeted her with a smile.

"This all for you?" he said in a rather high-pitched voice and what Landrien detected to be a New Jersey accent.

"Yeah," she replied, and he gave her the total. She scanned her credit card, signed the digital screen and waited for him to hand her the receipt. When she looked up, he was staring at her through bright blue eyes.

"You're Mrs. Moriset's daughter, aren't you?" The clerk handed her the bag and receipt.

She nodded.

An expression of regret sailed across his face. "I really was sorry to hear about what happened. She was one of the kindest people I ever met. Always talked to me like we were the best of friends when she came in to pick up Mr. Moriset's prescriptions. I didn't understand it at first. Folks usually just get what they come for, hand me some money, or tell me their prescription, and that's it. But Mrs. Moriset made a point to learn all the pharmacists' names and everything. She had a unique soul, your mother."

She just nodded some more and smiled. She wished she saw her mother the same way. The most she could muster up nowadays toward her mother was curiosity and a modicum of respect. "Thank you," said Landrien, stuffing her wallet inside her purse. She turned and walked away.

When she arrived at the house only ten minutes later, she rushed up to the bathroom and pulled out the pregnancy test. Luckily, she had to urinate almost as soon as she entered the house. She sat on the toilet and skimmed the instructions, trying not to think about what she would do if the test showed a positive result. *Think happy things, like Youtube videos about kittens. Good. Kitten videos are good.*

After a deep, steadying breath, she urinated on the stick and laid it on the sink. She did this all in thick silence, filled with a dread unlike any other she could remember. As she paced the bathroom a few times, her phone vibrated from her purse on the sink, but she ignored it. She went downstairs and poured a glass of orange juice. Once she finished a second glass, she returned upstairs to the bathroom. She did not look at the test lying on the sink.

Landrien paced back and forth, images of her and Jordan flashing across her mind: her and Jordan shopping for strollers and baby beds, Jordan standing over her as she lay exhausted in a hospital bed. She stopped and shook her head, as if she was trying to erase the images of this possible future. She closed her eyes for a few seconds, and a surprising calm drifted over her.

Holding her breath, she looked down at the test. In the time that she stood there and stared at it, Landrien made a decision. Whether it was the right decision, she did not know nor did she care. She threw the test in the trash and turned out the light.

As she crossed Chestnut Street and walked toward a towering gray brick building, she replayed in her mind the list of things she needed to accomplish today. Depositions from nine o'clock to four o'clock, call Darren to check in because sisters are supposed to do that sort of thing, have the conversation with Jordan, breathe. Sure, it was not a long list, but she had a busy day ahead of her, and the last item on the list was proving to be quite difficult.

"Spare some change, Miss?" called the old man in the wheelchair. He often sat outside her office building. As usual, he smiled at her and revealed a set of crooked, dingy teeth behind chapped lips.

She dug inside her pocket and handed him five dollars. He smiled and took the money in his gloved hand. She regularly gave him a few dollars and whatever loose change she could find in her pockets. Sometimes, she wondered what his life had been like before he became homeless. Or was he homeless? What event had led to his being here on Chestnut Street with a cup in his hand and a sad smile on his face?

"Thank you, Miss. Bless you." He bowed his head a little.

"Sir? What's your name?"

"Kenny. Kenny Muchmore," he answered, with an uncertain expression.

She introduced herself, almost too formally. "I hope I'm not being nosey. But do you mind if I ask whether you receive a disability check?"

"I get one every month, sure," Kenny admitted. "Ain't enough to cover my rent though."

Mentally, she checked off two facts: he was not homeless, and he was receiving some public benefits. He was better off than many other beggars, and this knowledge brought her a small bit of comfort. "You don't live in public housing or have a section 8 voucher?" she asked.

Kenny Muchmore shifted in his seat before he looked up at her with the same hesitant expression. After a moment, he responded. "No, Miss. The government took it from me years ago when my nephew who used to live with me, he got caught selling drugs out my apartment. They locked him up and kicked me out, even though I told them I didn't know nothing about my nephew's dealing. And it was the truth. These kids be into all kind of stuff they ain't got no business messing with. But it didn't matter to them folks whether I knew or not. You know how them folks are."

She listened intently to his heavy, accented voice and the bitterness in his tone. "Yeah, I know. You ever reapply for section 8 or public housing?" She stepped aside to let other people enter the building.

"Didn't know I could," replied Kenny.

"I think you can. I can find out for you if you're interested." She handed him her card, which he reluctantly accepted. "Our services are free. And just to be clear, we're not government attorneys. A lot of people mistakenly believe we are. We're a legal services, a nonprofit. If you want to reapply for housing benefits, just come in, go up to the second floor lobby, and ask for me. Okay?"

He nodded, staring up at her with some suspicion.

"Have a good day, Mr. Muchmore."

Smiling and feeling several pounds lighter than she had just ten minutes earlier, Landrien stepped inside the elevator and added another item to her mental checklist: visit Iris in public housing and talk to her about Kenny's situation. When Landrien entered her office, she hung her coat on the back of the door, stared at the pile of manila folders on her desk, sat down and went to work.

During the commute home that day, she cursed herself for failing to have the conversation with Jordan. She had planned to have the conversation over lunch. Yet, after half a day of depositions, she was exhausted. She supposed it would have to wait until the trip to Brooklyn on Saturday. This gave her at least a few days to script the conversation in her mind.

As she had done nearly every evening for the past couple of weeks, she reheated leftovers, sat alone at her dinner table and ate while listening to classical music. After washing the dishes and turning off the lights downstairs, she retreated upstairs and took a hot shower. She stood at the doorway of her parents' old room and looked around, not knowing why she stood there or what to think. Finally, she went to her room, where she set her alarm clock and got into bed.

Lying in bed, she fixed her gaze on the ceiling and thought about her life, about Jordan and Elena, about how much she missed her apartment. It was all over with Elena, of course. She had told herself that she was not upset about this, although Elena still haunted her thoughts daily. She switched off the lamplight and closed her eyes, watching as images of Jordan and Elena flickered across her mind. The images flashed like projections on a white screen: Jordan holding her, Elena kissing her shoulder, Jordan inside her. The images moved one after another as Landrien's hands slid under the covers.

With her eyes closed, she saw Jordan on top of her and Elena lying next to her. She fixated on this pair of images, and her hands moved with such vigor that her fingers began to ache until she released a low moan and shivered all over. Lost in shame and guilt, she covered her face and tears rolled down her cheeks, the frozen images fading, one by one. She turned onto her side and tried not to think about anything. After a while, it worked and she drifted to sleep and passed another night of dreamless slumber in the empty house.

NOVEMBER 28, 1980. Darren lost another tooth today, just as we sat down to dinner. It fell out onto the table. Bless his heart, he looked horrified. I couldn't help but laugh. While I went to the bathroom with Darren to clean him up and wrap the tooth in tissue, Anthony put five dollars under Darren's plate. Darren discovered the money when he was helping me clear the table later. Sometimes, I think I love Anthony, the way a wife should love her husband.

DECEMBER 1, 1980. I went to a bookstore today when I was out running errands, and I found an interesting new cookbook. It's a Tex-Mex cookbook. I couldn't help but think about how much I miss food back home. Food just isn't the same up here. I think I'm going to try a quesadilla recipe when I get home.

Anyway, I went to the new coffeehouse afterward, since the weather was sort of perfect for writing. Landrien was asleep in her stroller, and rain was pouring outside with no indication of letting up. Perfect writing weather. I've been trying to write again—poetry and stories, not cookbooks—but I can't really do it unless I leave the house. So I've been going to a coffeehouse downtown where it's not as crowded. But this new coffeehouse has more space and better coffee. The coffee doesn't taste so burnt like it does in all the other shops around this town. Anthony tells me I've become a snob about coffee, which is kind of funny since I never really drank the stuff until I moved up here.

Anyway, a few weeks ago, I was walking through the library, and I saw a poster about a poetry contest. I don't know if I have anything worth submitting, but Anthony says I should submit something anyway. Sometimes I'm so happy to have a husband who encourages me the way he does. According to Anthony, I should do whatever makes me happy, whether it's writing poetry, stories, cookbooks, or catering. I haven't gotten far with the catering business yet, but I'm working on it. I also haven't let him read any of my stories or poems yet. Maybe I don't trust his opinion. College professors rarely know good writing when they see it, and they have an annoying tendency to harp on about some truly horrendous "classic" pieces of literature.

Reggie was always a good judge of writing. But that's neither here nor there. He's gone. Once Lorraine was gone, my friendship with Reggie sort of faded. So many things have faded. Sometimes I miss Lorraine, her simplicity, her ability to love so hard. But life goes on, or so people say, and life is going all right for now.

The diary lay open on Jordan's lap, and he glanced at Landrien. "Have you read any of her poems or stories?"

"No," she answered, her eyes on the road as she passed a pickup truck. "I never knew she wrote anything, and I haven't come across any of her stories or poems. When I was growing up, she was just an okay cook who collected cookbooks and was always trying some new experimental recipe on us."

"But that was all Pamela…or Bell, right? The cooking and the catering part. That was just Lorraine keeping up the lie, I suppose," he mused.

"I guess so, or maybe all of that *was* her after a while."

He shook his head and reread the line where she referenced Lorraine. "She writes about herself as if she really is someone else, like she really isn't Lorraine anymore. 'I miss Lorraine, her simplicity…' It's so weird and fascinating. A psychologist would have a field day with these diaries."

"Probably."

"You want me to keep reading?" he asked.

"No. Not right now. Keep your eyes on the GPS. We're close to the last toll before we get into the city." She passed a slow moving minivan and crossed over to the right lane.

Jordan closed the diary, and they talked about New York and their plans for the evening. As she listened to him speak excitedly about the city—about how he had visited only twice and had seen nothing outside of Manhattan—her thoughts drifted to the conversation she needed to have with him about the pregnancy test. "We'll hit up Williamsburg tomorrow morning," Landrien assured him when he mentioned that he would like to see some bookstores and coffeehouses. By the time they crossed the Brooklyn Bridge, they were both leaning forward, trying to see the street signs.

"237 Monroe Street," she noted, driving along Bedford Street. The GPS on her phone instructed her to make a right turn onto Madison, which was a one-way. She drove a few blocks before turning left onto Marcy Avenue. Handing the phone to Jordan, she said, "Take a look at it and tell me how close we are."

Jordan leaned forward and squinted at the screen. "We're close. Maybe we should start looking for parking spots."

"Okay."

Moments later, she turned left onto Monroe Street. Each block was lined with brownstones and looked the same as the last block. Like most of New York, Brooklyn had a disorienting effect on her every time she visited and, as usual, she felt a little lost.

At last, she parallel parked between an old Volvo and a Ford Explorer and shut off the engine. The sun was out, and women and men wearing thin jackets or sweaters, strolled along the sidewalk, past black plastic bags of trash and red-bricked brownstones. It looked like spring had arrived a couple of weeks early, and New Yorkers appeared to be enjoying every second of it.

Several middle-aged black men sitting on a stoop nodded at her when she stepped out of the car. "How you doing, young lady? Looking like an African queen," beamed one man, who was probably twice her age. He wore a plaid Newsboy hat and smoked a cigarette while he leaned against the stoop, clearly attempting to convey an old school cool. She thought the overall effect was successful, and she cast an appreciative nod in his direction.

"Thank you. I'm doing all right," she offered, walking around the back of the car. She and Jordan started toward house 237.

"You take it easy now." The man flicked the ashes of his cigarette onto the ground.

"I will. You do the same," Landrien replied, with a last glance over her shoulder.

As it turned out, she and Jordan had parked only a few stoops away from the address. When they reached 237, they stopped and stared up at the brownstone. It looked no different than any of the other brownstones around it.

"Ready?" he asked and rubbed the back of her shoulder.

She straightened her cardigan and pants, and then turned to fix Jordan's tie. "I don't know why you decided to wear a tie under this sweater," she remarked, flashing him a smile. They both looked as though they had stepped out of a Banana Republic catalogue.

"What?"

"Nothing. You look good. Come on."

Without another word, they walked up the steep steps, and she pressed the doorbell.

A tall, freckle-faced man immediately opened the door. He stared at her, as if transfixed and unable to speak. He looked so much like the photographs in her mother's photo album that she felt like she already knew him.

"Hi, you must be Reggie?" she surmised after an awkward moment and extended her right hand. "I'm Landrien Moriset."

An equally tall white man with dark hair approached and stood next to Reggie. There had been no photographs of him, but Landrien thought Bobby looked as Lorraine had described him: thoughtful, an honest face, and exceedingly pale. Bobby smiled and shook her extended hand. She appreciated his firm grip.

"I'm Bobby Murphy. It's a pleasure to meet you." He coughed as if to cue Reggie to remember his manners.

Reggie held out his hand, and she shook it, disappointed that his grip was slack and hesitant compared to that of his partner.

"I apologize. I'm Reggie. Please, come in."

She smiled and then remembered Jordan, who was standing stock still next to her. "Oh, I hope you don't mind, but I hate traveling alone, so I brought a friend. This is Jordan Sheehan, my, ah, colleague."

A bit too formally, the three men shook hands and exchanged greetings. Following the men inside and down a short hallway, Landrien admired the calming colors of the walls, soft pastel yellows and greens. Despite the brightness of the house, it had a nest-like atmosphere that made her feel like she was far away from the city.

There were stairs to the right and a large reading room to the left. The reading room caught Landrien's attention and brought her to a stop. A smile curled her lips as her eyes swept the room.

Blues music sounded softly from a record player sitting on the top shelf of a tall bookcase. Another bookcase stood adjacent to the fireplace a few feet away, and two more rested against the opposite wall, each filled full with books. There must have been well over a few hundred books in this room, Landrien surmised. A glimmering stream of sunlight poured in through the sheer curtains of the floor-to-ceiling window between the bookcases. The oak floors glistened in the sunlight, which cast a gentle glow on the matching rocking chairs and small table sitting in the center of the room. Those chairs looked so inviting to Landrien. She found herself wanting to do nothing more than sit down there with a cup of coffee, open up a good book, and forget about everything else in the world. The reading room was meticulous, as if the slightest movement of one piece of furniture would throw the whole space into chaos. Whoever had decorated this house had a real artistic eye, Landrien concluded.

"Our library. Or, as I like to call it, 'Bobby's Sanctuary.'"

"I love it!" Landrien exclaimed, turning to the couple. "It gives me an idea for the family house."

"It was all Bobby's work, the decorating." Reggie gave Bobby a warm smile and nudged him.

"The library was my first project when we moved into this house."

Reggie gestured them away, however, and they followed him through the archway that led into the living room. It was more modestly decorated and contained a beige-colored leather lounging chair, a small wooden coffee table, and a beige leather sofa.

Landrien sat next to Jordan on the sofa and continued taking in the décor while Reggie reclined in the chair. Bobby stood up beside Reggie.

"Your home is so cozy—must've taken a long time to get it all just right. I just love all the colors. When did you move here?" asked Landrien.

"We moved here in 1997, right before the neighborhood started gentrifying. The woman across the street, she lived here ever since we moved in. She just sold her house for $850,000 a few months ago. We paid a fraction of that for this one. It's crazy to think about, but if we decided to sell and move to a cheaper city—since Reggie's been talking about going back South—we'd have a good chunk of money to add to our retirement." He sat down on the arm of the chair.

"Around the time we started looking for houses, Bobby had just got tenure and my attorney salary was pretty generous. Buying a house seemed logical. We lucked up with this one," Reggie added. His hand closed around Bobby's hand.

Bobby smiled at Reggie and then returned his attention to their guests. "First thing we bought for the house was that framed painting." He pointed toward the large painting on the wall opposite the sofa. The painting depicted a full moon shining over a small boat that floated in the middle of a vast body of water. The darkness and the moon gave the ripples of the water a glossy and vivid appearance.

"It's beautiful," Jordan marveled, staring at the painting. "It must've cost a pretty penny."

"We got a discount, you could say," Reggie smirked, looking at Landrien as though he was waiting for her to understand some implication embedded within this statement. She looked back at him blankly. "We bought it from Marie for $500. Our first donation to the youngest Moriset's college fund."

She stared at him with gratitude, her cheeks flushing red. "Marie painted this?"

Reggie shook his head. "No. Your mama did, back in Arkansas. She painted it during our last year there, but she never got around to framing it. She called this one 'The Spot.'"

"She painted?" Landrien's eyes widened.

"Not often. And I don't believe she ever painted anything else after we left Arkansas," Reggie replied.

"She never mentioned it in the diaries." Landrien marveled at the painting. "So she could've been an artist."

"She *was* an artist, at heart," Reggie declared.

"You said she never did it any more after she left Arkansas. How do you think that affected her?" asked Landrien.

He stared at her with an uncertain expression. "I'm not sure. I think everything that happened left a hole in her."

"Do you have any more of her artwork? I know she also did a bit of writing. Do you have any of it? I'm interested in seeing whatever you have."

"No. I'm afraid I don't. Pardon me if I'm out of line, but you act like this is some sort of research project, like you're interviewing me about some woman you've never met," said Reggie.

"I don't suppose I ever did meet her, not really. We weren't all that close," she admitted.

Reggie regarded her for a moment but then sat up straight and glanced at his partner. "Bobby, you mind putting on a pot of coffee? Or would y'all prefer sweet iced tea? I made it yesterday."

"Coffee is fine," Landrien answered. "With lots of cream and sugar."

"I'll take sweet tea," said Jordan. Reggie surveyed him and smiled as Bobby disappeared into the kitchen.

"Where are you from, son? Not many folks up here call it 'sweet tea.'"

"Georgia. My mom used to make it all the time during the summer. I haven't had any homemade in ages."

"Ah. A country boy. I thought I heard an accent when you introduced yourself. So you and Landrien work together?"

"Yeah, we're both lawyers," Landrien explained.

Jordan put his hand on Landrien's knee and patted it. "Plaintiff side, legal aid," he added.

Landrien noticed that Jordan's posture was rigid. He was nervous, she realized, and she could understand why. An air of intensity and power rose off Reggie like smoke, and it was unsettling, if not a little intoxicating. She knew he was a man who had no problem convincing others of his wisdom and integrity.

"Good." Reggie looked from Jordan to Landrien. She had the sense that he was reading her and trying to 'feel her out,' an expression her father often used. There was something distinctly cat-like about this man, she decided. Calculating was the word that came to mind. "Why weren't you and your mom close?"

The question caught her by surprise. "Huh? Oh. Well, I don't know. She didn't like me all that much, to be honest."

His eyebrows narrowed, and he appeared angry for the first time. "That's unfortunate."

She was not sure why, but for some reason this simple response satisfied her. Her posture slumped a little, and she relaxed. When Bobby returned with Jordan's glass of tea, Reggie began talking about her mother, whom they often referred to as Clem and sometimes referred to as Lorraine. It took Landrien a while to keep the two names straight in her head during the conversation. Bobby sat on the arm of the chair and joined in the conversation.

All the scattered pieces of her mother began to coalesce while the two men talked. They spoke about the two-day drive from Tennessee en route to Marie's house in Philadelphia, about how Darren cried for his mother and none of them knew how to make him believe the lie that Reggie had created.

Reggie stood up and walked to the window where he peered out and kept his back to his guests. "Within a week of our arrival in Philly, we had all—me, Bobby, Lorraine and Darren—moved into a house in Germantown. Renting, of course. Lorraine and Darren shared one room, and Bobby and I shared the other. It was a little cramped compared to all the space and country we'd been used to in Marie's house in Arkansas. But nobody complained. I sure as hell didn't complain. I think maybe we were all too scared to complain."

"Why?" she asked, moving forward to the edge of the sofa.

Reggie turned to face them. "Because of what we'd done, running off with Bell's son, switching Clem and Bell's driver's licenses to make everybody believe Bell had run off and Lorraine had died. The magnitude of what we'd done hit us during the drive up from Memphis. It was terrifying."

"How did you manage it? I don't understand why people didn't figure it out."

Reggie simply stared at her, and she saw a pain deeper than he could articulate. She decided not to press the question. Instead, Bobby answered:

"Bell was beaten until she was unrecognizable. Her whole body…it was like one big bruise. On one look, nobody other than her parents would have questioned whether it was the woman on the driver's license we left. And technology wasn't what it is now. We were lucky, no matter how awful that sounds."

"We weren't lucky. It was the seventies, and it was Arkansas. The racist white cops didn't give a shit," Reggie replied, in a venomously quiet voice. Bobby looked down at him with a sad expression but nodded in agreement. "We committed crimes, several crimes that could've landed us all under the jail. And, on top of that, we took Darren away from his family. All in some high and mighty belief that we knew what was best for him, that he was better off with us and that it was what Bell would've wanted. We were self-righteous fools." Reggie folded his arms across his chest.

"But maybe he *was* better off with you guys," Landrien wondered. "It's what Bell wanted, or at least that's what I read in Lorraine's early diary entries she wrote before the incident." She shot an eager glance at Bobby and then Reggie. "You don't think he was better off up here?"

Reggie turned and stared out the window at his neighbor's small patio. "Away from all the prejudice and hate down there? Yeah, maybe. But up here, told a lie all his life? I don't know. I don't know how that constitutes 'better.'"

"There's no one left from his original family. His grandparents and great aunt are dead. Bell's father died a few years after we left, and her mother followed sometime after him."

Reggie dropped his arms and stuffed his hands inside his jeans pockets. "They died never knowing the truth. No matter how you slice it, there's nothing right about that."

"I'm sorry, but I'm just curious. What *did* the police actually do? You did speak to them before you left Arkansas, right?" she asked.

"The police believed our story, without question," Reggie scoffed. "A black girl raped and beaten to death didn't warrant much investigation back then, or now. A missing black woman and her son was equally insignificant. It was so easy, so simple what we did. I think for a while it all felt like a dream. Clem was terrified for months that the police or somebody would figure it all out.

I think the fact that the police never figured it out, that they didn't even care, killed Clem's spirit. Unlike me, she'd always believed there was good in most people. But after everything that happened, that idealism of hers sort of slipped away." He paused and turned around to face them. He rested against the windowsill, with his hands still in his pockets. He looked at Landrien with a hard, bitter expression that unnerved her. "To answer your first question again: no, I'm not sure Darren or any of us were better off for what we did."

Bobby rose and put his arm around Reggie. For a while, the two men stood there, holding one another. Jordan and Landrien averted their gazes, feeling like intruders upon an intimate moment. She wanted to excuse herself to the restroom, just to get away from the two grieving men for a moment. She could not imagine what it must have been like to lose one's closest friends, one through a violent murder-rape and another through the psychological fallout of that violent crime. She figured it must have been damn near unbearable for Reggie, then and now.

"What about my mom's parents? My grandparents? I mean, they knew right?" she asked, hesitant to interrupt the silence.

"No. Not at first." Bobby held Reggie's hand as they released one another.

"Clem waited months before she contacted her parents and told them. We needed it to be real," Reggie explained. He returned to his seat, his eyes wet. "You never met them?"

Landrien shook her head.

"I'm not surprised," Reggie went on. "Not long after she told her parents, she distanced herself from them. Eventually, she distanced herself from everybody except

Marie. Her mama, Eve, is still alive. She lives in Maryland now with her two sisters. Remind me to give you her number later. Anyway, Clem cut everybody out of her life. It wasn't long before she got pregnant with you, got married and moved off to the suburbs. What little friendship we still had was gone by then." Reggie lit a cigarette he had rolled himself. He took a long drag from it and blew out smoke. With a wave of his hand, he tried to swish it away from Landrien and Jordan. "You mind if I smoke?"

"No, it's fine," she and Jordan assured him. The smoke was strong, and she quickly realized that it was a marijuana cigarette.

"She didn't even invite us to the wedding, you know?" Bobby lamented as Reggie handed him the cigarette. Bobby took a puff, offered it to Landrien and Jordan, who politely declined, and he handed it back to Reggie. "But we understood why. We didn't hold it against her."

"Speak for yourself." Reggie rolled his eyes.

"She was trying to start over, give herself and Darren a real life. It was understandable. I didn't like the way she went about it, but I understood what she was doing."

Reggie grunted. "What she was doing. You mean creating a fake heteronormative life that excluded you and me?"

"That life was her protection." Bobby looked reproachfully at Reggie.

"Look," Reggie interrupted, turning to Landrien, "surely you have some more questions, honey. But how about we take a break and grab some dinner? Y'all like sushi?"

"Sure," Jordan and Landrien answered.

Within the next ten minutes, the foursome was walking to the Kingston-Throop station and on their way to Williamsburg.

Sliding from under the covers that night, she grabbed her purse from the desk and crept out of the room. She drifted to the reading room, where she sat down in one of the rocking chairs, turned on the lamplight and reached inside her purse to pull out her mother's diary.

"Hey," came a deep voice that startled Landrien. She turned toward the hallway and spotted Reggie walking down the staircase. "Everything all right?"

"Yeah." The book rested on her lap. "I couldn't get to sleep."

"Guess it's contagious. What're you reading?" He sat in the rocking chair opposite her and crossed his legs.

"One of my mom's diaries."

"Ah, I see. So, what's it with you and Mr. Sheehan? Marie told me you were a lesbian."

Caught off guard by this question, she chuckled and shook her head. "I thought I was."

"Now, that's interesting. Care to explain?" Reggie leaned forward.

"When I was a teenager and during college, I dated women. Only women. The first person I ever loved in any romantic way was a girl. Her name was Amma. Incidentally, she was dating my brother at the time, until she dumped him for me anyway."

Impressed, he smiled, leaned back in the chair, and rested the back of his head against his palms.

"She was 15, and I was 13 when we met," she began. "Darren forgave me quickly and had another girlfriend within a couple of weeks. He was kind of popular with the girls in school, probably on account of being an athlete with a friendly face. So it wasn't hard for him to find a new girlfriend. They tended to find him. Anyway, Amma took me to her senior prom as her date. It caused a bit of a splash as you can imagine. Sort of a big deal, you know? She used to always talk about how she couldn't wait until I graduated, and how we would go to UPenn together. She told me we'd get a nice apartment together in West Philly. We'd meet more people like us, and we'd be happy. She killed herself a month after the prom."

"My God," he gasped, bringing his hands to his right knee that was crossed over his left knee. "Why?"

Landrien shrugged. "Buildup of dealing with her homophobic parents, I suppose. Her dad pretty much wanted nothing to do with her and her 'lifestyle.' He basically disowned her. And her mother was just as bad."

"But it was the 90s. She could've—"

"I know. She had a full ride to UPenn and everything. She could've gone to college almost anywhere, and I would've gone with her. I honestly don't think I'll ever understand why she did it. I suspect there was more going on than she ever told me. That's usually how it is anyway: people only let you in so much, only tell you what they think you need to know. It took me a long time to be close to anybody again. I dated lots of women afterward and a couple of men. And then I met Jordan."

"And he changed your mind about being a lesbian?"

"No," she said, staring at her hands. "He made me love him."

He sat up straight. "That's a strange choice of words."

"I don't know how else to say it."

Neither of them spoke. The oak floors creaked as floors in old homes often do, and there was the sound of a car door shutting outside.

"Can I ask you something, Reggie? Did my dad know all this? About my mom?"

"She probably told him eventually. As I said, Lorraine cut us off just before she married him. I suppose only those diaries or Marie know the answer to that question."

"I don't get it. She and my dad seemed like such a mismatch. I mean, especially considering how old he was compared to her. How did they even meet?" she asked.

"Through Bobby, actually. Well, through Bobby's brother, who was an English professor in the same department as your father. One weekend, me, Lorraine, and Bobby went to a party at Bobby's brother's house. A party full of English and history professors. (You can imagine how boring it was.) But that's where Lorraine met Anthony Moriset."

"That's it?"

"Pretty much. They met at the cheese and crackers table. And the rest is history. Next thing I know she's pregnant, and they're getting married."

"But how?" asked Landrien.

"You have to understand something. Lorraine was waitressing and bartending at the time. She wasn't the girl with the graduate degree in education anymore. She wasn't the girl from the middle class Memphis family. She was just plain old Bell, with no college training, no money, just a high school education and distant dreams of something better. And a single mother on top of all that. The old Lorraine, ultra-lesbian southernfied Lorraine we all knew as Clem, never would've looked twice at Anthony, and not just because he was a man. She would've thought he was too old for her. Fifty years old and never married, trying to flirt with a twenty-something year old woman. Although, he was very young-looking for his age. I'd imagined he was in his late thirties or early forties. Even for me it was off-putting, and I consider myself very open-minded, if you can't tell. Anyway, the old Lorraine never would have dated, let alone married a man almost thirty years older than her, and especially not a white man. She would've also thought he was overly introverted and boring.

But the old Lorraine was practically gone by then, and Anthony Moriset was an established man who could provide for her. I suppose the new Lorraine saw Anthony as a way out for her and Darren." He paused and seemed to ponder his next words. "Honestly, I think she had given up after all that had happened, after what had happened to Bell. Lorraine wasn't a fighter, you know. I realized that much later. Some people are fighters, natural-born fighters. But some people just want to love and be loved. Hell, I guess we all want that. I'm just saying the world's sort of divided into lovers and fighters. The problem is that sometimes love requires a fight, a willingness to be courageous in the face of a world so full of hate. But some folks are not built to fight. That was Lorraine. It took me a long time to understand it, and you better believe I've spent a lot of time thinking about this. She just didn't have it in her to fight anymore."

She thought he seemed a little broken as he talked about Lorraine.

"You're a lot like her," he added.

She smiled a little. "A year ago, even a few months ago, I probably would've told you off for suggesting that. But I don't know. All that I've learned about her, maybe I am a little like her."

"Just between me and you, the old Lorraine was a pretty amazing woman. I'm sorry you didn't get to know that Lorraine, but I guess that's neither here nor there. So," he paused and leaned forward, "now that we've got that out of the way, what do you say we see what's new in this diary?"

Landrien picked up the book on her lap, opened it to the marked page and read aloud the next few entries.

CHAPTER FIFTEEN

MAY 16, 1981. While I lay in bed next to my husband yesterday morning, I watched him sleep. He had pushed the covers down just below his chest and turned onto his back. I watched his chest rise up and down in a slow rhythm, just as I'm watching it now at three something in the morning. I thought about sketching him when I watched him sleep yesterday morning. I haven't drawn anything in years, not since Arkansas. He sure was a picture, a few dark curls of hair visible and creeping from under the blanket, his lips parted. Some of the hair on his chest is gray now. Usually, I make him shave it all off during the warmer months because I hate chest hair about as bad as I hate back hair. Men can be so hairy. Anthony never puts up a fuss about shaving it off, and, thankfully, he has no hair on his back. But if he did, he would get it removed for me with no fuss.

He does whatever I ask him to do, except cook. The man refuses to learn to cook, but he cleans up after meals and, along with the kids, takes care of most other chores around the house. That's only because a few months after we got married, I told him I wasn't his maid but his wife, and that I would not cook and clean every day while he sat around and did nothing like some sort of king. He straightened up real quick after that, and not a day goes by that I don't see a broom or dishcloth in his hand.

Maybe that's why I chose him, because I knew his devotion to me would make this choice and this life easier. He got to be the old man with the young wife, half his age, and in return he had to give in to most of my demands, if he wanted to keep me. It was a nice tradeoff. Marie told me it is best to make sure a man knows you have options and alternatives. "No marriage or relationship is the end of the road," she said when she found out her second husband was cheating last year. She had her own little affair a few months later, told her husband about it just to piss him off, and they're still married. "That road just keeps going. Besides, Robert knows it's cheaper to keep me," she said. Marie likes to talk in clichés sometimes.

I suppose I should consider myself lucky that I got somebody like Anthony.

This life has its difficult parts, though. Like sex. I don't like sex with Anthony unless I've been drinking. He knows this, and although he doesn't mention it to me, I can see that it hurts him. In bed last night, I told him I wouldn't mind it if he felt the need to see other women. He asked me what kind of a person did I take him for. I said, "A person with needs." You wouldn't believe how angry he got. It was the first time I ever really saw Anthony look angry, and it really was a little scary. There I was, trying to be loving and understanding, and he was mad at me for it. Anthony looked at me and said he would never see other women because he loved nobody else but me. After that, he buried himself in one of his literary theory books and didn't speak for the rest of the night.

I had only meant it out of kindness. We hadn't had sex in over six months. The last time had been back in August on the anniversary of our first date, and that had happened because I was drunk and wanted to show him I appreciated him. He doesn't understand what it's like for me to feel him inside me. It's repugnant. But it's not him. It's what he is, what he can't change.

Earlier this evening, I figured I'd make up for last night. I put Darren and Landrien to bed at eight o'clock, and I sat at the kitchen bar, opened my Tex-Mex cookbook and drank two glasses of wine before Anthony returned from work. I fixed him a plate of the smothered potatoes and grilled steak I'd cooked for the kids and myself. He ate in silence at the kitchen bar while I sat there drinking. I don't know if it was the alcohol or not, but I watched him grow more and more attractive as I drained a third glass of wine. The black stubble on his chin, the dimple in his cheek while he chewed, his eyes so bright and green, the black curls that dropped over his ears but grew outward like an afro. He called it his Jewish fro from his mother's side, his Jewish half. He looked at me awkwardly a few times while I watched him wash his dishes. Then, he kissed my forehead and went upstairs to shower. I finished off my glass of wine twenty minutes later.

When I got up to the room, Anthony was lying in bed and reading a book, a pencil behind his left ear, looking like an intellectual Paul Newman from Cool Hand Luke. (I don't know why I'm telling you all of this, but I need to paint a clear picture, so bear with me. I need you to understand why I did it and what's happening to me.) He really was a little breathtaking, lying there on the bed in his boxers with his shirt off. For a man his age, I'm always so surprised by how well he has preserved himself. Of course, when Anthony's not working or writing, he's jogging, at least during the warm months. And he's a nut about eating healthy.

Standing at the doorway and looking at him, I was ready, maybe even excited about the prospect of being close to him. I hadn't felt that way about any man but

Reggie, but that was years and years ago, and I'd quickly gotten over it.

Yet the longer I stood there, even beneath the haze of the wine, some part of me still was not really up to the task, at least not until I crawled into bed, and he held me and kissed me like he had completely forgotten his anger from the previous night. He reached over to turn out the lamplight, but I turned it back on. If I was going to do this, I needed to see all of him.

Do you know how difficult it was for me to look at him and feel all of his maleness against me? I don't know why I felt this way. We had done it many times before, but it had never felt natural. Do you know what I had to tell myself for the first few minutes? "This is what mothers do. This is what I have to do for my children, for you." I repeated that in my mind until it became a steady refrain. But then something happened. Something pushed that refrain to the back of my mind, and I'm telling you, I could not hear it any more. I could not hear it for the sound of our lovemaking. Isn't that what you used to call it? 'Lovemaking?'

Today of all days, I should not be feeling like this or writing these words. I should not feel this strange sense of contentment. It feels wrong, somehow, and odd that I may have discovered love again exactly four years from the day that I thought I had lost it for good.

Landrien followed Jordan up the dim stairway to her old apartment. When they reached the third floor and he walked inside the apartment, she hung back in the hallway.

"You coming in?" He tossed his coat inside the hall closet and glanced at her.

"I think I should probably just head home—I mean, back to Phoenixville."

Jordan watched her stare at her feet. A nervous and shy Landrien was an unusual sight. "What's up with you? You've been weird ever since we left New York."

"I figure since we're still trying to work through some things, we should take it slow. Set some boundaries." She stopped when she thought about the two pregnancy tests in her bathroom trash back in Phoenixville.

Holding her hands, he led her into the apartment and shut the door. "Look, I don't care about all the bullshit before. It's done. Let's just start fresh."

She shook her head.

"What's wrong?"

"I took two pregnancy tests last weekend, Jordan," she confessed, as quickly as she could before she lost her nerve.

His eyes widened. "You're pregnant?"

"I thought I was. I took two tests to be sure."

He folded his arms across his chest and glared at her. "You seem relieved or something."

"I *am* relieved. You know I don't want children. I don't want to be a mother. We talked about that. But when I thought I was pregnant, I realized if I had to have anybody's baby, it might as well be yours. You understand what I'm saying? I'm no good at all this sentimental stuff. I'm just saying I love you." She looked as though verbalizing such words had required great effort.

"Thank you," he said, after a significant pause.

She wished she could decipher what those two words meant at that moment, but instead of trying, she kissed the side of his face and opened the door. "I'll see you at work." She retreated down the narrow staircase before he could offer any response.

***

That night, she lay in bed and stared at the ceiling while her thoughts drifted aimlessly from her mother's diaries to work. When she glanced at the clock, it was half past midnight, and she considered going downstairs to grab a late night snack. In the next moment, however, Bell appeared, and Landrien nearly fell off the bed in fright.

"Shit," Landrien cried, holding her chest and sitting up. "A little warning would be nice. You scared the hell out of me. Why are you moving like that?"

Bell swayed her head back and forth, her shoulders and arms following as the orange dress fluttered around her thighs, and her long braids swished around her face. Smoothly, she danced across the room in some imitation of ballroom dancing, and Landrien watched out of curiosity. Accepting that all of this had reached a new level of weirdness, she leaned against the headboard and observed Bell in silence.

"How was your trip?" asked Bell, her semi-sheer orange dress fanning like bright flames as she danced around the room.

"Good," Landrien replied.

"You were thinking about your life just now and possibly getting a cat. I like cats," Bell noted, as usual changing the subject with no warning.

"How do you...oh right, you're all spiritual and omnipotent." Over the past few weeks, she had learned to relax around Bell and now found amusement in the fact that she spent many of her evenings talking to a woman who had died over three decades ago. If Landrien's life had been dull and uneventful before she moved to Phoenixville, it certainly had taken an interesting turn since then.

"Omnipotent?"

"All-knowing," explained Landrien.

Bell shook her head. "No, I ain't all-knowing. I don't know most things, just some things here and there. So why'd you stop taking pictures?" asked Bell. She was crouching and thrusting her hips left and right.

"I don't know. After Amma was gone, it just didn't seem worth it anymore." As she said this, it suddenly seemed like a poor excuse. She had spent her whole childhood obsessed with cameras and pictures, and her father had bought her one camera after the other. Why had she stopped taking photographs? Reggie had not stopped doing what he loved, neither had Bobby and Jordan. Reggie loved activism, and he had made it his life. Bobby loved home life and his relationship with Reggie. He had made his relationship and his home into a work of art, or damn near. Jordan loved writing, and he spent every weekend buried in it. *Why did I stop?*

"She was your inspiration, wasn't she?" asked Bell, still dancing slowly with her arms spread out.

Landrien nodded. The more she thought about it all, the more she felt like a sentimental loser. "But there's no point now." She lay on her back and stared up at Bell. "I don't have time for anything else at the moment, let alone relearning photography. I just need to focus on getting this house in order and on my work."

"You're so much like Clem. She also liked to make excuses. Just like you, she spent too much time thinking, lost in her memories. Get out of your head for a while and look around you. There's plenty of things and people with stories to tell." Barely moving anything other than her hips now, she hummed something that Landrien eventually recognized as an old Bobby Blue Bland song that her mother used to play while cooking. She appreciated Bell's grace and rhythm. There was elegance and something just a little dirty in every twirl and hip thrust.

Once Bell stopped, she rested against the window and closed her eyes briefly. Her chest heaved up and down, and she clutched her stomach, smiling all the while.

"Did you dance before? Professionally, I mean."

"No." Bell shook her head, still attempting to catch her breath. "But my mama was a dancer when she was in her twenties. Then, she had me and moved back to Arkansas and found Jesus."

"Where did she live before?"

"Chicago. She got some training with a black theater group there in the forties and did a few shows at little black-run community theaters. Chicago was a good place for a performer back then, if you were the right color. Of course, my mama wasn't the right color. She used to say she wished she could move to D.C. or New York, where I guess there was a stronger black theater community. I don't know. Being a black performer was hard everywhere, I suppose.

Anyway, she turned thirty, got married to a factory man who didn't have any love for art—bless his heart—and then she got pregnant, he got laid off, and they came back to Arkansas where all his family was. Since her mama had passed away, her pa wasn't no count, and she didn't have siblings, I guess she didn't feel like she was leaving too much behind in Chicago. I always wondered how Mama supported herself in Chicago before she met Pa, though. She never told me, and I know her folks didn't help out. She swore she never regretted coming back to Arkansas or giving up her dream of dancing and acting. I ain't too sure I ever believed her. Life changes, and you just gotta adapt.

She did what she had to do. She was a good woman, even though I don't think she knew it."

After a few minutes passed in silence, she figured Bell had said all she would say for the moment. "Tell me about your trip to New York," Bell went on, abruptly. Happy to fill the awkward silence, she launched into an abbreviated description of the trip. Bell lay at the edge of the bed and listened, asking questions here and there but mostly remaining quiet and attentive. When Landrien finished, Bell asked, "Why did you leave out the parts about you and that boyfriend of yours?"

"Because I'm not up for talking about Jordan right now. All I can say is it's complicated."

"All right. But can I just make a point, a little point?" Bell insisted, and Landrien nodded for her to continue. "He seems like a decent man, not bad looking either. Consider how you'd feel if he wasn't around anymore. That's all I'm gonna say."

Landrien chuckled. "Relationship advice from a ghost."

"I don't think I'm a ghost, honey."

"Okay," Landrien smiled. "Then, what are you? A poltergeist?"

"Of course not," Bell exclaimed.

"Right. Well, speaking of what you are, I'm just wondering are you going to be around indefinitely? Because I was thinking if I carried out Mom's wishes—read the diaries, lived here for the one-year period—I might not see you anymore. You know, like in the movies, where the spirits hang around because they or the other main character have some sort of unfinished business?"

"Do you want me to go?" asked Bell. She stood up and looked down at Landrien.

"No. Actually, I like you being here, as crazy as that sounds. This house is kind of spooky, well spookier anyway, when you're not around."

Bell smiled and sat down again. They talked for a while longer about nothing in particular until Landrien finally yawned and lay back on the bed. "Good night," she told Bell, who had perched at the foot of the bed. Landrien pulled the blanket up to her shoulders and immediately fell asleep.

The next day at the office turned out to be a slow day as Landrien plunged through deposition transcripts and began working on questions for the deposition of her client's former supervisor. She felt increasingly unprepared as Friday's deposition approached and as she poured through the documents they had received about her client's supervisor. The supervisor was a real piece of work, she concluded, flipping through the documents and shaking her head as the details got worse and worse.

After two cups of coffee and two fruitless hours of trying to brainstorm questions and structure the deposition, she gave up and pushed the task onto Jordan, who took it begrudgingly. "Look, I can get the motion to compel done, and you can work on preparation for Friday's depo. This supervisor's going to be the toughest person to break, especially because he knows he's already dug himself a hole he can't get out of. I'm thinking the depo last week with the human resources lady is gonna feel like a short jog compared to this one. Did you see the shit he said in that email to the human resources lady? I mean, he actually referred to Jennifer as a 'lazy spic.'" Landrien stood in the doorway of Jordan's office. "The man's a racist twat. But, really, what kind of moron puts shit like that in writing?"

Jordan sat behind his desk, glasses pushed down onto his nose, papers and folders scattered across his desk. Not looking up from the papers spread out in front of him, he said, "A really racist moron. He definitely was looking for any excuse he could find to can Jennifer, and he was dumb enough to spell it out in an email. I wish all horrible supervisors were that dumb, would make life a lot easier for us. And look at it this way: if he's as awful and mean as he seems on paper, they won't want him to go before a jury. So, good for us, I say."

"Yeah, for sure. That's exactly why you should be the one to depose him on Friday," she suggested, and his right eyebrow went up in surprise.

"Why?"

"The man's going to shut down as soon as I open my mouth. Think about it, Jordan."

Indeed, Jordan appeared to be thinking deeply for a moment and then nodded. "Because you're a woman."

"And not white. I'm hardly any better or more worthy of respect than Jennifer in his mind."

"Okay. You're right." He nodded after he mulled over her words. "You're right."

"Yeah, I know. Have fun," she replied, just before she turned out of his office.

"Yeah, you bet," Jordan joked.

When she returned to her office, she began working on the motion to compel, hoping to force Jennifer's employer to turn over prior disability discrimination complaints other employees had filed against the company. She had to write a brief for the motion, and it was mind-numbing, tedious work, although she preferred writing to dealing with the deposition right now. With great effort, she made herself focus on finishing the brief, so she could file it by the end of the week. Throughout the afternoon, she repeatedly glanced at the clock on the computer, only to find a mere twenty or thirty minutes had passed each time she checked. *Mondays. Fucking Mondays.*

Eventually, five o'clock arrived, and she wasted no time getting of the office. She told herself that what was unfinished could wait until tomorrow. At least she had drafted the motion and brief, called a few other clients and got to work on a new case. That was something, she told herself.

On the train, she sat and read some more of her mother's diary entries. Many of the entries were detailed accounts of banal daily tasks—such as taking Anthony's suits to the drycleaners, buying another cookbook, trying a new recipe, celebrating Landrien's or Darren's birthdays, or just reminiscing about her past. Her mother seemed to reminisce a lot, Landrien noticed, and after a while, all the reminiscing became rather monotonous. It was as though her mother had spent her life judging her present by her past. She seemed to have assumed that her present never could live up to the idyllic past. This was rather a sad way to go through life, Landrien concluded, vowing to not repeat her mother's mistake of forgetting to live.

Upon arriving at home, she reheated some roast chicken and potatoes, sat at the table and ate in silence as the sun set. She expected Bell to show up and join her, but by the time she finished the last potato, Bell still had not put in an appearance. She shrugged, drained the remaining water in her glass, got up and cleaned the dishes.

Standing at the archway leading into the living room, she surveyed the space until her gaze landed on the spot at the bottom of the stairs. She saw her dead mother lying there, eyes wide, night scarf wrapped around her head. But the image faded in an instant, and there was only the floor and the dark spot on the wall where her mother had rested her oily head. Right then, she decided she would visit the hardware store tomorrow after work to buy some paint to redo the living room and dining room. If she was going to stay in this house, she might as well make it comfortable.

Another thought took shape: she would take some before and after photographs of each room she redecorated and repainted. She would make a project out of it. Of course, she did not remember how to develop photographs, and she needed to buy all the chemicals and film. It occurred to her that it did not matter in this current age of digital photography that she had forgotten how to develop photographs the old-fashioned way. Besides, maybe her old photography books contained some instructions. She learned it once. She could learn it again.

As she stood there in the quiet living room and her thoughts raced, there came a knock on the door. When she peeked through the blinds, she saw Rona standing on the porch with her hands on her hips. Rona wore a thin cardigan and a dark red dress that dropped to her knees and flared, and she looked positively anxious. Rona, Landrien had realized, was a lonely woman with children who never visited her. She felt a little sad for the woman sometimes.

Although she was not interested in having company, she took a deep breath and opened the door. "Hey." She pasted a smile on her face as she opened the screen door. "How's it going?"

Rona beamed. "Oh, pretty darn good. I just wanted to come over and check on you. Mind if I come in?"

"No. Of course not," Landrien lied, stepping aside as the woman strode in.

"I don't mean to bother you, child. I just feel like I owe it to your mother to check on you once in a while. How have you been?" Rona went toward the sofa and sat down, looking up at Landrien who still stood in front of the door.

"Well. I've been well. I went up to New York this past weekend."

"Oh yeah? What for?" Rona removed her cardigan and placed it across her lap. Her movements seemed stiff and suggested she was nervous about something. She had noticed Rona never seemed comfortable around her lately.

"Just to talk to some old friends about a woman named Lorraine. Did my mom ever mention a woman named Lorraine to you?" She had not intended to broach the subject with Rona, but she also knew she would not regret asking the question. Something told her that Rona knew more than she let on and that she was dying to spill some secrets.

"She did. It was during one of our knitting nights. Once in a while, especially after your father passed away, Pam would tell me a lot about people and things from her past."

Landrien approached Rona and sat in the armchair next to the sofa. "What did she tell you about this woman?"

"Let's see," Rona considered, leaning forward and running her hands through her gray-white hair. "Well, it's hard to recall." Rona stared at her wrinkled, freckled white hands that were resting in her lap, and she hesitantly glanced up at Landrien. "She was a woman Pam knew a long time ago and lost touch with, I guess. They were close. Pam was never real specific about it. That's about all I know."

"No it's not," Landrien surmised, trying to sound as polite as possible. "I might not know you that well, Rona, but I can see from a mile away that you're not telling me everything. And since I know you liked my mom and care about me, I'm assuming you're trying to protect me or my mom's memory. So, let me just get right to the point: I already know more than you think about my mom's weird past. What I really want to know is what my mom told you about this woman. I'm less interested in the woman herself, and more in what my mom thought of her. Does that make sense?"

Rona gazed warily at Landrien.

"If I make us a pot of coffee and reheat a banana nut muffin for you, will you talk?" coaxed Landrien.

"Yes. Thanks. I'd appreciate that," Rona replied, with a none-too-pleased smile.

Landrien got up and disappeared into the kitchen, where she quickly made a pot of Ethiopian coffee and reheated an overpriced vegan muffin she had gotten from the market a few blocks away. She cut the muffin in half and put each piece on a separate saucer. When she returned to the living room, she found Rona standing near the fireplace and holding a framed photograph of Darren sitting on the front porch. Her father had taken it right after Darren had won his first soccer game in middle school. The pride on her mother's face as she draped her arms around Darren expressed itself in a rare, wide grin. Landrien sat the coffee and saucers on the end table between the sofa and armchair.

"She always talked about how much she'd wanted to be a good mother and how much she'd failed." Rona placed the framed photograph back on the mantel and turned to Landrien. "I don't think she failed, and I told her as much. She produced a lawyer and a police officer. How many parents can say that?"

"Well, in that case, whether or not she failed depends on your view of lawyers and police officers. To some, that would make her a complete failure. But, to be fair, I'm a civil rights lawyer, which makes me a little less detestable. Just to be fair." Landrien resumed her seat in the armchair. She glanced up at the gray-haired old woman and sipped her coffee.

Rona chuckled and took her place on the sofa, where she sipped the dark coffee and took a pinch of the muffin. She looked up at Landrien a few minutes later and appeared more relaxed, although still hesitant. "Look, your mother was a good woman. I just want you to know that. I think she did her best with you and your brother, and she wanted you to understand that."

"I mean no disrespect, but just out of curiosity, how do you know that? How do you know she did her best? You weren't around when we were children, Rona."

"Well, just look at you. You're a fine, smart woman, and your brother's a good man as far as I can tell. That doesn't come from bad mothering, I can tell you that," declared Rona, matter-of-fact.

She knew from Rona's stern stare that she probably should not question the woman's opinion of her mother. "Fine, okay. But whatever it is you have to say, quit trying to soften the blow by telling me how great my mom was. I appreciate it, but you don't have to do that. So, back to this woman named Lorraine?"

Rona cleared her throat while she regarded Landrien with a hint of disapproval. "Pam never said much about this woman, Lorraine. Not until one Saturday afternoon, when I came by. She'd left the front door unlocked, so I just walked in. Your father had just gone into the hospital for his prostate surgery, and Pam had come to gather some of his things to take back with her to the hospital. I had walked over to bring her a peach pie to take with her. You know how your father liked peach pie. Well, I found Pam on the back patio, talking to herself and saying something about Lorraine being gone."

Landrien remembered her father's fondness for peach pie, for almost any fruit pie, in fact. The memory made her smile. Anthony Moriset had made peach pies every Christmas and Thanksgiving. It was about the only thing he ever cooked, and he cooked those pies to near perfection. It warmed her opinion of Rona to learn that the woman had known of her father's love for peach pies and had been thoughtful and caring enough to make one for him just before his surgery. He never recovered from the surgery and seemed to deteriorate afterward. To make matters even worse, during those years, his Alzheimer's had gotten so bad that he hardly said a word to anyone. Yet his face always lit up when Landrien brought him a peach pie during her visits. The last peach pie she had baked was one for his seventieth birthday, and she had sat on the back porch and ate it with him. The two of them ate an entire pie. A few months later, after she began law school, he went to sleep one afternoon and never woke up again.

Landrien sat forward, a sudden realization hitting her like a boulder. She smiled with satisfaction. *Bell appeared to Mom, too. It's not just me.* "She was talking to herself, you say?"

"Yeah. Nobody but her was there, and she was talking, saying that Lorraine was gone. 'Long gone' were her words, if I remember right. She said something like, 'Will either one of us ever have any peace'? Now, I couldn't figure out what that meant, and I never asked her. I only remember the words because they were so odd. It didn't make sense. I started to interrupt her, but then she clutched her chest and got quiet for a while. She was holding a dress against her chest. I just stayed put and watched her. I figured with all the stress, she was just going through a spell." Rona took another sip of coffee.

"What color was the dress?"

Rona seemed taken aback by the strangeness of this inquiry. She stammered for a moment. "Orange, I believe. A shimmering sort of orange."

Landrien reclined back in the chair and sighed as cool relief swept over her. She even smiled, to Rona's general dismay. "Thank you."

Still perplexed, Rona went on, "I think she was mentally unstable, maybe depressed and hallucinating. There was no one there but her. Maybe the thought of losing Anthony brought it all on, or maybe it was always there. I have no idea. She never talked to me about that day. All I know is, like I said, she did try to be the best mother she could be to her family."

"She wasn't hallucinating," Landrien mumbled under her breath, glancing down at her cup. For a second, she was hardly aware of Rona's presence.

"What?"

"Nothing." She turned toward Rona. "Nothing.

Rona regarded her with concern. "Anyway, all this is to say, I think Pam was very unhappy, and it had something to do with this woman, Lorraine. I don't know how to say this politely, but I think she might've been, you know, *that* way. Gay." Rona whispered the last word.

Landrien laughed, unable to contain herself, but stopped as soon as she caught the horrified expression on Rona's face. She tried to make her face as serious and understanding as possible as she locked eyes with Rona.

"It's okay, Rona. You're right. She was really unhappy, and she was gay or at least bisexual," she said, stifling the urge to laugh at Rona's wide-eyed gaze.

"You knew?"

"I figured it out," Landrien replied, and this time Rona burst into laughter.

Rona held her stomach, and the laughter seemed to relieve her of something she had held in for a very long time. "Good Lord, I figured I was the only one who even thought it," the woman exclaimed. "I couldn't ever pinpoint why I thought she was, you know, gay, but I always just knew. You know how sometimes you can just tell? Of course, I didn't care one way or another, and I sure wish she'd been comfortable enough to tell me. Oh, how lonely it must've been for her, keeping it all hidden. And I felt so bad about you and your brother not knowing. Poor Pam."

How did Rona figure it out? Landrien wondered. She scanned her mind for any lesbian or bisexual stereotypes that her mother had exhibited, but she could think of none that fit her mother, other than a slight tomboyish demeanor—the way that she preferred jeans and tennis shoes and hardly wore jewelry, abhorred nail polish and bit her nails. Despite any of these stereotypical qualities, she never had considered her mother anything but a conservative, God-fearing heterosexual suburban housewife. Finding out that her mother was once a non-religious lesbian from the sticks of Arkansas and Tennessee had upset her entire memory of the woman, so much Landrien had begun to question the accuracy of her own memories.

She pondered all of these things during the rest of the conversation with Rona, until her thoughts strayed to another related topic. Although Rona said she could sometimes "just tell" that a person was gay, she seemingly had not picked up on Landrien's sexuality. *Mom made me straight, in her mind and in the minds of her friends.* As she thought about this, so many notions began to take shape in her mind, and she realized that she finally understood her mother.

She and Rona spent the remainder of the hour sipping coffee, eating muffins and discussing her mother. When Landrien walked the woman out to the porch and turned back into the house, she shut the door and leaned against it, her thoughts returning to the earlier part of her conversation with Rona. *I guess seeing dead folks sort of runs in the family.* Half bent over, she laughed harder than she had for many months. The laughter came out in waves, shaking her whole body. How relieved she felt to know that Bell's presence was not merely a hallucination! After all, she reasoned, what were the chances that she and her mother would have the same exact hallucination?

Just before Landrien pushed all thoughts of Bell and her mother aside, she added another item to her mental to-do list: find that orange dress.

CHAPTER SIXTEEN

APRIL 4, 1991. I beat Landrien yesterday. I don't know how long it lasted, and all I could hear was the belt and her hollering. But I was sweating once I finished, and she was staring at me with nothing but hate in her eyes. The moment I dropped the belt, I knew I deserved that look, too. I also know that someday she will understand and maybe even forgive me. She will see what I am trying to show her, and if she doesn't, she'll pay the price. All brave women pay the price for their bravery in the end.

Before you judge me, let me make something very clear: I refuse to stand back and watch it happen all over again, not after all I've sacrificed to give her and Darren a normal life. That is the only reason I can offer for why I am so hard on her. She deserves better from this world than what we got from it. Of course, I can't stand being the source of her pain, and sometimes I wonder if I'm going about this the wrong way. But if I have to beat some sense into her to keep her away from Amma Shepherd, I will do it, no matter how much she hates me for it. I won't let her be like me.

When Anthony came in from work a couple hours later, I guess she told him what happened. He was furious. Without so much as a word to me, he packed up her bags and sent her to Marie's for the weekend. Anthony never hollers at me, never even raises his voice. But as soon as he got back home from dropping Landrien off at Marie's, he snapped and said a lot of hurtful things. I admit I deserved most of it. He even threatened to leave me and take Landrien with him if I ever laid a hand on her again. I have no doubt that he'll make good on his threat. His anger was like nothing I had ever seen from him.

I just don't know what to do anymore. Anthony doesn't understand how mean this world can be for a woman. Being a woman is hard enough without adding extra burdens on top of it. I can't let her be like me.

Landrien rested on the sofa and reread the entry. As she did, she watched more pieces of the puzzle that was her mother meld together into a melancholy but cohesive image. Nothing could excuse her mother's behavior, but she had to admit that it sure was nice to have an explanation for it all. There was some logic in the madness. That was worth something.

After a glance at the clock, she bookmarked the page, closed the diary and placed it on the nightstand. She turned out the lamplight and minutes later passed into a dreamless slumber.

Many nights over the next several months, transpired in this fashion. She filled her nights with recollections from her mother's diaries—rereading some entries on occasion to fill in gaps here and there—while she passed her days either working at the office, out taking photographs, or redecorating the house. She painted the living room walls sage green and shined the wooden railings of the staircase. The brown iron frame bed in her room was now white, set off against tan and sage green walls. She dedicated a weekend to repainting each room, including the downstairs half bathroom, and the two full bathrooms upstairs. With each room she completed, she made a list of furniture she should get rid of or update. She took photographs of every room of the house and repainted each room except the one that had belonged to her parents. For some reason, that room seemed out of bounds.

As time rushed by in a flurry, Landrien could not be certain what changed more quickly, the months and seasons or her feelings about living at 4516 Belmont Road in Phoenixville. She welcomed the change.

When Darren visited one weekend to pick up some items from the storage room, he found his sister suited up in raggedy jeans and an oversized paint-stained t-shirt, her hair grown out and pulled back into a short ponytail. She had a brush drenched in green paint in one hand and the other hand on her hip. Nineties alternative rock music blared from the sound system she had just bought for the new flat screen television. He looked from her to the half-painted walls to the plastic covering the hardwood floors. "Landrien?" he called over the music, and she turned to him with a smile.

"Why don't you pick up a brush while you're here?" she hollered, lifting her arm and gesturing him over to assist her. She fully expected Darren to decline blithely, kick back on the sofa and turn on the television. Yet to her surprise, after he took off his shoes, Darren picked up a brush and painted alongside her for at least an hour.

Afterward, they collapsed onto the sofa, ordered Chinese and watched television. She eventually passed out against his shoulder, and he enjoyed a couple of hours of HBO. He left by early evening but returned a few more times over the next couple of weeks to help his sister paint her room and one of the bathrooms. Whenever he was not there to keep her company, Bell lingered and either talked to Landrien about life in Arkansas or else danced about the room. She noticed that Bell seemed quite happy nowadays and figured that the sunny, warm weather might have contributed to the change.

"It's still early," Bell said one evening, after Landrien washed paint off her hands and concluded her work in the downstairs bathroom. "You could run over to that boyfriend of yours. He misses you."

She dried her hands on a towel and glanced over her shoulder at Bell, who stood in the doorway. "And you're saying that because you know that he misses me, or are you just guessing?" asked Landrien, with a raised eyebrow.

"Mostly, I'm just guessing," Bell admitted.

"Well, I'm not running anywhere other than to the kitchen to pour myself a glass of wine. Do you realize this house almost feels like home, finally? I just want to relax and soak it all in." Landrien removed a bottle of Moscato wine from the refrigerator and poured some into a coffee mug. When she returned to the living room and sunk into the sofa, she turned up Prince's *Purple Rain* soundtrack and kicked her feet up on the table. Sipping the bittersweet wine, she closed her eyes and listened to music and the occasional sound of cars passing along the street in front of the house.

Bell had sat next to her, and they both leaned back. "I'm glad you're here."

"Likewise," replied Landrien, with a glance in Bell's direction.

This had become her weekday evening ritual: some housework, reheated leftovers, and then sitting in the living room with Bell and listening to the creaking of the floors or whatever other sounds sometimes disturbed the silence of the house. On clear sky days, she sometimes went for a jog or a brisk walk around the neighborhood. When the weather was less appealing, however, she might turn on a

Pilates DVD for an hour and spend thirty minutes after that lifting weights in the basement, half of which she had converted into a very small fitness center, fully equipped with a weight bench and a wall-mounted pull up bar. She had transformed the other half of the basement into the darkroom of her teen years, partitioning it off from the fitness area with a room divider she had found at IKEA. With Bell's encouragement, Landrien racked up a bill at a local photography store—purchasing a safelight, all the necessary chemicals, as well as photo paper—and forced her brain to relearn traditional darkroom photo development within a few weeks.

She had resigned herself to the possibility that Bell would always be there, that Bell was in some way connected to the house the same way her mother was connected to house. She rarely asked Bell about Arkansas any more. Instead, they talked about Darren sometimes, and Bell often would linger and watch during Darren's visits, which became more frequent. At other times, Bell lounged about and hummed a tune while Landrien cooked or painted.

As spring quickly flowed into summer, she saw more and more of Bell, who seemed to emanate peace and tranquility. She inquired about Landrien's second visit to Bobby and Reggie during mid-June, happy to hear that Landrien had developed a friendship with the two men. "Take Darren with you the next time you go up to New York. He should know them too," said Bell while they sat on the back porch one afternoon, awaiting Jordan's arrival.

Hot wind came in bursts as clouds passed away to reveal a vivid blue sky and a blazing hot sun. Landrien, wearing short shorts and a tank top, leaned back in the recliner patio chair and read the last of her mother's diaries.

It had taken longer than she had expected to read all the diaries. She was glad to have arrived at the end of the journey through her mother's sad memories. "Yeah, I'll talk to Darren about it next time."

"When's that boyfriend of yours supposed to get here?"

Landrien glanced at her watch. "In a few. We're celebrating my promotion, among other things."

"There's a lot to celebrate, isn't there?" Bell stared up at the bright sky.

Landrien thought about this question for a moment. "I suppose so."

During the past few weeks, Landrien had begun settlement negotiations on Jennifer's employment discrimination case and moved into her new position as Senior Staff Attorney. Jordan was ecstatic about the news of her promotion and his newfound status as her subordinate. On the home front, Landrien finished repainting the whole house except for her parent's room, and replaced much of the furniture in the house. She had spent most of her time either alone and working on the house, having coffee or grocery shopping with Rona on Sundays, or furniture shopping at antique stores with Marie, who had a special eye for interior decorating. She had seen very little of Jordan outside the office. To put it plainly, she had been a very busy woman.

Although she was trying not to admit it, she was a little bored living in the family house so far away from the city. The mellow lifestyle in Phoenixville felt so new and uncomfortable that at times she was sure she would sell the house as soon as the one-year period ended.

"I sort of miss barhopping with Elena and Jordan, the spontaneity of the city, you know," she told Marie on one occasion while they were out shopping.

"You can still do that." Marie examined a pastel yellow lamp.

Sometimes Landrien thought she might remain in the house and forget her life in the city. After all, there was safety and tranquility in this small town. She realized she had lived in the city for so long that she had forgotten what it was like to hear nothing, to feel safe leaving her door unlocked on occasion, to not have to deal with the unpleasant and ever present smell of garbage. She even was considering cultivating her green thumb eventually and starting a garden in the backyard. *Hell, I've got a backyard now, might as well use it*, she thought, remembering that she did not have even a patio when she lived in the city. Small-town living was easy, and easy might be boring, but easy was all right. Well, sometimes, anyway.

She observed Bell, who was sitting on the steps of the porch and staring out at the yard. A cookbook lay open next to Bell. "Hey." Landrien sat up.

"Yeah?" Bell asked.

"Is she all right?"

Bell chuckled and shook her head. "Honey, I wouldn't know. She's dead, and the dead generally ain't got that much to say."

"You seem to be an exception to that rule," noted Landrien.

Bell shrugged. "Well, I guess you got a point. I never much believed in anything to do with heaven or hell. I just figured you die, folks remember you, and that's that."

"Then why are you here?" Landrien asked.

"I don't know. Maybe I'm not. I don't think it's got anything to do with heaven or hell, though."

"You mean, maybe this is all in my head?"

"Who knows. All I can say is I suppose Clem's just fine now. I don't know why she wouldn't be. The dead ain't got no worries." Bell spoke in her usual matter-of-fact tone and regarded Landrien with sympathy. "You remember her. I believe you even respect her now, right? Ain't that all that matters?"

Landrien thought about this for a moment and nodded. "Why you ask that anyway?"

"She just seemed so sad in the end. I never noticed, you know. But she was depressed. I think maybe she was always depressed."

"Yeah. After I died, Clem was a broken person."

"I never noticed it when she was alive. If I had, maybe I could've done something."

"Listen, Landrien," Bell replied, standing up and approaching her. "Ain't nothing you can do for a broken person but love them."

But I didn't really love her.

"Of course you loved her," Bell insisted and smiled at Landrien's frightened expression. "Love is a hard thing to do. Some folks get it right. Others spend their whole life trying to get it right. Nobody gets it completely right. We just do it because we got no choice but to do it."

Landrien turned away and wiped her face, hoping that Bell thought she was rubbing her eyes because of allergies. "They should make a book full of your little words of wisdom. You would've been a great mother."

Bell smacked her lips. "I know. I always thought so myself."

They both laughed and fell back in their chairs, and they stared up at the cloudless sky, feeling no need to interrupt the silence that expanded between them.

Jordan walked onto the back porch a while later. Landrien immediately looked up at his cheerful face. She greatly appreciated that he had let his beard and moustache grow in a little. No grown man should be walking around without a little bit of facial hair.

"I heard talking."

"I was on the phone with Marie."

"No you weren't. Your phone's on the dining room table." He bent down and kissed her forehead.

"Fine. But it sounded less crazy to say I was on the phone."

"Yeah, it did, but I'm past trying to figure you out any more. If you're crazy, you're the most functional crazy person I've ever met. Besides, I've seen too much weird shit in this house to not believe that maybe it is a little haunted." He sat down in the chair that Bell had deserted the moment he arrived.

"Not haunted. Just a little 'inhabited' is all," she corrected him.

Jordan smiled. "Whatever you say. Why don't you and I go 'inhabit' the kitchen? I bought everything we need to make jambalaya and hot water cornbread."

"You know how to make jambalaya? And what the hell is hot water cornbread?" asked Landrien, to which Bell, who was now sitting on the porch stairs, looked at her in dismay and disappointment.

"Something that's gonna blow your mind. Come on." He stood up, took her hand and led her inside the house.

***

After they finished dinner, Jordan washed up the dishes while Landrien returned to the back porch. She went out into the yard and peered at the sky. There must have been a billion stars up there, shimmering like glitter on black silk. The wind nipped at her exposed shoulders. She had slipped into a sleeveless lavender dress just before they had sat down to dinner. Her feet were bare against the cool grass, but she hardly noticed the chilly breeze or the chill bumps rising up on her arms. She stood completely still and gazed up at the world above her.

A cold hand touched her back. "What're you up to?" said Jordan, standing behind her and resting his chin on her shoulder. His breath still smelled of the sweet wine they had had with dessert.

"Nothing, just felt like stepping outside."

He wrapped his arms around her waist while they stood there in the middle of the backyard, staring up at the sky and talking about nothing in particular.

Later, they tidied up the living room, dining room and kitchen and retreated upstairs to bed. Wasting not a minute more, they fell into one another's arms and had a wild kind of sex they'd had when they first met so many years earlier at a house party.

"Hey," Jordan yelled over the music, with a smile that Landrien instantly trusted. Until his interruption, she had been sitting alone on the sofa and watching the other guests. As she looked up at the man who had disrupted her people watching, she surveyed his dark hair and black framed glasses with only faint interest. She thought he looked a little like an awkward young Dustin Hoffman from his *Lenny* days, slightly boyish and nonthreatening. "I'm Jordan. Is anybody else sitting here?"

She shook her head disinterestedly and muttered, "No." She did not offer him a smile. Instead, she resumed scanning the crowd and people watching while trying to ignore what she considered to be truly horrendous eighties pop music. Meanwhile, Jordan took in her appearance with increasing curiosity, from the shaved head and sparkling nose ring to the dangling hooped earrings and sun tattoo on her left upper arm. She wore a black tank top and tight-fitting blue jeans that were a little too long for her.

"How do you know Lauren?" he asked. Forever a fan of eighties new wave music, he bobbed his head to "Blue Monday" and tried to appear relaxed.

"We went to law school together," she explained, her gaze resting on a couple who had been sitting in a corner across the room for the past several minutes. She noticed now that the taller man was working his hand up the other man's leg, and the man seemed not to mind.

"Oh." Jordan's eyes widened. "I work with Lauren at the legal services downtown, but I do employment cases. So I don't see much of Lauren other than when she throws a party. Where are you working?"

"At a law firm, defending corporate assholes. I'm planning on quitting as soon as I get the nerve," Landrien grumbled, turning to him and not breaking the slightest smile. "I'm bored. You?"

He raised his eyebrows. "Uh, with the party, or with life?"

Landrien smiled, and he wondered if he ever had seen a more infectious smile. "With the party."

"Oh. Yeah, a little, I guess," he stammered.

She regarded him with curiosity. "You wanna get out of here?"

His eyebrows might have retreated into his hairline. "Uh, yeah. All right," Jordan answered, and the two of them made their way toward the exit.

On that snowy February night, Landrien took Jordan to her apartment where she wasted no time seducing him, and he wasted no time resisting her. They never made it to her bed.

Now, on another night several years later, they only made it as far as the bedroom floor. As they lay awake on the cool floor, naked and wrapped in one another's arms, they recalled that first night and talked until they drifted to sleep.

When Landrien woke up the next morning, she was lying in bed, the sheets draped across her waist. She reached for her cell phone on the nightstand, but her hand landed on a small black case sitting on top of a red envelope. Struggling to focus her sleepy eyes, she picked up the box in one hand and the envelope in the other. The case contained the silver engagement ring he had given her almost a year ago. She stared at it thoughtlessly for a long time before she turned her attention to the envelope. On a thin piece of parchment paper, Jordan had written, "When you're ready."

She wiped sleep out of her eyes and continued to stare at the letter and the ring. The sun streamed through the curtains, and an aroma of eggs and bacon clung to her nostrils. Soft music that sounded like 80s new wave was playing from somewhere downstairs. She fell back against the bed, the envelope and the box still in her hands, and she was overwhelmed by an unfamiliar feeling of...what was it…contentment, perhaps? Things were not supposed to go this right in her relationships, or so she always had told herself.

After a while of lying there, thinking about Jordan's offer and about her life, she put the box and the letter back on the nightstand. She rose, went to the bathroom and cleaned up. When she arrived downstairs, she found him in the kitchen, pouring two cups of coffee. He was shirtless and wearing snug-fitting jeans. It was a sight she could get used to seeing every morning.

She approached him and gave him a nudge in the back, just before she kissed the back of his neck. "You look like a much older, much more attractive, Abercrombie model."

"An Abercrombie model? You do know that's the opposite of a compliment, right?" He glanced over his shoulder at her and grinned.

"In this case, it's not," she assured him.

He chuckled as he flipped a pancake and glimpsed her hand. "There's a cup of coffee for you." He nodded toward the orange mug sitting alongside a cup of milk and a box of raw sugar. "I see you're not wearing the ring."

"The thing is I'm flattered, Jordan. Really. But I'm not ready," she said gently and poured milk into her coffee.

He removed the pancake from the skillet and placed it on a plate.

"I shouldn't have said yes when you proposed," she added.

"But you did."

"I did, and it was short-sighted. I don't even know if I'm the marrying type. Besides, I'm a little fucked up, Jordan, and I don't want to put all my drama on you."

He picked up the two cups of coffee. "Maybe. But just so you know, I do think you're the marrying type, and I'm sort of into you because you're a little nuts."

"You should see a counselor about that last bit," she replied, smiling as she took the orange mug, and they proceeded toward the dining room.

"I'm looking into it," he joked, and they both laughed.

He had set the table with plates full of scrambled eggs, bacon and grits. They sat down and talked some more while devouring every morsel of food on their plates.

Once they finished, Jordan washed up the dishes, and Landrien disappeared into the basement. Before she came out of the basement, she called him to the dining room and asked him to close his eyes and count to ten. She emerged at the basement doorway as he reached ten. Standing a couple of feet away and peering at him expectantly, she wore a shimmering orange dress with spaghetti strap sleeves. The dress dropped low over her breasts, hugged her narrow waist and stopped just above her knees.

"Wow." He gaped at her.

"It's her dress."

"Whose? Your mother's?"

She shook her head. "Bell's. I spent the last couple of months looking for it. I looked everywhere." She ran her hands over the dress and looked down at it.

"What made you look for it?"

"Something Rona said, but never mind that. I never put it on until now. I kept feeling like I shouldn't, you know?"

He looked her over, caressing the beard stubble on his chin and pinching his bottom lip between his teeth. "Well, I'll say one thing. That dress looks like it was made for you."

"Trust me. It's way more beautiful on Bell."

"Wait. This is how you see her? Wearing this dress?" asked Jordan, folding his arms.

"Yeah. You remember that night in the kitchen? I said she was there, a woman in an orange dress, and I asked you if you'd seen her? This was the orange dress. I first realized the dress was real when I saw the picture in the photo album. The picture I showed you, with her standing in front of the old house? The picture was sort of faded, though, so I couldn't be sure it was the same dress she was wearing in the kitchen. But when Rona said she saw my mom holding an orange dress and talking to herself on the back porch—"

"Talking to herself?"

"Talking to Bell, clearly. Rona didn't know that. But my mom was definitely talking to Bell and holding this dress. That's when I figured it had to be here somewhere, and I was just hoping I hadn't thrown it out with the stuff I gave to the Goodwill. Thank goodness it was just packed away in the basement, in a box of Mom's old purses that I hadn't given much thought to. She had so much shit, Mom did. I never realized she was such a hoarder. I mean, I'm still sifting through some of her belongings and trying to figure out what to do with it all. Anyway, this dress was the first thing Mom ever gave Bell, back in like 1975. She wrote about in her diary. It's vintage."

"Wow."

"And all the times I've seen Bell, she's wearing this dress. It's unreal. I don't even know what to do with it." She approached the mirror that hung on the wall next to the fireplace, and Jordan followed her. They both surveyed her reflection, and an idea struck her. "Run to the basement and get my camera tripod. It's next to the dryer," she ordered him.

"Why?"

"You'll see!" She hurried toward the staircase and up to her room to retrieve her Nikon camera. In the closet, she rifled through the box of diaries until she found the photo album. Between the cover and first page, she had inserted the photograph of Bell standing in the country and wearing the orange dress. She grabbed the photograph and returned downstairs to find Jordan standing next to the sofa with the tripod. "Come on," she said, leading him to the back porch. The sky was partly cloudy with a fair amount of sun. It was perfect.

She set up the tripod and camera so that it faced the back of the house and stood about ten feet away from the back porch. Examining the photograph of Bell, Landrien tried to memorize every aspect of the background and composition. Next, she repositioned the tripod and changed the aperture to blur the background a little. She repeated this a few times in silence while Jordan merely stood back and watched.

At last, she set the ten-second timer, positioned herself about five feet away from the tripod and stared at the camera. The sunlight broke through the clouds and forced her to squint, but she did not mind because she remembered that Bell appeared to be squinting in the old photograph. While she took a few more of these shots and adjusted the aperture and shutter speed, Jordan hung to the side and continued to watch her. She took shot after shot until she finally turned to Jordan and beckoned him to her.

He was still shirtless and wearing only jeans. As Landrien examined him, he looked increasingly amused and somewhat embarrassed. "Okay." She took Jordan by the arm and positioned him a few feet in front of the camera. He stood with both hands at his sides while she went to the camera tripod and snapped several test pictures of him. After she made some adjustments, she snapped more pictures of him, instructing him to look this way and that way rather than at the camera the whole time. Within a few minutes, Jordan got into it. He placed his hands inside his pockets and stared intently at the camera with his lips slightly parted and a stony gaze that he believed was sexy. Holding back her laughter all the while, she took a few more shots of him.

"Now, I want you to take a few photos of me." Before he had the opportunity to protest, she handed him the camera and explained some of the features. "Tell me what you want me to do, and I'll do it. You're the one in control, okay?"

"I like the sound of that." He stepped back and held the camera to his face.

Landrien grinned. "Don't get too cocky."

Overexcited like a little boy with a new toy, Jordan took several shots before she was ready, and she scolded him for catching her off guard. He laughed and took a few more shots. After taking a dozen or so shots and instructing her to stand here and there and put her hand here and there, he said, "All right. I think I'm out of ideas."

"Cool. That's good enough. We're done." She took the camera, collected the tripod, and they retreated inside the house.

"What now?"

"You're gonna help me develop and print these."

"In the darkroom? Awesome." He happily followed her down into the basement, where she assigned him the task of getting the equipment—trays, tongs, and chemicals—out and ready. From there, she filled a tray with developer, another with stop bath, and another with fixer. She explained the importance of each chemical solution to Jordan, who turned out to be the perfect pupil.

They spent most of the afternoon developing and printing the photographs.

After that weekend with Jordan, Landrien carried a camera everywhere she went. When she went to work, she carried her smaller Nikon with her, but when she went elsewhere on the weekends—around Phoenixville, to visit Reggie and Bobby in Brooklyn, to the Jersey shore with Jordan, hiking with Darren and Irina—she carried her old SLR with her. She even traded in her smartphone for one with a higher quality camera. She took pictures of everything because, for some reason, she began to see stories in everything. She saw stories in soggy cigarette butts on the sidewalk, in mountains of black trash bags lining the neighborhood streets in Brooklyn and West Philly, in the lighthouses of the shore, in the trees broken and fallen by late summer thunderstorms, in the stray cat chasing a defenseless bird along the street. She saw so many stories and so much beauty. It disturbed her that she had not seen it all before.

One September evening, she left her office and ran into Kenny Muchmore, whom she had not seen for several months. He was outside her building and panhandling as he used to do. "Hey, Mr. Muchmore. How've you been? Adrien down in housing told me she got you set up on a section 8 voucher a while back."

He nodded, with an unusually warm expression on his face. "She did. I'm living down south now, in a row house off of Snyder and Passyunk. It's a lot more space than I had before and cheaper with the voucher. I can't thank you and Adrien enough for what y'all done for me."

"I'm happy to hear it. I was wondering where you were the last couple of months," she replied.

"Oh, I was down in Virginia last month. My last aunt passed away. Stroke. I stayed down there for a few weeks, just got back a few days ago. I been spending some time at the homeless center up the way, volunteering some of my time to help out with the cooking and things. One of the girls up there say she might be able to help me get a paying job at the shelter before long. So, I just been putting in work, that's all."

As she studied his dark eyes in his heavily lined face, she saw a spark of confidence and certainty there that she had not seen in him before. She had an idea. She had been having a lot of those lately. "Mr. Muchmore, this is gonna sound weird. But can I photograph you real quick? Just a few pictures?"

"Uh," he said, caught off guard. "For what?"

"No real reason. I'm into photography, as sort of a side hobby," she explained, digging inside her purse. "I've just started getting back into it."

"Lawyer and a photographer. Hmm. I can't see why you wanna take a picture of *me*, though. I ain't what you'd call photogenic or nothing."

"You might not realize it, but there are a thousand stories in your eyes alone, Mr. Muchmore. As weird as that might sound."

If his dark face could have flushed, she was sure it would have been bright red at that moment. He averted his eyes nervously and smiled. "That's real flattering, Miss Moriset. I done heard a lot of things. But I can't say I ever had anybody say that to me."

"I'll make you a deal," Landrien offered. "I'll develop and frame a photo or two just for you. You can consider it a housewarming gift from me. What d'you think?"

Kenny Muchmore smiled some more, his eyes still averted, and he nodded. "All right then."

She put her bag on the ground, pulled out her camera and without much thought began taking pictures of him. She squatted and moved around him and took frames at various angles, hoping to get as much of the street in the background as possible. He rolled his wheelchair this way and that way to accommodate her position suggestions. In a pure and unaffected manner, he looked stoically at the camera sometimes, and at other times, he stared at his hands or in another direction. He was natural and conveyed an effortless grace in his demeanor and gaze as he took a drag of his cigarette, blew out smoke and looked toward the street or else at the camera with a look that expressed contentment tinged with deep pain.

After taking at least twenty shots of him, she turned off the camera and tucked it inside her bag. "Promise me something, Mr. Muchmore. You'll keep me updated about your work at the shelter and your housing. If you need any legal help or just want to tell me some good news, you'll drop by my office. Yeah?"

Kenny nodded. "You're a strange woman, you know. I still can't figure why you even took a second glance at me that morning all them months ago."

"You always had a smile for me, Mr. Muchmore. I appreciated that."

"Well, I'm glad you did take an interest that morning."

She smiled, not sure what else to say. "I'm gonna get started on these pictures this evening."

"All right. I'll be looking forward to that framed picture, too."

"You bet. In about a week or so, I should have it. If I don't see you out here, come up to my office."

"All right now. You have a blessed day, Miss Moriset," said Kenny Muchmore.

"You do the same." She waved just before crossing Chestnut Street. Landrien smiled all the way to the subway station, anxious to get home and develop the photographs.

CHAPTER SEVENTEEN

Landrien stood in the center of her parent's bedroom and, with a heavy sense of anxiety, sat two paint drums on the floor next to her feet. She stood there, preparing to paint the walls pastel yellow, preparing to paint over the memories of her parents, memories that had settled into every crack and corner of the room. She looked over her shoulder at Bell, who lingered in the doorway and watched her.

As she gazed around at the walls, she took a deep breath and visualized how she wanted the room to look. The room was mostly vacant. Other than removing most of the furniture and books, she had avoided altering the room. When she had first moved in, she had taken all of her mother's books and belongings, packed them into boxes and placed them all either in the basement or in the storage room. Only the bed—still covered with her mother's favorite floral quilt and pillows—and the three empty bookcases remained in the room. The bookcases had housed her mother's cookbooks and many of her father's academic books. Darren had taken the chest and drawers, along with the nightstand and chair, months ago.

She closed her eyes for a moment and recalled the occasions when she had found her father sitting in the rocking chair next to the window, and the time when she had found him sitting in the chair and reading a Toni Morrison book and she had asked him about love. As she thought about her father, she wondered if she should paint the room. He seemed to live on in that room, in every crack and dusty corner. Why not just leave the room as it was, she wondered?

Once she opened her eyes, though, she sighed and bent down to open the bucket of paint. *It's just a damn room.* Without further hesitation, she poured the yellow paint into a plastic pan, drenched the roller brush in it and went to work on the walls.

After she finished painting the walls, she swept the floor and dusted the bookshelves. She removed the curtains from both windows and replaced them with white venetian blinds. A headache began to brew at her temples as the fierce odor of the drying paint clung to her nostrils. She turned on the ceiling fan and cracked the windows to air out the room, but half an hour later, the bitingly cold December air forced her to close the windows.

Cold and suddenly sleepy, she went downstairs to put on a pot of coffee. She had bought a new Guatemalan dark roast at the organic store the other day and was eager to try it. She switched on the stereo in the living room, put in one of Marie's classical piano CDs and returned upstairs shortly with a mug of coffee in her hand.

Landrien pulled three boxes out of her bedroom closet and dragged them to her parents' old room. She had stored her old book collection and some of her father's old books in two of the boxes. The third box contained her mother's diaries. On the smallest bookcase, she arranged all of the novels in alphabetical order by the authors' last names. She placed the photography books and her father's nonfiction books on the next bookcase. The two boxes of books filled all but one row. On the bottom row, she laid out her mother's diaries, dusting some of them off as she removed them from the box.

The two-shelf bookcase remained empty. She picked up the dusty old photo album, put it on top of the empty bookcase and opened it to a random page that contained photographs of Reggie and her mother.

Landrien went to her room, opened the top drawer of her nightstand and pulled out two recent photographs she had developed but not framed. One was a photograph collage of the living room before and after she had redecorated it. She took these two photographs and the old SLR camera her father had given her when she was a kid. She placed the two photographs side by side on the first row of the empty bookcase and put the camera in the center of the bottom row. In terms of décor, it was minimalist and plain and not necessarily inspired, but she decided it was the best she could do right now.

Finally, she carried up from the basement several framed photographs, two at a time, and sat them on the floor in her parents' closet. In all, she brought up six framed photographs she had taken recently and developed. She had developed some of the photographs digitally, while others had been developed and processed in the darkroom. She could not decide which style of photography she liked best. The lazier side of her preferred the ease of digital photography and found fiddling around in the darkroom rather boring sometimes. Yet she was amazed at the quality of the photographs she was able to develop and print in the darkroom. She wondered which one her father would prefer.

Once she brewed another pot of coffee and refilled her mug, she sat down on the sofa and reread her mother's will. She had glanced at it several times over the last few weeks as the one-year anniversary of her mother's death rapidly approached. Although she was not certain that she wanted to remain in the house, she had realized that she did not want to return to her apartment and, therefore, had turned over her apartment lease to Jordan. Her mind wandered among all of her options as she stared at the will. After a few minutes, however, she slipped the will back inside a manila envelope and sat it on the coffee table. Leaning back against the sofa and closing her eyes, she took a drag from her e-cigarette.

"Darren, what are you doing here?" Landrien opened the door and stepped aside to let her brother in. He was shivering and holding a paper bag in one hand. "The least you could do is call, you know."

"As if you're so busy," he teased, smiling and planting a kiss on her cheek.

He stepped out of his boots and took off his coat.

"You want some tea or some coffee? I can make a pot," Landrien offered, taking his coat and hanging it in the closet.

He declined and made his way toward the living room, where he dropped onto the sofa, and crossed his legs. "This couch is new. I like it."

"I got it a few weeks ago. What's in the bag?"

He regarded her for a moment, as if hesitant to answer. "Something I found in Mom's nightstand," he said and poured the contents of the bag onto the coffee table. At least a dozen greeting cards—holiday and birthday cards— lay scattered on the table as Landrien leaned down to get a closer look.

"All the cards I sent her. She kept them," Landrien muttered, running her hands over the cards. "I didn't even think she'd opened any of them." She picked up one card and read it, then another and another. As she read each card, her smile widened and her eyes watered. She picked up the pile of cards and held them against her chest, forgetting that Darren was there. "Thank you."

"You're welcome," Darren replied, snapping Landrien out of her daydream.

She turned to him at once and nodded. "Thank you," she repeated.

A long silence passed between them. After she placed all the cards back inside the paper bag and sat the bag on the coffee table, she sat down next to him on the sofa and stared at nothing in particular.

"So how have you been anyway?" he asked.

"All right, I guess." She looked at her brother. He had grown a bit of facial hair lately and, as usual, was wearing a woolly turtleneck. She faced him as she folded her legs underneath her.

"So, anything new on your end? Or did you come all this way just to check in on me and drop off these cards?" she asked, offering him a clove cigarette, but he declined. It was time to give up smoking for good, and she was intent upon thoroughly enjoying her last pack of cigarettes. She savored every drag. When Darren didn't answer her question, she stared at him over the top of her glasses and concluded that he was concealing something.

Unable to take any more of the silence, she stood up and said, "Come on. Let me show you something."

"What?"

"Just come on," she urged him, walking toward the stairs and blowing out smoke. She switched on the hall light as she reached the stairs, Darren following close behind her.

Once upstairs, she stopped at the doorway of their parents' old room and switched on the light. The room was almost as empty as it had been days before, but now black and white framed photographs hung about the walls, and the bed was gone. Landrien, with the help of Rona's son who was visiting for the holidays, had moved the bed to the storage room next to the carport. She had placed two rocking chairs in the center of the room and between them a floor to ceiling lamp that curved over in the shape of a lowercased letter "r." A gray ottoman sat in front of each chair.

"Man, this is nice," Darren exclaimed, gazing around the room. "Sort of like a library or reading room?"

"Something like that. I like to think of it as a reading gallery."

He approached two framed photographs on the wall between the windows. "It's got a nice vibe to it. I'm feeling it. And these pictures, they're stunning."

"Thanks. I was hoping they made sense in here."

He glanced at her and saw her flushed cheeks. "Wait, are these yours?"

She smiled and nodded.

"Get outta here. For real? I didn't know you'd gotten back into photography. That's what's up." He returned his attention to the photographs, pointed at one and asked, "Who's this guy here?"

"He's a man who used to stand outside my office building sometimes, panhandling. His name's Kenny Muchmore. Isn't he a natural?"

Darren nodded, his gaze fixed on a black and white photograph that depicted Kenny sitting in his wheelchair on a busy Chestnut Street and blowing out cigarette smoke, his eyes half closed, and a bright yellow taxi visible in the background. The yellow taxi provided the only color in the black and white photograph. "I think this one's my favorite."

"Mine too," she said, staring at the photograph.

"Have you sold any of these?"

Landrien shook her head.

"Have you thought about it? I bet some folks would pay good money for them."

"Maybe."

He drifted to two more photographs on the adjacent wall, and Landrien remembered how nice it used to feel when he admired her photographs. It was he who had encouraged her to take photographs of Amma, and she had given many of the photographs of Amma to him—not the best ones, of course. She wondered if he still had those photographs. "This is a nice picture of Jordan, too. How have you two been lately?" He threw a stern look at his sister. In the photograph, Jordan stood off center, barefoot and shirtless in front of two maple trees, with his hands in his pockets and his head slightly cocked to the left as he squinted at the camera.

"We've been all right. Good, actually."

"Whoa. This dress..." He pointed at the framed photograph of Landrien wearing Bell's orange dress. "Where did you get it?" He turned sideways and shot her an accusatory look.

"I found it in Mom's stuff."

Darren looked at her for a moment, anger etched in every line of his face, and she could not fathom what had brought on the sudden shift in his mood. She got ready to ask him what was wrong, but his expression went flat at once, and he turned to the photograph, moving closer to it and running his fingertips along the glass. "It belonged to Bell," he said, almost inaudibly.

Landrien's hands dropped to her sides, and her eyes darted to his face. She took a step toward him. "You know about Bell?"

"I do." He did not look at his sister. "Mom told me about her when Dad died. Bell was my biological mother." He spoke in such a matter-of-fact tone that it both unnerved and infuriated her.

"Why didn't she tell me?" she asked, trying her best to subdue her anger.

He shrugged. "I'm sorry, sis. I sort of came over here to talk to you about that, actually. Over the last few weeks, I got to thinking maybe I should tell you, after all this time and the few things you've told me about the diaries. I don't know why I didn't want to tell you before. It's just that Mom didn't want you to know, and I'm sure she had her reasons, whatever they were. I think she wanted to make sure that we had a real sibling bond or something. But she told me because she said I had a right to know about my real mother. Obviously, I was mad at first—who wouldn't be—but I understood, you know. Bell died and left me with Mom. It wasn't anybody's fault, really."

"What all did she tell you about Bell?"

"Bell died when I was only a couple years old. She was from Arkansas, and she and Mom were friends," he answered.

Landrien regarded him with pity—and, though she hated to admit it—felt a certain satisfaction that her mother had indeed kept some parts of the story a secret, even from Darren. Feeling compelled to do what she knew she should have done months ago, she took a deep breath and said, "Sit down, Darren."

Without a word, he sat down in one of the rocking chairs and looked at her. She sat across from him and started from the beginning of the story of Bell and Lorraine, filling in the gaps that their mother had left in the story. When she finished, Darren sat lost in his head for a while. She was not sure if she detected shock or general amusement on his face, but he smiled at last.

"So, Mom was a lesbian? Hmph," To Landrien's general amazement, he shrugged. He did not ask about the men who murdered Bell, and for some reason, this relieved Landrien.

"Probably bisexual."

"Like you?" he asked.

"Like me, yes. She loved Dad, after a while, anyway. She even told him about her relationship with Bell. I'm assuming she also told him you were Bell's son. And he was okay with her sexuality and everything. Isn't it crazy?" She rested against the wall and smiled at her brother.

"You found all that out in the diaries?"

"I did. She wrote everything down, it seems. I guess it was the writer in her. She had so many secrets. It's strange to think she and Dad had such a complicated marriage, but it worked for them."

Darren nodded and smiled, staring at his sister.

"What?"

"She sounds like you, sis."

"Yeah, maybe a little," she admitted as the two of them rose and exited the room.

Darren grabbed her by the shoulders and pulled her into a hug. "I missed you, sis. We gotta do better about this staying in touch thing."

"Yes we do." Landrien rested her head against his shoulder as they stood there. "We really do."

***

On New Year's Eve the following week, Landrien sat at the dining room table alongside Jordan, Darren and Irina. Marie, Bobby and Reggie sat on the opposite side, and were having a loud disagreement about Eric Clapton, whom Marie appreciated but Reggie considered a knock-off of true blues artists. Eric Clapton's cover of Muddy Water's "Hoochie Coochie Man," which had sparked the disagreement between Marie and Reggie, played softly from the living room. Bobby enjoyed a glass of wine while watching Reggie and Marie's argument grow more and more heated.

Meanwhile, Irina and Darren helped themselves to more dessert, which consisted of a peach pie and strawberry cheesecake Landrien had made, and a sweet potato pie prepared by Reggie. Jordan and Darren had brought two bottles of wine.

"Landrien, honey, this house is simply beautiful. I don't know how you found this color for the walls in here. But it is just amazing," said Reggie, an inebriated smile on his face. Apparently, he and Marie had concluded their discussion about Eric Clapton. Marie was pouring herself some more wine.

"Thanks, but I can't take credit for the walls. That's all Marie's doing. She did some mixing and experimenting, and I just let her have at it because I don't have the first clue about painting and mixing colors."

Reggie toasted Marie, and both of them drunkenly sipped their wine and went back to talking about music. Landrien noted that she would have to make sure neither of them got behind a steering wheel later. She needed to check upstairs and make sure she had laid out enough blankets and bathroom towels for everyone. She was not accustomed to being a host, but she had to admit she rather enjoyed it.

As she thought about this and sliced off another piece of sweet potato pie, Jordan leaned over and brushed his lips against her neck. "You look beautiful," he whispered, and she grinned.

"Hey, Marie, when's your date gonna show up?" asked Darren, looking at his watch. Marie had informed everyone that her date, some engineer named Ahmed, who was from the United Arab Emirates and very rich, would be arriving late due to a prior engagement with his family in West Philly.

"He texted me that he's on his way from his sister's house. Why are you so eager to meet him anyway, Darren?" she asked, with a sassy look at her nephew.

"Because I'm gonna need to check him out and make sure he's not up to no good. No prior records. No scandalous background," Darren explained. He winked at Marie and forked some cheesecake into his mouth.

"Well, I'm planning on him being up to no good and scandalous tonight, if you know what I mean," declared Marie, her shoulders bouncing as she laughed.

"Eww," Landrien exclaimed. "No, that is not for my ears, Marie. Way too much information."

Marie grinned and shrugged. "Old people got needs, too, honey."

"Speaking of relationships and such, what's up with you two?" asked Darren, proving once again that tact was not his forte. He looked at his sister and glanced at Jordan, whose smile faltered.

"What d'you mean?" Landrien thought about the ring and the envelope on her nightstand upstairs. She looked sideways at Jordan and back at her brother, who wore a smirk as he sipped his red wine.

"You know what I mean. You're engaged. Then, you're not engaged. I'm just saying. Are you gonna get married any time this decade?" Everyone around the table had fallen silent, watching Landrien and Jordan with undisguised anticipation.

Jordan squeezed her hand under the table just before he leaned forward and kissed her. "Maybe," said Landrien to her brother while she and Jordan held one another's gaze. She turned back to Darren and the rest of her guests. "Maybe not."

After another tense couple of seconds, Darren laughed and finished off his glass of wine. "Damn. You know how to make a man wait for you."

"Yes, she does," Jordan agreed, slicing his cheesecake and kissing Landrien's cheek.

"You do you, honey," Reggie interjected, and Bobby nodded. The two of them raised their glasses once more to toast Jordan and Landrien. "I made this one here wait, too." He and Bobby smiled at one another, not bothering to disguise what was on their minds.

"All right, all right. Enough." Landrien laughed, slapping away Jordan's frisky hand that was under the table and inching up her thigh. "Since I have everybody's attention," she went on, catching a glimpse of the wall clock above the back door. "It is exactly seven minutes before the new year. I want to remind everybody that at midnight, we're going out onto the back porch for a toast and then we're going up to the reading gallery for an unveiling of some amazing works of photography by yours truly. So fill up your glasses now and let's make our way to the back porch." She rose, picked up her plate and headed toward the kitchen. Jordan followed her.

"Don't worry about it. What Darren said in there, don't worry about it."

Landrien looked at Jordan and put her plate in the sink. "I'm not." She opened the refrigerator and took out the second sweet potato pie that Reggie had brought. "I'm not worried."

"Okay."

She put the pie on the countertop and closed the space between her and Jordan. "I'm not worried because I'm still here and so are you, and we're happy. Right? I'm not going anywhere." She pushed his hair behind his ears and met his gaze as his lips slowly parted into a smile. "So what do you think about cats?" asked Landrien.

"Better than dogs," Jordan answered, not missing a beat.

"Good." She kissed the back of his hand, held it and picked up the sweet potato pie with her free hand before they exited the kitchen. "You're coming to the animal shelter with me next week," she told him, thinking about the gray and black kitten she had seen at the Phoenixville Animal Shelter a week earlier and wondering what name might fit it.

When they arrived in the dining room, she placed the pie on the table, and Reggie immediately cut himself a moderate slice. "Two minutes to midnight," Bobby announced, with a quick glance at his watch.

Hurriedly, everyone filled their glasses with more wine and rushed to the back porch. Reggie stuffed half a slice of pie in his mouth, and Bobby grabbed their wine glasses.

Snow had fallen the day before, but on this night, the clouds had cleared out and stars filled the sky. Jordan stood behind Landrien on the stairs, one hand on her waist and one hand holding a glass of wine. She spotted Bell standing a few feet away near the willow tree. Bell regarded the party of people with an approving smile, and her orange dress shimmered under the moonlight. She gave Landrien a curious nod and walked away, as she did so often nowadays, rarely stopping to talk anymore.

"So, you think you're gonna stay here for good?" asked Marie. She came forward and stood next to her niece.

"I don't know," Landrien hollered over the noise of the others counting down the last ten seconds to midnight. "I could say 'sure,' but who knows what I'll think tomorrow."

"Just taking it day by day, huh? Well, I think living here suits you, niece."

Landrien smiled and considered the strange year she had had at 4516 Belmont Road. "Yeah, you might be right."

While everyone cheered the beginning of the New Year and raised their glasses in salute, Landrien thought about the woman in the orange dress. She wondered if Bell would be there in the morning or the morning after that. Then, she looked around at her family and friends, and thought about all the wine and dessert she planned to consume once everyone returned to the dining room, and about all the dancing and conversation that would ensue, and for the moment she had no complaints.

About the Author

Berneta L. Haynes was born and raised in Little Rock, Arkansas but has lived everywhere from Missouri, England, Iowa, Chicago, and Philadelphia since age eighteen. She is the author of several publications, including articles and short stories. Formerly an environmental attorney, Berneta is a public policy professional in Atlanta, Georgia, where lives with her husband and fellow writer. She is currently working on her upcoming sci-fi series and blogging joyously. Social butterflies can follow Berneta on Twitter @BernetaWrites. If you enjoyed this novel, please leave a review at your favorite retailer's website and share on Twitter or Facebook!